Body Wave

Body Wave

Nancy J. Cohen

KENSINGTON BOOKS
http://www.kensingtonbooks.com

Library of Congress Card Catalogue Number: 2002103431
ISBN 0-7582-0068-4

First Printing: December 2002
10 9 8 7 6 5 4 3 2 1

Printed in the United States of America

ACKNOWLEDGMENTS

With many thanks for sharing their knowledge and generously giving their time to answer my research questions:

Dr. Bart Baca, Director of Aquaculture Programs, Oceanographic Center, Nova Southeastern University

Phyllis E. Kolianos, Curator and Historical Society Manager, Tarpon Springs Area Historical Society

Chapter
One

"If you succeed, I'll sell you my half of our jointly owned property," Stanley Kaufman offered. "You'll double your rental income and get rid of me all in one swoop."

Marla Shore gave her ex-spouse a sardonic grin. "Oh joy. All I
have to do is solve a murder which *you* may have committed."

"You've been wanting to get me off your back. Well, this is your
chance. Don't make a hasty decision you'll regret later."

Dressed in his high-powered attorney suit, Stan appeared out of
his element in the stark confines of the city jail. Marla's gaze trav-
eled from the painted gray concrete floor to the metal sink and toilet
unit at the opposite end from where they stood. The room stank of
urine and stale sweat. A built-in bench qualified as the sole piece of
furniture; residents didn't stay long in a holding cell. Fluorescent
lights lit harsh angles on walls that pressed too close. Gray scored as
the operative color, coating the solid door with its secured viewport.
It seemed the wrong choice in a place where society drew definitive
lines of justice.

Stan would have to hire his own partners if he was actually
charged with murdering his third wife, Marla thought. "Why do you
think I can find Kimberly's killer? You've got money. Engage a private investigator."

"You've solved cases before," Stan replied, his hazel eyes glinting as though he didn't want to admit she'd done something right. "Obviously, you're more on the ball than that detective friend of yours, Lieutenant Vail. He'd like to bust my ass."

"If it weren't for Dalton, I wouldn't have been allowed to see you," she snapped, her glance flickering contemptuously at Stan's thin black hair brushed off his forehead. It reminded her of how many times he'd brushed off her accomplishments over the years. Ever since their divorce, Stan had never let Marla forget how much he'd done for her. Even now, despite her ability to manage her own hair salon, she couldn't believe the man regarded her capable enough to do him a service.

"Maybe we haven't gotten along in recent years," he said in a half-apologetic tone, "but we had something once. For old times' sake, give me a break."

"Tell me what happened, and then I'll decide," she said, striding to the bench and plopping herself down. She avoided the seat's encrusted crud so it wouldn't soil her khakis.

Hands folded behind his back, Stan paced purposefully like a trial attorney. "I'm a sound sleeper. You remember, don't you? When I fall asleep, I don't even hear the lawn men trimming hedges outside our windows. This morning, I awoke at my regular time, seven o'clock. Kim usually gets up earlier and has a cup of coffee waiting for me. I couldn't smell it like I normally do, but her side of the bed was empty, so I figured she'd be downstairs."

He halted, shoulders slumping. "I should have known something was wrong, because I couldn't hear her moving around the kitchen. Kim was a good wife. A good wife," he repeated in his habitually annoying manner. "She always had my breakfast ready on time." His resentful glare told Marla how she'd never met his expectations when they were married.

"Go on," Marla grated, suppressing her irritation.

"I was still in my pajamas when I reached the foyer. Our stairway is just a few steps from the front door," he explained. "Kim was lying on the floor. I called her name, but she didn't respond, and her body was awfully still. I couldn't imagine what had happened. Did she trip and fall down the stairs? In a terrifying flash, I thought she must have broken her neck until I saw the blood. It had seeped out like fingers of a river."

His eyelids squeezed shut, and a tremor rippled through him. Seconds ticked by while he regained his composure. When he opened his eyes, pain glistened in their depths.

Surprise slashed at her. She hadn't realized Stan could feel so deeply about anyone. Rising, she embraced him in a quick hug, startling both of them. While she cursed Stan for his arrogance, she didn't wish upon him this type of suffering. Grief was a difficult burden to carry alone. "Tell me more," she said encouragingly, stepping back a few paces.

He drew in a shuddering breath. "I-I knelt to see what I could do. I turned her onto her back, but it was too late. Too late. She'd been stabbed in the abdomen. It must've hit a major organ. I'll never forget the look in her eyes—terror mixed with astonishment." His voice faltered. "I-I froze, Marla. For the first time in my life, I didn't know what to do."

"You called the police."

"Yes. Somehow I stumbled into the kitchen. It crossed my mind that I should wash my hands." He turned them palm up as though to show her the stains. "Instead, I grabbed the phone and called the cops."

"What did you do until they arrived?"

"I don't remember." He squinted as though trying to force memories into his brain. "Before I knew it, uniformed officers were pouring into my house."

"So you opened the door for them."

"No, it was unlocked. The officers let themselves in after ringing the bell. I was too numb to respond."

"Where did they find you? In the kitchen?"

"Hovering over Kimberly's body. I'll admit it doesn't look good for me, babe."

"Maybe an intruder entered the house and Kim surprised him. Do you think robbery was a motive? If you could prove things were stolen—"

"Nothing was missing. The cops asked me to check before I got dressed." Stan's gaze held genuine bewilderment. "I can see why they believe I did it. Blood on my pajamas is damning evidence, but I-I touched my wife when I tried to save her. What was I supposed to do, leave her lying there bleeding to death? I don't know how we're going to clean up the mess on the floor."

From his use of the joint pronoun, Marla realized he hadn't come to grips with his loss. "Did the police find signs of forced entry?"

"N-No, that's the peculiar thing. The windows were secure, and our other exterior doors were locked. There weren't any footprints on the ground, either, and the sprinklers had been on earlier."

"So when the cops confronted you, there were no signs anyone else had been in the house, and you had blood on your clothes."

His face darkened. "Hell, Marla, whose side are you on? Things may not have been perfect between us, but I'd never hurt Kimberly. You know how I abhor violence. When you and I were married, I never mishandled you in anger. Never."

Not physically, no. But you're skilled in throwing verbal darts that can wound.

"What do you want me to do?" she asked him, intending to speak to Detective Vail to get his viewpoint.

"Help me, Marla." He spread his hands toward her. "The police don't believe me. Find out who killed Kimberly, and I'll sell you my half of our rental property at a reasonable price."

"Are you willing to put that in writing?"

"Why? You don't trust me?"

Her lip curled in a cynical smile. "Well, Stanley, let's just say I like to protect my investments."

His spine stiffened. "If that's what it takes. Will you do it?"

His voice echoed in the high-ceilinged room, and it struck a chord within her heart. When they'd first met, Stan had pulled her out of a morass so deep, Marla feared she'd never emerge into the light again. Didn't she owe him the same favor?

"I'm surprised you have such faith in me, but yes, I'll check things out," she replied. Her nature wouldn't allow an innocent man to be convicted. No matter how much she loathed Stan, injustice wasn't tolerable.

On the other hand, she didn't discount the possibility that he might be guilty. In that case, this could be a ploy to distract attention from himself. She'd look for evidence, and if it pointed toward Stan, he'd lose her sympathy pretty quickly. But that possibility was later down the road. Marla knew quite well she enjoyed solving mysteries because they provided spice in an otherwise routine life. She sought the challenge, despite Detective Vail's warnings to steer clear of his domain. Maybe it was the challenge of matching wits with him that entertained her.

Several paths opened in front of her, and she leapt at the nearest one.

"What did you mean, things weren't perfect between you and Kimberly?" she demanded.

Stan shrugged. "I set her spending limits, but Kim always exceeded them with her credit card. We had our minor disagreements, that's all. When she behaved herself, we were as close as glue to paper. Why did she have to get herself killed?"

Anger is a natural part of the grieving process, Marla reminded herself, biting her tongue. "Would you like me to contact your partners?"

"I've already phoned them, thanks. Your detective friend made an exception by allowing me to call you, too."

"Really? How kind of him."

Stan cleared his throat. "So tell me how you'll proceed." His gruff tone belied the imploring look in his eyes.

Despite her sympathy, it amused Marla to hold the upper hand. "I suppose I could attend the funeral. I've never met any of Kim's relatives. How are you going to make arrangements if you're in jail?"

"I'll get out on bail as soon as I have an arraignment. But I don't think it's a good idea for you to attend the funeral. I have a better plan. An intruder isn't the only possibility. Kim's murderer might have been someone she knew. You can start with her family."

Marla knew little about Kim's background. Why would she? Kimberly had been Stan's secretary when he'd been married to wife number two, Leah Kaufman. Marla had believed Stan would finally be happy with Leah since they had two lovely children. But he was a man who'd never be satisfied, because Kim had seduced him right under his wife's nose. Leah had been the one who'd initiated their divorce. Now Kimberly was dead. Stan had achieved a brilliant career, but he'd been unsuccessful in the marital arena. At least he couldn't be accused of lacking a taste for variety, Marla thought spitefully. She fingered her chestnut hair, curled inward at chin length, musing over the differences in his choices of wives. At five feet six, she didn't quite match Stan's height. Leah's short auburn layers suited her petite figure, while Kim had been a busty, blue-eyed blonde with a model's long legs. Marla's eyes were cocoa brown; Leah's were almost black. Maybe Stan would go for a green-eyed, raven-haired beauty next.

The grid over the viewport slid open. "Ma'am?" said the attending officer.

"I just need a few more minutes," she pleaded. Relieved when the woman nodded, Marla returned her attention to Stan.

"Kimberly's family lives in an exclusive compound in East Fort Lauderdale," Stan explained, plowing a hand through his hair. "They're rich, you know. Their investments involve coffee plantations in Costa Rica and South America. Miriam Pearl, Kimberly's grandmother, requires a daily nurse. They've been advertising for an aide so the nurse can take Sundays off. You're free on that day of the week. You'll apply for the job so you can check things out from an insider's viewpoint. Her family has never met you, so you won't be recognized."

Marla's spine stiffened. "What? You want me to apply as a health aide? I have no background for that kind of job."

Even as the words left her mouth, she imagined herself undercover investigating Kim's murder and a thrill of excitement spiraled through her. If she really wanted to play the part, she could consult her friend Jillian, a seasoned actress. Jill had plenty of experience pretending to be someone else.

"You can do it," Stan said encouragingly. "Kim's mother, Stella, and her aunt Florence live on the grounds. So does her uncle Morris and his family, plus assorted servants."

"Any sisters or brothers?"

"Nope."

"Her father?"

"He passed away, leaving the bulk of his wealth to Stella."

"What about the old lady's nurse? She'll see right through me. I'll have to ask her for instructions on what to do."

"In all likelihood, Agnes will be gone by the time you arrive on Sunday morning. Don't worry so much, babe. You're good about caring for people." *Just not about me,* his sour expression implied. "It can't be so difficult to watch over an old woman for a day."

"I don't understand why you suspect one of Kimberly's family members."

He shifted his feet. "First of all, Kim may have opened the door for someone she knew. Secondly, who stands to gain from her death? One of her relatives, that's who." He lowered his voice. "Kim is . . . was due to receive an inheritance from Grandpa Harris when she reached the age of thirty. She'd just turned twenty-six last month on January tenth, meaning she still had four years to go. With her out of the way, one of her relatives gets her share."

"So you think she was murdered for her money."

"Why else?"

"I can think of other reasons," Marla muttered, recalling the blonde's nasty attitude the few times they'd met. Marla wasn't the only one who'd resented the woman. Another person came to mind immediately, but she didn't mention her theory to Stan.

"I'll see what I can learn," she promised, touching his arm. "How will I contact you?"

"I'll get out of here when the judge sets bond. You can reach me at the office or at home." He leaned toward her, eyes glistening in a manner that made her uncomfortable. "I really appreciate this. I know I haven't been agreeable lately, but that's because you don't need me as much as when we were married."

I don't need you at all now, pal, except for that rental property. Marla was accustomed to his arrogant, condescending manner. Having him request her help threw her off guard. She almost liked him better when he was in a vulnerable position.

"I'll handle it, Stanley. I'm sorry you have to suffer this indignity." Her gesture encompassed the jail cell.

His gaze locked on hers, and he reached out to stroke her cheek. His touch brought back memories best left forgotten. "I care about you, Marla, even after all these years."

She stepped back abruptly. "Don't push it, Stan. Be grateful I've offered to help you and leave it at that. Good luck with the judge." She strode to the door, where she knocked loudly to draw the guard's attention.

Upstairs, she walked briskly into Lieutenant Dalton Vail's office, knowing he anticipated hearing the results of her interview. After Stan's unnerving influence, it was a pleasure to see the lines of concern on Vail's face as he rose to greet her. Sharp angles defined his features, set off by bushy eyebrows and thick, peppery hair parted to the side. Feeling empowered, Marla boldly kissed him on the mouth.

"What was that for?" he asked, a smile creasing his craggy face.

"You're a refreshing change from Stan," Marla replied, appreciating Vail's two-sided perspective on life compared with Stan's blurred distinctions. At least with Vail, you knew where you stood: he valued truthfulness rather than deception. Dalton stated what was on his mind, at least as far as she was concerned. Stan's motives were more questionable.

Vail's smoky gaze raked her, then he grasped her shoulders. The warmth from his hands seeped through her cashmere sweater. "Would you like to try that again for the benefit of my colleagues?" he asked in a husky tone. His glance darted to the open door through which the cubicles beyond were visible.

Marla realized Dalton's aim was to pair them publicly as a couple so she'd be forced to commit to him. He'd become especially intent on this goal after her fake engagement to Arnie Hartman had ended. Come to think of it, Marla already had acting experience pretending to be Arnie's fiancée, so maybe posing as a nurse's aide wouldn't be so difficult. Not that she'd tell Vail her plan. She could imagine his explosive reaction.

Another kind of eruption came to mind as he pressed his body closer. His touch left her weak-kneed and on a hormonal rush, but she wouldn't be swayed from her purpose. "Stan didn't do it," she said, disentangling herself. "I believe him. I've never seen the man so upset."

Vail sighed as though he'd expected that response. "Murderers kill *because* they're upset. What did he tell you?"

"Probably the same things he reported to you." She strolled to a bookshelf and picked up a toy police car from a collection of miniature vehicles. Dust coated its surface, making her wonder who cleaned his office. "Stan woke up around seven, went downstairs, found his wife stabbed to death in the front hallway. He tried to revive her, got blood on his hands, stumbled into the kitchen to call the police."

Vail snorted. "Don't you find it hard to believe he heard nothing while his wife was attacked?"

Marla faced him, refusing to be intimidated by the stubborn thrust to his jaw. Tall and imposing in a sport coat and tie, he wore an authoritative air that fit as tautly as his jacket. "Not if Kimberly had let someone she knew into the house. Since the door was unlocked, that seems logical."

"Have you considered that Stan is playing upon your sympathies, and through you, he hopes to throw me off track?"

Marla smirked at the absurdity of the notion that Dalton could be thrown off track. "You? You're like a bloodhound running after a piece of fresh meat, never put off from the scent. He's afraid, Dalton. The evidence looks bad against him, and he knows it. He wouldn't have asked for my help otherwise." She returned the miniature car to the shelf. "If you brought Stan in this morning, why did it take so long for him to call me? I didn't hear from him until three o'clock. He's lucky I was home; Monday is normally my day to run errands."

"Processing a crime scene takes time, and so does questioning a suspect. His attorney didn't make it easy for us."

She noted the gleam in his eyes. "I'll bet you enjoyed interrogating him."

"The man hasn't treated you well. I did him a favor by letting you into the cell block."

"No, you didn't. You're hoping I've learned something new. Stan suspects one of Kimberly's relatives may have bumped her off to inherit her share of the family fortune. You'll be speaking to them, I presume."

"I'll question anyone associated with the deceased. That's my job, remember? Not yours. What did Kaufman want you for, honey?"

Marla was so taken aback by his use of the endearment, mostly because she felt he meant it, that an answer tumbled from her lips. "He wants me to find Kimberly's killer," she said, stopping herself before she blurted out the rest of Stan's scheme. "What about friends and neighbors? I really don't know much about their life together."

He crossed his arms, eyes narrowed perceptively. "I don't either, not yet. I'll attend the funeral to see who shows up."

"I suppose you'll canvas the area to see if any of the neighbors noticed strangers in the vicinity."

"I know my duties, thanks. Why do I have the feeling you've got something up your sleeve? You've given me that same look before, and I don't like it."

Uncomfortable from standing in one place for so long, Marla crossed the room to lean on his desk. "I owe him, Dalton. I don't expect you to understand, but I feel an obligation to the man. He was there for me when I needed him, and now it's his turn."

Vail groaned, passing a hand over his face. "Oh no, he's got you wrapped around his little finger like ribbon on a package. Well, I need you, too. Brianna's thirteenth birthday is in March. When are you going to help me plan her party like you promised?"

"I've been meaning to check into different places around town. Did your daughter mention how many kids will be coming?"

His face folded into a perplexed frown. "The list tops thirty and keeps growing. A lot of her friends are having fancy affairs for their bat mitzvahs, so Brie wants to do something different from an ordinary party. In the meantime, next week is your birthday. I'll pick you up at seven-thirty that night. We'll meet Arnie and Jill at the restaurant." His voice lowered. "February fourteenth is Valentine's Day. That makes it special for us."

"Yeah, I'll be thirty-five. Another year older."

"That's not what I mean."

"Oh? Tell me more."

"You'll see when the time comes."

Marla swallowed. Going undercover to investigate Kimberly's death beckoned as a more appealing option than dealing with Dalton's hints. If her intuition was right, she wasn't the only one with something up her sleeve.

"Stan wouldn't look so spiffy in prison garb," she said to change the subject. "I'd hate to see him convicted if he's innocent, so I hope you'll keep an open mind where he's concerned. I assume you're planning to keep me informed about your progress on the case."

"That depends."

She could swear his tightened lips were stifling a smile. "On what?"

"On my progress with you, sweetcakes."

Chapter Two

Marla decided to visit Leah Kaufman before the police interviewed her. She wanted to assess the woman's reaction to the news of Kim's death, and this afternoon held no other plans except for completing chores. Thus when Marla exited the police station, she steered her white Toyota Camry toward Coral Springs, where Leah lived.

Fifteen minutes later, Marla glanced at the address she'd copied from a phone book at the gas station. Leah's house should be down a side street just past the City Center, off Coral Springs Drive. Getting lost cost her another ten minutes. The turnoff for Leah's residential development was just before Wiles Road, and she'd gone too far. When she finally identified the correct house number, her heart quickened. A brick red Chevrolet Lumina sat in the driveway.

Marla emerged into the cool February air, wishing she'd brought a jacket to wear over her olive cashmere sweater and khaki pants. A cold spell had lowered temperatures into the fifties. Her lips pursed as she strode the short distance to Leah's front door. While she liked the seasonal change in wardrobe, her body preferred warmer climates. Winters where the thermostat stayed around seventy degrees, as they often did in this part of Florida, were preferable. Under those conditions, she could enjoy the balmy sea breezes while others endured frigid weather up north.

A single step brought her to the front door. It was adorned by a half-moon crystalline glass insert guarded by cobwebs. The white ranch-style house had midnight blue shutters that matched the door of a two-car garage. Landscaping consisted of ixora hedges with bright crimson blossoms. *Red, white, and blue: how patriotic.* She rang the doorbell, shifting her handbag to the other shoulder. Although she'd met Leah a couple of times, this was her first visit to the woman's house.

"Who's there?" cried a female voice from inside.

"Marla Shore." In case Leah didn't remember her, she added, "I want to talk to you about Stanley."

Leah swung the door open. Her charcoal eyes regarded Marla with surprise. "Hey, there. I suppose you'd better come inside. We're letting the cold air into the house." Leah patted the apron she wore over a shift dress. Exhaustion showed in dark circles marring her pale complexion.

You could use a deep-conditioning treatment, Marla thought, observing Leah's limp layers of short auburn hair. She stepped gingerly around a tricycle parked in the front hallway, while shrieks of children's laughter rang in the background. "Am I interrupting your dinner preparations?" she asked, sniffing the spicy aroma of spaghetti sauce.

"The pot is simmering. What's this all about?"

Marla faced her. Nearly an inch and a half taller, she was dismayed to feel their difference in height was more due to Leah's slumped posture and dejected manner than to skeletal structure. *Oh joy, wait until she hears what I have to say!*

"Uh, how are the kids?" she asked, to delay the inevitable. Her glance swept the Chinese motif furnishings in the living room. Most outstanding was an ebony lacquered screen with mother-of-pearl inlays depicting Japanese ladies in kimonos chatting by a gazebo. Their porcelain faces held more life than Leah's wan expression. She'd looked better the last time Marla had seen her, right after her divorce from Stan about two years ago. Were times that tough that she seemed so downtrodden?

Leah gave a small smile. "Keith is fine. He's in third grade this year, and Emily is in first. That helps me a great deal since I don't get out of work until three o'clock."

"I see." Marla shuffled her feet awkwardly. "Does Stan ever see them?"

Leah grunted. "He comes by, but it's not often enough. Look, I can spare a few minutes to sit down. Would you like a drink? I'd just poured myself a glass of merlot."

"That would be great, thanks." Marla sat in an armchair and waited patiently. She heard voices, presumably from the kitchen, where Leah must have been quieting her kids.

A few moments later, Leah returned, wineglasses in hand. The two children followed, and she introduced them. Keith looked like a younger version of his father, with black hair and hazel eyes. Emily had an angelic face framed by a halo of reddish gold hair. Both of them wore *schmattes*, clothing Marla would have consigned to the local rummage sale.

"Finish your game in the family room," Leah advised them. Obediently, they scampered off. After handing Marla her glass, she sat on a weave-patterned sofa.

"They're beautiful children," Marla began. Crossing her legs, she sipped her wine. The fruity liquid slid down her throat, leaving an astringent aftertaste.

"Stan has always been good about child support payments," Leah admitted, clutching her goblet, "but it's never enough when you have two kids to raise. I need health insurance and other benefits, plus I contribute toward my mother's support. It's been a struggle."

"Does Stan share custody?"

"He didn't request custody, said it would crimp his style. I think Kimberly was the one who didn't want the burden."

Diving into the opening, Marla said gently, "Kimberly is dead. Someone killed her early this morning."

Leah stared at her, eyes intent like a seagull searching for prey. "Are you for real?"

Marla nodded. "Stan's been arrested. The cops discovered him bending over her body, his pajamas covered with blood. Stan claims he came downstairs and saw her lying there. He turned her over to see if he could help her, but she'd been stabbed. I'm so sorry, Leah, but I felt it would be better for you to hear the news from me rather than a stranger."

"I don't believe it. Stan wouldn't kill anyone," Leah murmured, her eyes glazed. "Kimberly . . . dead? How horrible!" A few moments of heavy silence passed before Leah spoke again. "I can't say her departure saddens me."

"I understand how you must feel," Marla said soothingly. "Kim was a thorn in my side, too. Stan and I owned some property together, and he kept pressuring me to sell so he could use the proceeds to move. Kimberly wanted a house on the water."

Sharing confidences might encourage Leah to talk. Sipping her drink, she waited for the woman's response.

"Kim had been his secretary, you know. I popped into the office one day and caught them doing it on Stan's desk. My dreams for the future evaporated in that instant."

"How so?" Marla leaned forward.

Leah averted her gaze. "I'd always wanted to be a stay-at-home mom. College was just a means to an end for me. I didn't expect to work the rest of my life. Stan and I were a good match. He handled our finances, made the major decisions. I didn't want to manage those details, so I was glad he took charge."

"You complemented each other," Marla said. It hadn't been that way between her and Stan. When she'd met him, it was just after Tammy's death. Marla had been a nineteen-year-old babysitter when the toddler she was watching drowned in a backyard swimming pool. She'd panicked when the girl's parents threatened to press charges. Stan was a member of the law firm Marla had consulted. Her vulnerability appealed to his need for dominance, and they'd been attracted to each other like positive and negative ions.

Rising from a pit of self-recrimination, Marla strove to prove herself a worthy individual. That wasn't possible under Stan's demeaning influence. She'd found redemption by attending cosmetology school, opening her own salon, and working for the child-drowning-prevention coalition. As she regained self-esteem, Stan's dictates lost their power to sway her.

"The best thing I ever did was to leave Stan," she confessed, placing her empty wineglass on a table. "It must've been terribly difficult for you, especially with the children."

Leah, who'd been lost in her own memories, lifted eyes blazing with animosity. "I hated Kimberly. That bitch stole my husband and ruined our marriage. Life will never be the same."

"I think Stan is telling the truth. He said the front door was unlocked, and Kim might have let in someone she knew. Do you have any idea who might have had reason to kill her?"

Leah's mouth curved in a wicked grin. "Other than me? Her death leaves my children as Stan's main beneficiaries. If he doesn't remarry, that is."

Marla snorted. "Ha, I wouldn't count on it. Stan's an easy one to criticize others, but he doesn't recognize his own failings. If you ask me, I think he's afraid to admit he's growing older. You'll see, he'll shack up with someone younger than Kimberly next."

"He'd better not! Stan visits the children once a month," Leah said, answering Marla's earlier question. "He tells them about adventure trips he's taken: white-water rafting, hiking the Appalachian Trail, skiing in the Alps. We should have had the money he spent on those extravagances!"

"So the man likes to live dangerously."

"He holds on to his youth, like you said. My kids need a father who is around for them. If not for Kimberly—" Her voice cracked, and she halted.

"It takes two people to tango," Marla said quietly. "Stan let himself be seduced. If not Kimberly, another woman might have come along."

"Maybe so, but I still blame her. A decent woman wouldn't get involved with a married man." A triumphant gleam entered her eyes. "Kim got what she deserved."

"Did you ever meet any of Kim's family?" Marla relaxed against the upholstery, feeling light-headed from the wine. Food would be welcome, she thought to herself, salivating at the aroma of cooking onions and peppers.

Leah finished her drink and put her glass next to Marla's. Rising, she stretched. "I heard they were wealthy, but I never encountered her relatives. Why would I?"

Marla shrugged, then rose to face Leah's shorter figure. "I told Stan I'd ask around to learn if someone had a motive."

Leah propped her hands on her hips. "Wait a minute, how do you know all this if Stan was arrested?"

"He called me, and I went to the station. I was allowed to see him in his cell. I'd helped the police with a couple of cases before," she added for an explanation.

"So I'm the first person you chose to interview?" Leah's brows furrowed angrily.

"You and I were closest to him, Leah. I felt I should tell you about Kim's death."

"Does Stan feel I had anything to do with it?"

"No, of course not. He doesn't even know I'm here."

Leah glared at her. "I'm not sure if I should be grateful or upset by your visit."

"I was hoping you could help me."

Leah edged toward the door, signaling an end to their conversation. "You might want to talk to Gary Waterford. He was dating Kim when she took up with Stan. Gary wasn't happy that she chose to leave him for richer prospects. I think he runs an air-conditioning business down in Dania."

"Okay, thanks."

A loud shriek came from the back of the house followed by a crash and a prolonged wail.

Leah's jaw tightened. "Now what?"

"You've got enough to keep you busy," Marla commented. "I appreciate your taking the time to see me."

Leah swung open the front door and gave her an appraising glance. "Yeah, well, Kim couldn't have chosen a more convenient time to die."

"Huh?" Marla stepped over the threshold.

"Never mind. Kindly give Stan my regards and tell him to come see the kids when he gets out of the clinker."

"Sure. Please say good-bye to the children for me." Her gaze shifted inadvertently. "And if you have some free time, drop by my salon. I'll give you a complementary cut."

On the way home, she reviewed their dialogue. All she'd learned was that Leah hated Kimberly for the woman's intrusion into her idyllic life. Leah and Stan had been perfectly suited for each other. Too bad Stan's inadequacies had kept him from recognizing that fact. Apparently, his will named their children as his beneficiaries after Kim. How convenient for Leah that Kim had dropped out of the picture. As for Leah's last remark, maybe that's what she meant.

Marla would have to talk to Gary Waterford another day. Spooks was home waiting for her to let him outside, plus she was hungry. Stan had promised to call tomorrow regarding the nurse's aide position, assuming his arraignment took place as expected. So there was nothing more she could do about this affair tonight. Today had been an emotionally exhausting episode. She needed to recover her equilibrium before showing up for work in the morning.

Spooks greeted her with wild barking. She stroked the poodle's cream-colored hair until he calmed, then she let him outside. Her meal consisted of a heated meat-loaf dinner in front of the TV. Newscasters made brief mention of the murder in East Fort Lauderdale of a prominent attorney's wife. Stanley Kaufman had been detained by the police for questioning, although he claimed an intruder was responsible. Marla cringed when his name was mentioned, imagining the smear on his reputation. Unpleasant memories surfaced of her own ordeal after Tammy drowned, and she vowed to help clear his name.

Deciding to do the dishes later, Marla let Spooks back inside before calling her mother. Anita lived in a housing development about fifteen minutes away.

"What kind of *mishigas* is this?" Anita cried when Marla revealed Stan's plan. "Like you don't have enough to do? You're *meshuga* if you get involved with such an idiotic scheme. Stan must be off his rocker."

"I've never seen him so upset, Ma," she said, repeating what she'd told Vail. "Stanley sure as hell wasn't so bothered when I left him!"

Anita clicked her tongue. "You weren't very nice to him at the time, if I recall."

"Nice! All he did was put me down and tell me how much I needed him. He didn't want me to succeed on my own. If it weren't for Tally, I'd never have had faith in myself to go back to school."

"Your best friend is a jewel, but she might have steered you back to college."

"Two years of undergraduate studies was enough for me to see that wasn't my calling. You wanted me to be a teacher. After what happened to Tammy, working with children was the furthest thing from my mind. I love being a hairdresser and making people feel good about themselves. Anyway, this is an old discussion."

"Maybe Stan is hoping to rekindle your romance."

Marla laughed aloud. "Heck, Ma, he's just using me."

"So why are you getting involved? Won't your detective friend disapprove?"

She shifted her position. "He would if he knew about it."

"You know, I'm starting to like him. He was quite charming when we met at Taste of the World. When am I going to meet his daughter?"

"At her dance recital this spring, remember? I bought you a ticket since you like ballet."

"Oh yes." A moment of silence. "I got the impression things were getting more serious between you."

Marla imagined her mother sitting at the kitchen table in her two-bedroom house, touching up her red fingernail polish. "I haven't gone out with anyone else lately, if that's what you mean."

"What about your other male friends? I know Arnie Hartman is still seeing Jill. He's quite smitten by her. You missed a good chance there, you know. Arnie has a good business with Bagel Busters, and it's in the same shopping strip as your salon."

"I love Arnie, but he'll never be more than a dear friend. As for

Ralph, he quit working at the body shop and went back to school full time. Besides, he got himself a live-in girlfriend."

"What about Lance, the computer expert?"

"We keep in touch."

"Well, then, Marla, you should move ahead in your relationship with Dalton Vail. If I were you, I'd tell him about Stan's scheme before you fall flat on your face. Trust is an important issue between two people who care about each other."

"He shares his insights with Brianna, not me."

"You told me his twelve-year-old daughter is sharp for her age. They must be very close since his wife died."

"So where do I fit in?"

"You're not family, *bubula*. And he's not really supposed to talk about his cases."

"If I tell Dalton about the nurse's aide job, he'll forbid me to get involved. I hate how he tries to control my actions like Stanley did."

"For heaven's sake, Vail is not the same type of man! He respects your accomplishments. He's afraid for you, that's all. You should be glad he has a protective nature." Her voice lowered. "It's special when you meet a man who admires you and wants to keep you safe."

She'd never heard that peculiar tone in her mother's voice before. "Ma, what are you saying?"

"Just that I understand."

"No, there's something more here. What's going on?" A memory jolted her. "Didn't you say a while ago that you had news to tell me?"

"Look, I gotta go. Ethel is at the door. Tonight is our Hadassah meeting to plan the regional education day."

"Wait, Ma," Marla said but broke off when she heard the click on the other end of the line. Darn, why did she get the feeling Ma was hiding something from her? Would Michael know anything about it? She dialed her brother's number in Boca Raton, but no one answered. His family must be out to dinner. Ask Cousin Cynthia to find out the scoop? No time. Besides, now someone was knocking on *her* door.

"Who is it?" she called from the foyer.

Spooks yipped in the hallway, but his lack of frantic barking told her it was no stranger.

"It's Moss. Are you decent, mate?"

"Of course." She swung the door wide to smile at her elderly neighbor. "Is Emma okay?" she asked about his wife, instantly concerned.

The white-haired gent nodded, his seafaring cap bobbing on his head. "I wrote a new limerick and wanted you to take a look before I add it to my collection."

Marla took the paper from his hand and gestured for him to enter. "Have you submitted your poems yet like I suggested?"

Moss shuffled his feet. A wiry fellow, he had leathery skin from so many years in the sun. "I'm waiting until there are enough verses for a book. But I still go to that writing group at Barnes & Noble. Emma comes with me, says it gets her out of the house."

Marla nodded wisely, suspecting Emma's excuse was her means of encouraging Moss to show his literary efforts to other writers. Her gaze drifted to the paper, and she read aloud:

I went with my wife to the store
We bought veggies, fruits, and more
Until I glanced at the prices
And said we have a crisis
We need to start keeping score

"Tell me about it," Marla remarked. "This sounds like good advice for everyone. It seems as though my grocery bill rises each time I go to the supermarket."

The old geezer chuckled. "Maybe you should stop buying those gourmet baked treats for your pooch."

"Holy highlights, I should say not! Spooks deserves them. He's home alone all day waiting for me to return from work. It's worth the extra cost." She handed Moss back his paper. "This is super. Show it to your writing buddies."

Beaming with pleasure, Moss took his precious page and left

Marla with a smile on her face. After cleaning the dishes, she phoned her best friend, Tally, who'd left a message on the answering machine.

"Marla Shore, what kind of a mess did your ex-husband land in? I saw the report on the news."

Seated at her desk in the study, Marla rolled her eyes. *Here we go again*, she thought resignedly, then proceeded to tell Tally everything, including her plans to go undercover.

"Wow, that sounds like fun. A fancy estate on the east side of town, huh? Can I come, too? Maybe they need an extra maid on Sundays. I'm a whiz at dusting!"

"I don't think Ken would be happy if you were gone all day." Her stomach full, Marla felt like crawling onto the couch with the newest copy of *Modern Salon*. Tally wasn't about to let her off so easily, though.

"You'll need references if you apply for the job. Give them my name. I'll say you take care of my mother during the week. They don't have to know Mom lives in New Jersey."

"I could always consult Jillian for acting lessons," Marla commented wryly.

Tally laughed, an infectious peal. "After your pretend engagement to Arnie, I don't think you need lessons from anyone! Have you told Dalton?"

"No, I haven't. Arnie and Jill are meeting us for dinner a week from Wednesday for my birthday. Maybe I'll bring it up then, but only if I get accepted for the position." She waited to see if Tally would mention her birthday. They hadn't made plans together yet, and Tally usually treated her to lunch.

"Is it Valentine's Day already next week? Oh, my. How time flies. Well, let me know what happens after Stan calls you tomorrow. Bye!"

Marla stared at the dead receiver in her hand. Was it her imagination, or did Tally sound a bit breathless? Paranoia might be afflicting her, but she sensed Vail and her mother weren't the only ones with something cooking on the back burner.

Chapter
Three

At work on Tuesday morning in the Cut 'N Dye Salon, Marla was subject to curious stares from her staff, who'd seen the local news reports. She had no choice but to describe her visit to Stan in the city jail. Sometime during today's full schedule, she hoped to squeeze in a phone call to Gary Waterford, Kim's former flame.

At the station on Marla's left, Nicole Johnson teased a client's hair. "So Stan is supposed to be released today?" Her ebony ponytail bobbed with her movements. The sleek stylist's gaze glowed with the same warmth as her cinnamon skin.

Marla paused, curling iron in hand. "That's assuming he gets an arraignment with a judge who sets bond."

She glanced at her client, Babs Winrow. The woman had shared secrets with Marla in the past, and Marla instinctively knew Babs could be trusted.

"Stan wants me to sound out Kim's relatives regarding possible motives," she confided in a low tone. "He thinks Kimberly might have been murdered for her inheritance. I'll tell you, it nearly bowled me over when Stan asked for my help."

"Why wouldn't the man consult you?" Babs said, snickering. "You're better at solving murders than the cops. Thanks to your efforts, Ben Kline's killer is behind bars. After Ben got his head bashed in, all of us on Ocean Guard's board of directors were under suspicion. Not only did you save our fund-raiser, but you also cleared our slate. Detective Vail should be glad you're on his side! What does he say about your involvement with your ex-spouse? Don't you have a thing going with him?"

Marla's face flushed, and she resumed curling Babs's blond hair. "We see each other occasionally. I wouldn't say either of us is committed. We're just getting to know each other better."

Liar. What would you call that little scene in his office? Kissing the friendly officer?

"Dalton hopes Stan will confess his guilt to me," she continued. "He won't be thrilled if he finds out what Stan proposed."

"What's that?" Nicole asked, leaning in her direction. "I get the distinct impression that you're about to plunge into hot water again. Wasn't it enough when Jolene drowned in that whirlpool last month?"

Marla gripped the curling rod tightly. "I owe it to Stan. He was there when I needed him."

"Girlfriend, he never lets you forget it. Now spill the beans. What does that louse want you to do?"

"Marla, another applicant is here," Giorgio announced. The handsome Italian stylist waved toward the front desk.

"Give me ten minutes," Marla sang out, hastening to finish Babs's coiffeur. She'd confide her plans to Nicole later, when they had a moment alone.

The salon was short several staff members, since Miloki had left to open her own place, taking along their shampoo assistant, manicurist, and another stylist. Marla still had to find a permanent staffer for the front desk, and now she had the added burden of interviewing for skilled professionals. Sighing, she put down her implements on the counter and accompanied Babs toward the front. Facing the plate-glass window was a seating arrangement with six chairs and a table that held a platter of bagels and cream cheese with chives.

Marla spotted a man hunched by the coffee machine and walked over to introduce herself. "Hi, I'm Marla Shore, salon owner. How can I help you?"

He straightened, and she took a step back after having a clear glimpse of him. The man was a better applicator of makeup than she. Even with the embellishments, his skin had a sickly gray pallor made worse by overly bleached hair with the consistency of straw. She resisted the urge to wrinkle her nose and instead plastered a polite smile on her face.

"I'm, like, applying for the job." He pointed to his scrawny chest encased in a stained T-shirt. "Call me Joe."

"Which job? We have three openings." She couldn't imagine him in any of the positions.

"For the stylist. That pays the most, don't it?" His watery blue eyes peered at her in a manner that made her uneasy.

"How long have you been doing hair?" she asked, skepticism creeping into her tone. She ignored his remark about money.

"Like three years, baby."

Marla bristled. "Are you licensed?"

He glanced away briefly. "Sure I am."

"Are you working somewhere else?"

"Yeah, but it's not cool. I need to find new digs."

"Are you flexible about hours? We need someone for Thursdays from one until seven since we're open late that day; Fridays from nine to five, and all day Saturday."

He shifted his feet. "Can't do Saturday. That's when I meet my buddies at Culver Beach."

She compressed her lips. "Well, I'm still interviewing other applicants. If you'll write down your name, phone number, and where you're currently employed, I'll get back to you by the end of the week."

As soon as he left, she felt as though fresh air swept through the salon. "What is it?" she asked Giorgio, who was doubled over.

"Culver Beach," the gay hairdresser said between fits of laughter. "That's where you bathe nude. It's down near Hallandale."

Marla rolled her eyes. "Just out of curiosity, I'll call that place where he works now. I have another phone call to make anyway." She had a few spare minutes before her next customer arrived.

Inside the storeroom, she lifted a telephone extension and dialed the phone number Joe the applicant had given her.

"Manny's Dry Cleaning," intoned a bored female voice.

Marla hung up, her curiosity satisfied. The man named Joe had lied to her. Scratch him from the list. She'd looked up Gary Waterford's home number in the phone book last night, so now she punched in the code and waited anxiously while listening to a ringing tone. No one answered. *Of course not, he's probably at work.* Didn't Leah say Gary owned an air-conditioning business in Dania? She pulled out the Yellow Pages. Several places were listed. She'd have to call each one and ask for Waterford.

"Marla, Andrea is here!" called Giorgio's voice.

"Okay, I'm coming."

Hours passed before she was able to conduct further research. At five o'clock Marla was finally free. Her last client had canceled, and she was finished for the day. She had meant to catch up on ordering supplies and dealing with the leak in the laundry room, but those chores were shuffled aside when Stanley Kaufman strode through the front door of her salon.

"Marla!" he cried, marching purposefully toward her. From his moist hair, clean-shaven jaw, and freshly laundered shirt, she could tell he'd gone home and showered.

"What are you doing here?" she demanded. Stan had never set foot in Cut 'N Dye before.

He planted himself in front of her, oblivious to the sudden hushed silence in the room. His intent gaze bored into hers. "We need to talk. I have information for you."

Oh, yeah. The nurse's aide position. Conscious of her staff's attention, she gestured to him. "I'm done here. Let me get my purse from the back room, then I'll join you. Nicole, would you mind locking up?"

Nicole's bright grin made her jaw clench. By now, her staff regarded Marla as a source of ongoing entertainment. Last month it was her fake engagement to Arnie. Before that, she'd had a relationship with a killer. Now Stan complicated matters. All she needed was for Vail to walk through the door!

Be careful what you wish for, girl.

In the storeroom, she scribbled down the phone numbers for the different air-conditioning businesses in Dania and added Waterford's home number. She'd reach him either way, unless Stan wanted her to call off the hunt. Maybe that's why he was here. Marla felt a brief stab of disappointment. She hadn't realized how much she'd anticipated another challenge.

"Want to grab something to eat?" she asked him once they were outside. The cold air hit her like a freezer blast, and she buttoned her brown suede jacket, wishing she'd brought a scarf. The weak afternoon sun added little warmth. Darkness would come swiftly. She'd prefer to be home by then, and Spooks needed to go out. Hopefully, they'd make this fast.

"Nice salon you set up for yourself with my money," Stanley remarked, brushing a piece of imaginary lint off his shirt. The cold temperature didn't seem to bother him, probably because he was so full of hot air.

"Thanks to our divorce settlement," Marla retorted, "I was able to achieve something worthwhile in my life, which is more than I can say for our marriage."

"That's your fault. You should've been happy being married to a rich attorney. I gave you everything you wanted."

"You didn't give me respect. You made me feel I owed everything to you, which I did at the start. That's the only reason I'm helping you now. But you refused to let me grow when I needed to become someone better. It's clear you never truly understood me."

A pained expression entered his hazel eyes. "Yes I did, babe. And I still do. You're trying to erase your guilt over Tammy's death. If you'd have been a proper wife, you might have redeemed yourself by giving me a family."

"Leah gave you a family, and where did it leave her? You let that woman seduce you."

His face purpled. "Don't speak of Kimberly in that manner."

"She used you, Stan, just as you use everyone to satisfy your ego." Uncertain if she still wanted to help Stan, she decided to hear what he had to say before making any hasty decisions. "Shall we go to Bagel Busters?" she snapped. Arnie Hartman, the proprietor, was a special friend. She relied on his concern in times of trouble. *So how come I let him act protective, but I can't tolerate that attitude in Dalton Vail?*

"Good enough for me," Stanley muttered. Taking her elbow, he meant to steer her in that direction, but she shook him off. "My God, you're touchy." The look he gave her could have shriveled a snake.

"Keep your hands off me." How had she ever let him talk her into this? The schmuck didn't deserve her attention. Maybe she should charge him a consulting fee.

The idea lurked in the back of her mind while she took a seat opposite him in the deli. "Is Arnie here?" she asked Ruth, a waitress.

The older woman smiled. "Sorry, honey. He ran off to pick up Jill from work. She had to get her tires changed."

A strange sense of abandonment claimed her. How dare Arnie desert her in this hour of need! He'd been spending much of his free time in Jill's company lately, she realized with a twinge of jealousy. Well, that had been her choice. Despite Arnie's urging to the contrary and their false engagement, Marla hadn't wanted their relationship to progress beyond friendship.

She ordered a full meal, intending to milk Stan for a free dinner. "So what's this information you have to share?" she asked him after Ruth left to get their drinks.

Folding his hands on the table, he leaned forward. A lock of black hair fell across his brow.

"I spoke to Stella, Kim's mother. We were discussing Kim's funeral, and I asked about the nurse's aide position. They're still interviewing people and haven't found anyone satisfactory."

"Tally said I could use her for a reference, pretend I'm working for her mother during the week. I feel guilty about lying, though."

"How do you think undercover cops conduct investigations? You're helping to find a murderer."

Marla tucked a strand of hair behind her ear. "Why are you so convinced one of Kim's family is guilty?"

"A lot of money is involved. A lot. Kim and I made a prenuptial agreement. In the event anything happened to her, Kim's family retains her share of Grandpa Harris's trust fund, although I think the trust itself is set up that way."

"What if something happened to you first?"

He regarded her with a steady gaze. "My kids inherit my savings and pension funds. I'm not a total nudnik, Marla. I take care of my own. If you had let me—"

"Let's not go down that road again." She slouched back when Ruth brought their beverages. Just what she needed. A cup of hot coffee would revive her brain for a few more hours. Taking her time, she added cream and sugar while contemplating what to ask Stan next.

"How do I get an interview for the job?" she asked after sipping the strong brew.

"Here's their phone number." Stan gave her a piece of paper. "The old lady rules the nest, but she's grown feeble. Florence, her eldest daughter, is the one who interviews prospective employees, so ask for her when you call. God, I can't stand how those sisters bicker constantly. When Florence and Stella are together in the same room, it can drive you nuts."

"Why is that?"

He shrugged. "Stella dabbles in craft projects, which Florence thinks are frivolous wastes of time. Florence is hung up on society functions. The two of them don't see eye to eye on anything. Then there's the other reason they don't get along." Leaning forward, he lowered his voice. "Florence was in love with the man who became Stella's husband."

"Really?"

To her disappointment, he didn't elaborate. "Their brother, Morris, lives at the complex with his wife and sons, but he's engrossed in the family business. None of them ever approved of me because I earned my way up the rungs instead of being born into wealth. They're a bunch of snobs."

"How delightful," Marla murmured.

Their meals arrived, and she ate her corned beef sandwich in silence, savoring the greasy potato latkes that accompanied the dish.

Stan played with his roast beef, cutting the meat into fine pieces and pushing them around on his plate. He didn't eat with his usual gusto, reminding Marla that he was in mourning.

A surge of sympathy engulfed her, but she steeled herself against it. "How about our agreement?" she said, putting down her fork. "I want proof that you'll sell me your half of our rental property."

A grimace crossed his features. "I figured you'd bring that up. Always interested in serving your needs first, aren't you?"

"I can say the same thing about you." Grabbing her mug, she accidentally sloshed a dribble of coffee on her blouse. Heat flushed her face while she mopped the spill with her napkin. Hearing a rustle of papers, she glanced up.

"My partners prepared these documents. I suppose you'll want your attorney to look them over."

Marla's eyes widened as she scanned the contents. "This is highway robbery! What kind of a schlemiel do you think I am? I can't afford to pay that much!"

Stan sneered. "My price goes along with the property appraisal. You want to call off the deal, it's fine with me. In fact, I'll pay you that amount for your share. Just think what you can do with the money: buy your car when the lease expires; pay off the mortgage on your townhouse. What do you say?" He stuffed a piece of buttered roll into his mouth.

Marla slammed her hand on the table, not caring that several patrons glanced at her in disapproval. "I say, *dershtikt zolstu veren!*" You should choke on it.

"Tch, tch. Not nice, Marla."

"If you want my help, you'd better play nice with me. This cost is too high."

Her resolve must have shone through her expression, because he grunted resignedly. "Very well, I'll give you a discount, but you have to earn it."

She pushed away her plate, no longer hungry. "Consider it my retainer fee as your private investigator. I want new papers delivered tomorrow. I won't trust you until you sign them."

"Hey, you think I'm stupid? I'm not signing anything until you turn in Kim's killer to Detective Vail." His wily gaze penetrated hers. "Let me amend that statement. I'll sign, but with an option to cancel within thirty days. If you don't bring in a suspect by then, our deal is off."

"Thirty days? Ha! A piece of cake."

Like a punctured balloon, his expression deflated. "Kim made the best chocolate cakes. The best. I can't believe she won't be bustling around the kitchen anymore."

"I'm sorry, Stan." Her anger evaporated in the face of his grief.

A flicker of something else flashed behind his eyes. "Yeah, well, in one way you could say she got what she wanted."

"What does that mean?"

He pursed his lips. "A bird who tries to fly with clipped wings ends up on the ground."

"Excuse me? I'm not following your train of thought."

"Never mind." He shook himself, as though mentally resurfacing. "Let me know what happens when you contact the Pearls. Kim's funeral is set for Thursday. Her family will sit *shivah* afterward at their place. I'll be receiving visitors for the required three days at my house. That includes the day of the funeral, according to my rabbi. So don't expect to be interviewed for the job until Sunday at the earliest."

"That works for me. Oh, I told Leah what happened. She'd like you to stop in and see the kids."

"Thanks, Marla. For everything." Rising, he threw some dollar bills on the table and waited while she pulled on her jacket. At the cash register, he paid their check.

"That was a simple meal," he said to her outside in the parking lot. "It was almost like old times, sitting across from you at the dinner table."

"If I recall, you preferred places with a dress code. But you're right; after things went bad between us, we argued our way through every meal just like tonight. I'll be seeing you, Stan."

"Wait a minute, let's say a proper good-bye." Taking her elbow, he directed her toward a darkened corner. "It's your birthday next week, and I want to give you an early present for being so helpful."

He drew her close before she realized what he intended and kissed her full on the lips. Marla was so astonished that she didn't pull back. He must have taken that as encouragement because he deepened the kiss, arousing memories she'd rather forget. Once upon a time, she'd craved his touch. Now it merely reminded her of past mistakes. She tolerated his embrace only because part of her wanted to comfort him, knowing he ached inside with grief. Maybe a passionate kiss was his way to reaffirm life in the face of death.

No, this wasn't right. While one arm tightened around her, his other hand snaked to her breast. What was the man doing? Bracing herself to push away, she froze when heavy footfalls sounded from behind.

"Here you are," Dalton Vail announced. "I've been looking for you."

Whirling around, Marla swallowed at the grim expression on his face. Behind her, Stan cleared his throat.

"Which one of us do you mean?" Stan demanded with a hint of bravado.

"I wanted Marla, but maybe you're staking a prior claim?"

Marla glanced from one to the other, feeling as though they stood on a battlefield. Stan returned her glance, his eyes speculative. Surely he didn't believe she still felt some attraction toward him? Her gaze swung to Vail, who'd traded his signature suit for jeans, a flannel shirt, and a black leather jacket. His mood appeared as dark as a level-one hair color.

Stan raised his hands. "I ended my claims long ago, unless Marla's had a change of heart. I think she knows what she's been missing. Or does she get it from you?"

"That's none of your business," Vail grated.

His fist clenched, and Marla feared they'd come to blows. But the detective reined his temper, no doubt saving it to take out on her later.

"Well, I was just leaving," Stan said, backing away. "Bye, Marla."

"What's going on between you and Kaufman?" Vail demanded after Stan's car squealed from the parking lot.

Marla shivered in the cool night air. "It was a friendly kiss. He didn't mean anything special by it."

"The two of you seemed pretty snug."

"That's because he surprised me. Don't worry, Stan doesn't affect me the way you, er, I mean . . ." She moistened her lips, aware he watched every movement. "S-Stanley is grateful because I'm helping him out."

"Really?" His tone held a dangerous edge. "I'll drive you home, and then you can tell me all about it."

Chapter Four

"It wouldn't be a good idea for you to come to my house," Marla said after she'd unlocked her car door.

"Why not?" A beam of light from a street lamp shimmered on the silvery highlights of Vail's dark hair.

Marla's breath came short at his nearness. Facing him, she leaned against her car, the driver's door unopened. "You're working on a case that involves me. It isn't smart to mix business with pleasure."

"Is that what we're doing?" He lifted his arms to pin her in place against the vehicle's metal body.

"You're too close, Dalton."

"Am I?" He nuzzled her neck, inhaling as though he enjoyed her scent.

"I intend to prove Stan is innocent."

That jolted him. Abruptly, he stepped back. "Just what is it you've agreed to do for him?"

She drew in a deep breath. Trust had to begin somewhere, didn't it? "Kimberly's grandmother employs a daily nurse. The woman needs a day off, so Stan said I should apply for the position of health aide on Sundays. It shouldn't be so hard to look after an old lady for one day. Stan believes one of Kim's family members might have bumped her off to gain her inheritance since they had a prenuptial agreement. I'm supposed to snoop around the estate. In return, Stan will sell me his half of our jointly owned property."

"Hmm. Having an insider there could prove useful."

"You mean you're not angry?" An imaginary weight lifted off her shoulders.

"Would it stop you if I disapproved of this masquerade?"

"Not really."

"I still think Stan has his own motive and is trying to throw us off track."

"Undoubtedly you'll be investigating that angle." She couldn't believe his easy acceptance. "What do you say we exchange information?"

"Sure."

She tugged on her skirt. "You've never been so agreeable before. You're always warning me to stay away from your cases."

His eyebrows raised. "Marla, you advised me at Taste of the World that I have to let you take risks. That goes for our relationship, too. I won't be able to tell you everything, but I'm sure you know that."

"Yes, I do."

"Good. I'll interview Kim's friends and neighbors, in addition to the relatives. Let me know if you get the job caring for her grandmother."

"I will." She hesitated. "Good night, Dalton. Someday soon I'd like to cook dinner for you and Brianna."

"Sounds great." He gave her a quick peck on the mouth, nothing like the hot kisses she'd anticipated.

Just as well, Marla thought during the drive home. Why start something they couldn't finish, at least not now? Too many issues still divided them, and while part of her wondered what might have happened tonight if she'd accepted Dalton's company, putting off that scenario presented a more comfortable option.

Friday rolled around before Marla could think about Stan and his problems again. Two quick phone calls set her weekend schedule.

She arranged for a job interview with Florence Pearl on Sunday morning. Meanwhile, Gary Waterford agreed to meet her at his workplace around six o'clock.

She located Waterford's Air-Conditioning Emporium in downtown Dania, past the antique district and a few doors from Jaxson's Ice Cream Parlor on South Federal Highway. Fortunately, the street wasn't crowded for a late Friday afternoon, and she found a parking space with little effort.

Wearing a tangerine sweater and black corduroy slacks, she strolled along the sidewalk, casting a longing glance at the restaurant. Maybe she'd run in there later for a quick meal. Established in 1956, Jaxson's had the best foot-long kosher hot dogs with grilled onions. And don't mention the homemade ice cream! Visions of a hot fudge sundae with coffee ice cream and mounds of whipped cream swirled through her mind. Why worry about a few extra calories? This counted as walking exercise, right?

All thoughts of food vanished when she pushed open the door to Waterford's business. A chemical odor like burning wires entered her nostrils. Wrinkling her nose, she surveyed the display of mechanical parts lying haphazardly on the grimy floor.

"Yo, how ya doin'?" drawled a lanky young man behind the counter. He pushed aside a section of newspaper he'd been studying and gave her a blatantly admiring glance.

"I'm looking for Gary Waterford," she said, shifting her handbag strap to the other shoulder.

"That's me." He smiled, revealing a row of uneven white teeth that would benefit from braces.

Marla appraised him. Bleached blond hair covered dark roots in an unkempt style that needed a couple of inches snipped off the ends. Stubble on his square jaw was either a permanent fixture or else he hadn't bothered to shave. She dropped her gaze to his sweatshirt and well-laundered jeans. Combined with the grease stains on his rough-hewn hands, his manner suited a laborer more than a desk jockey. Was this why he had appealed to Kim? His primal aura of raw masculinity would have been a direct contrast to her willowy beauty.

"How can I help you?" Waterford said.

She fumbled for a way to begin. "I'm Marla Shore, and I've come to talk about a former friend of yours."

"Who's that?" The look he gave her implied they couldn't possibly share a common acquaintance.

"Kimberly Kaufman. I understand you knew her before she married."

"Yep, that's right."

"You were dating her, I believe?"

"That's my business, lady. Who sent you here?"

"Leah Kaufman. She was Stan's wife when Kim became involved with him."

"I remember. What's the matter? Is Kim all right?"

Darn, she'd hoped he already knew. This wouldn't be easy. "I, uh, have some bad news."

"Tell me!"

She fortified herself with a deep breath. "I'm so sorry; this may come as a shock. Kimberly passed away over the weekend. I thought you . . . someone might have told you."

His face drained, and he took a stumbling step backward. "I don't believe it."

Marla glanced away, imagining what it must be like for police officers who had to tell families tragic news on an ongoing basis. "She was killed. Stan asked me to talk to people who knew her. I visited Leah, and she gave me your name."

"Where the hell do you fit in?" His voice was angry, as though it were her fault that Kim had died.

She gave a small smile. "I was Stan's first wife. Look, I know you need time to assimilate this, but the police may come to question you. I thought I'd give you fair warning."

His eyes bulged, and he glanced briefly at the newspaper open on the counter. Marla sidled nearer, catching a glimpse of the page listing Gulfstream horse races before he snatched it out of sight. Being closer gave her the advantage of noticing peeling paint and an accumulation of grime. None of the parts on display appeared to be in prime condition, making her wonder if Waterford struggled to maintain his business. In South Florida, that didn't seem likely considering air conditioners were in constant need of repair. So why was Gary here instead of out in the field? Maybe he had other employees, or else he mismanaged his funds. That might account for the air of desperation she sensed from his nervous mannerisms and the decaying surroundings. One other possibility sprang to mind: this business served as a front for a more nefarious activity.

"I don't get it," he said, shaking his head. "Who would hurt Kim?"

"That's what I hope to find out. Do you know if she still maintained any of her old friendships?"

His gaze shifted uneasily. "How should I know?"

"Since you'd been so close, I thought you might have kept track of her."

"I haven't seen Kim since we broke up."

She pounced on the opportunity his words offered. "You must've been terribly upset when she left you."

His eyes blazed. "Sure, I was pissed. We were hot together, but I wasn't good enough for her. She chased after that fancy-pants lawyer who gave her all the things she wanted. Kim's grandpappy was rich, but her grandma holds the purse strings. Their money is all tied up in a trust. Kim was too impatient to wait for her share."

"So you admit Kim went after Stan with the intention of breaking up his marriage?"

Waterford lumbered to the other end of the counter, picked up a gauge, and attached it to a piece of machinery. "She had ambitions, and I wasn't part of 'em."

"So at what point did she tell you good-bye?"

"As soon as she got the job in his office. Kim planned to worm herself into his bed. I told her the guy sounded like a real tight-ass, but she laughed. With his ego, she felt it would be a breeze to seduce him, and then she'd be on easy street. But Kim was wrong." He paused, glancing at Marla. "She should've bailed out sooner."

Marla leaned against the counter. "What do you mean?"

"The bastard didn't treat her right. Kim didn't tell hardly anyone because she was afraid."

Her pulse accelerated. "Afraid of Stan?"

"You got it." His gaze narrowed suspiciously. "How did you say she was killed?"

"Stabbed to death," Marla said quietly. "Stan found her in their foyer early Monday morning."

Gary glared at her. "I hope she didn't tell him. I told her not to mention it because of what he might do."

"Mention what?"

"That she was—" He caught himself, stopping with a choking cough. "She was going to walk out on Kaufman," he finished, although Marla got the impression he'd been about to say something else.

"Kimberly was planning to leave Stan?" Now it was Marla's turn to stare. Could this be true? If so, how would Stan have reacted when he discovered his wife's intent? Or did he even know?

"I thought you hadn't seen Kim since she went to work in Stan's office, and that was nearly two years ago."

Waterford stiffened. "That's right. I wanted nothing more to do with her after she gave me the shaft. I, uh, heard about her from a mutual friend."

"Name?"

He hesitated, bouncing on his heels. "Look, don't tell no one I talked. Lacey Mills is her name. If you see her, you'd better not mention your visit here."

"Why?" Marla sensed undercurrents racing through their conversation, and tried to focus on them. *Bless my bones, I'm getting more like Dalton every day.* What happened to the trusting individual she used to be?

"Lacey likes me, and she'll get jealous if she knows we were talking about Kimberly."

"But Kim is dead." *And why would Lacey be jealous if you haven't seen Kimberly for two years, pal? Something doesn't ring true here.*

"Lacey and Kim were friends. You should tell Lacey what you've told me."

"Sure. Can you write down her phone number for me?"

He scribbled the woman's address, handing Marla a grease-stained paper. "Have there been any arrests?" he asked.

"Stan has been detained for questioning."

"Figures he'd do it, especially if he knew." His glance darted nervously toward the door. "You didn't tell him you were coming here, did you?"

"No, I didn't. You seem anxious."

"Kim told Lacey about his temper. Wouldn't want the man coming after me next!"

"Stan wants to find the person who killed his wife, that's all. I promised to help him."

"Good luck. You may not have far to look."

As she left the shop, Marla hoped her faith in Stan was not misplaced. Doubts assailed her, not only about Stan, but also about her own motives for wanting to prove him innocent. She hadn't heard from him after their last encounter, but that was expected. Kim's funeral was Thursday, and he'd been sitting shivah since then.

Driving home from Dania, Marla felt an urge to confront Stan but resisted the impulse to stop at his house. If any of Kim's relatives were there, she'd ruin her cover story before getting the chance to present it.

Opportunity arrived on Sunday morning when she went for the interview with Florence Pearl. Kim's family lived in a reclusive compound located in an older section of East Fort Lauderdale. After finding a mailbox with the address, Marla turned down a heavily wooded road. She arrived at a circular driveway curving in front of a two-story mansion of antebellum motif. Painted white, with tall columns, the house featured a wraparound brick porch; wide, curtained windows; and mahogany doors. A separate guest cottage stood off to the side along with two garages, each holding four bays. Live oaks, sea grapes, and Queen palms graced grounds enhanced by bougainvillea and hibiscus bushes.

Fragrance from a Hong Kong orchid tree reached her nostrils as she emerged from her Camry into the cool February air. After putting away her keys, she smoothed down her navy suit, hoping she looked adequately professional. Glimpsing her reflection in the car window, she checked her apricot lip gloss. Her hair remained softly curled inward at the ends.

Marching resolutely forward, she pushed the doorbell and listened to chimes cascading through the house. Barely moments later, the door swung wide, and a middle-aged man wearing a black sport coat and tie bid her to enter.

"You must be Miss Shore. I'm Raoul, one of the staff." He spoke with a clipped accent that she couldn't quite place. "Please follow me to the library. Your interview will take place there."

Marla followed his stately figure, her gaze inadvertently drawn to the bald spot on his head. *Sorry, not much I could do about that, unless you parted your hair on the other side where it's thicker.*

She shook herself mentally, remembering she wasn't here in her capacity as a hairdresser. *You're a nurse's aide,* she admonished herself silently. *You take care of old people for a living.* That was partially true, considering her elderly clientele. Young professionals mostly populated the area in Palm Haven where her salon was situated, but she took care of her share of senior citizens. That was why this shouldn't be such a tough job, assuming she was offered the position.

They entered a room lined with bookshelves stretching from a cherry inlaid floor to a bead-board and tray ceiling. Furnished with leather armchairs, a massive desk, and assorted lamp tables, the library had a cozy, warm atmosphere. It smelled like furniture polish, pine, and wood smoke, the latter coming from a fireplace blazing at the opposite end.

She'd just begun wondering why Florence had chosen this somber room instead of a sunny parlor to interview her when in stalked a tall, grave man dressed in a charcoal suit. He walked right up to her and stuck out his hand.

"I'm Morris Pearl. I understand you're applying for the job of taking care of my mother."

What happened to Florence? Gripping his palm, Marla prayed he didn't notice the perspiration beading her upper lip. "Er, yes, I heard you had an opening for Sundays when the regular nurse takes the day off."

Morris stepped back as a heavyset woman clomped into the room. "This is Agnes. She stayed this morning so she could help me assess your qualifications. Agnes has been caring for my mother Miriam for eight years."

Oh God. How could she deceive this woman, whose ocean blue eyes regarded her warily? "Nice to meet you," Marla murmured, assessing the newcomer. Agnes wore her prune-colored hair secured in a bun, the severe style accentuating her long nose. Guessing her age to be mid-fortyish, Marla mentally created a softer hairdo that would make her more attractive.

"You have references, I suppose," Agnes stated, her gaze flickering over Marla's suit. Her eyes narrowed, as though she wondered how an aide could afford such stylish attire.

"Of course." Marla had written out a skimpy résumé that showed her working in a friend's hair salon as a shampoo assistant before taking the false job with Tally's mother. It also mentioned her stint at Westside Regional Hospital where Marla had once volunteered to style hair for a charity event.

Agnes scanned the paper, then gave it to Morris, who seemed content to let the nurse handle the interview. He was more interested in examining Marla's legs. "Miriam requires help with her daily needs," the nurse explained. "Are you prepared to provide that level of care?"

"I'm well experienced at tending to the needs of elderly ladies," Marla answered confidently. "Besides physical care, patience and praise go a long way toward making my clients comfortable. I think you'll find my performance is highly satisfactory."

"Miriam can manage her meals, but she doesn't move well. Arthritis, you know. You'll have to help her shower and dress; take her in a wheelchair if she wants to go outside, read to her, and administer her medicines."

"No problem."

"Your salary requirements?" Morris demanded, his hooded gaze revealing nothing of his opinion.

Anticipating this question, Marla had consulted her mother, whose disabled friend had a full-time companion. "Ten dollars an

hour. That's less than you would pay an agency." She addressed
Agnes. "Did you have someone cover for you before on Sundays?"

"I've rarely taken time away from my duties. Miriam and I have a
close rapport, and she relies on me to look after her. Unfortunately,
urgent personal business requires my attention. You'll have to come
at eight in the morning and stay until eight at night on Sundays. I'll
be taking Wednesday evenings off, too, so we'll need you then as
well."

"I-I thought the job was just for Sundays," Marla stammered.

"If these hours are not convenient, this interview is over," Morris
snapped.

"I didn't mean to imply—"

"Can you or can you not accept these terms?"

"Well, yes," Marla said, her heart racing, "but I have another
obligation for this Wednesday. I didn't realize you'd be expecting
me then. Can we change the date for this week?"

"I suppose so," Agnes said grudgingly. "I don't dare leave Miriam
by herself."

Morris gestured. "You're forgetting that my sisters and I are here.
If you really need to take this Wednesday off, we'll watch over her."

"No, that's all right, sir. I'm just concerned that Miriam gets the
special attention she needs."

"We've had a death in the family," Morris explained to Marla, "so
things aren't well organized right now. Why don't we make it for
Thursday next week? We'll expect you to wear a white uniform
when you report for work."

Marla glanced at Agnes, who wore slacks and a pullover sweater.
Did that mean the nurse was already off-duty?

"You can run off now, Agnes," Morris said, answering Marla's
silent question. "Miss Shore will begin at once."

Marla nearly dropped her handbag on the floor. "Now? But I'm
not ready . . . I mean, this was just supposed to be an interview. I
thought you said you wanted me to start on Thursday."

"It doesn't matter that you're not in uniform today," Morris said.
"Come upstairs, and I'll introduce you to my mother."

"B-but what do I do? Agnes, aren't you going to instruct me?"

"I already did." Agnes paused. "Good luck, Miss Shore. May I call you Marla?"

"Of course."

The woman's gaze cooled. "A word of caution, Marla: Mrs. Pearl is a special lady, and I care deeply about her. See that you follow her orders explicitly. If she has any complaints, I'll hear about them. I may be an employee here, but I report directly to Miriam. She'll listen to me if I advise her to dismiss you."

Chapter
Five

Marla stood in the center of Miriam Pearl's bedchamber, staring at the shriveled woman lying in a queen-size canopy bed. After muttering a quick introduction, Morris had left her to her duties. The old lady peered at her with sharp black eyes, a diminutive figure among volumes of bedcovers.

Laying her purse on top of a dressing table, Marla approached the matriarch. "I'd like to get started. What shall we do first this morning?" she asked, wondering how old Miriam was and if she retained her wits.

"My glasses are on the nightstand," Miriam rasped. "Give them to me so I can see you better."

Marla complied, waiting patiently while Miriam inspected her. The collar of her suit itched in the stuffy, warm atmosphere. The heat must be turned up to eighty degrees, she thought, sucking in a dry breath of air.

"Nervous, are you? You're sweating," the old lady pointed out with a smirk.

"It's awfully hot in here. May I open the drapes and lower the thermostat? I think you'd be more comfortable."

"My body is thin. I'm always cold."

"Perhaps what you need is a hot bath. Did you have your breakfast yet?"

Miriam shook her head. "You have to call downstairs, dearie. Dial number eight on the phone, and ask for Kathleen. She'll bring it up. I take my pills with meals."

"Oh, right." Her responsibilities included administering medications. Unfortunately, the nurse had been in too much of a hurry to provide details.

A quick survey of the room revealed an absence of medicine bottles, so Marla headed for the lavatory, a spacious area nearly as big as her bedroom at home. *I'd spend hours in here if this were mine,* she thought enviously, admiring the sunken bath and separate glass-enclosed shower. A gleaming bidet caught her eye. Although it was the first she'd seen, her mother had described the European device.

She found the medicine containers lined up like soldiers on parade atop a marble vanity. Checking the labels, Marla frowned. They made no sense to her at all. She'd have to ask Miriam which ones she took in the morning.

She reentered the bedroom just as a middle-aged woman with silver-streaked auburn hair entered bearing a laden tray. She wore a maid's uniform, so Marla assumed this was Kathleen.

"Hi, I'm Marla Shore. I'll be taking care of Mrs. Pearl on Agnes's days off."

Kathleen grinned, her face transforming into an impish expression. "Aye, and it's a blessing to get a breath of fresh air in this place." She spoke with a pleasant lilt as she placed the tray on a portable table in front of Miriam.

"Would there be anything else you'll be needing now, madam?" Kathleen asked the old woman.

Miriam grimaced at the items on her food tray. "Not in here, but I noticed the silver on the sideboard downstairs needs polishing. See that you get to it today."

"Aye, madam." The maid exchanged glances with Marla, raising her eyebrows slightly as though to commiserate.

"Speaking of fresh air," Marla said after Kathleen had left, "let's brighten up this room. It's gloomy in here."

"Don't do that!" Miriam exclaimed when Marla drew apart the curtains. "The sunlight will fade the fabrics. Besides, we're in mourning." Her hand trembled as she lifted a spoonful of oatmeal to her lips.

"Here, let me help you." Marla rushed over to tuck a napkin under the woman's chin. "Mr. Pearl said you'd had a recent death in the family. I'm so sorry."

"My granddaughter Kimberly was murdered." Miriam stated it matter-of-factly, but an expression of pain crossed her wrinkled face.

"How horrible." Marla pulled up a chair, then proceeded to spread jam on a slice of whole wheat toast. The old lady set aside her spoon as though she'd lost her appetite. "Now listen, you have to eat in order to gain strength, Miriam. Tell me about your grand-daughter while you finish your cereal."

Miriam's expression hardened. "She was a beautiful girl, but fool-ish. I'd hoped to avoid the mistakes I made with my daughters, but it didn't work in her case. Kim didn't have a pragmatic bone in her body. If she hadn't rushed into marriage with that lawyer, she'd be alive today."

"Oh?"

Miriam squinted at her. "Talk to my daughter Stella. She'll tell you more."

"When was the last time you saw Kimberly?"

Miriam swallowed a spoonful of oatmeal Marla held to her lips. "It had been a while. We didn't get along too well."

"That's a shame."

"It's partially my fault. The girl was born with a silver spoon in her mouth, and she expected to breeze her way through life. I was afraid she'd become vapor-headed like my Stella." Glancing at the door, the old lady lowered her voice. "It's a good thing Morris has brains. He runs the family business and does a damn good job. Neither one of my girls is capable."

"I'd hoped to meet Florence today."

"She went to Stan's house to ask about getting back some family albums."

"Stan was Kimberly's husband?" Marla asked in an offhand man-ner.

Miriam nodded, taking a sip of tea. "Kim was excited about writing up our family genealogy. If only she could have put the same devotion into training for a career. I've insisted my grandchildren learn how to support themselves, because I won't have them ending up useless parasites like Stella and her sister. Kim wasn't too happy with me the last time I saw her alive." The old lady sniffled and pushed her tray away.

"You didn't eat enough," Marla chided, rising.

"I lost my appetite. Get me my pills. I take a diuretic, heart medicine, and blood thinner in the morning."

Marla entered the bathroom. Her confused glance surveyed the collection of containers. "Do you know the names of each medicine?" she called out.

"Bring them here." Miriam glared at her when she returned. "I thought you were a nurse even though you're not in proper uniform."

"I'm just an aide."

"Well, I can tell by the colors which ones I need. Open them up, and we'll see."

Marla struggled to twist open the childproof cap. When her first attempt failed, she squeezed harder. "Is it always this difficult?" she mumbled, feeling like a klutz.

"Oh, for God's sake. Don't you know anything? Morris!"

"Wait, I'll do it. Please don't summon your son." Gritting her teeth, she pushed down on the cap and jiggled the top until it loosened. A breath of relief escaped her lips. She managed to open the other containers, and they sorted out which pills Miriam had to take.

"Run my shower, dearie. There's a stool inside that I sit on. You'll have to scrub the parts I can't reach."

Bathing hour stretched into two while Marla fumbled to follow Miriam's instructions. At last the matriarch was dried and powdered. Escorting her into the adjacent room, Marla wiped a trickle of sweat from her neck. She could use a shower herself. Although she'd suggested giving Miriam a hair wash, the old lady had declined. Instead, she'd ordered Marla to use a pumice stone on her feet. Marla hadn't done a pedicure since training, and wearing a suit while leaning over in the steamy shower had been an ordeal she'd rather not repeat. Now she had a backache from the effort.

"Get me a clean nightshirt from my drawer," Miriam demanded, panting as she sat on the edge of her bed in a terry robe. Exertion had left her short of breath, and Marla feared harming her delicate state of health any further. Nonetheless, it wouldn't do the woman any good to lie in bed all day.

"How about putting on a slacks set? It should have warmed up outside by now. I'd like to take you out for some fresh air." Maybe she'd meet the other family members. One thing was certain: her investigation wouldn't get anywhere if they were confined to quarters.

"It's freezing out!" Miriam exclaimed. "Agnes said I'd catch pneumonia if I go outside in this weather."

"Oh, come on, we'll bundle you up. A change of scenery will be good for you."

"Who says? You can read to me until the news comes on TV."

"Listen, I'm in charge of you today, and we're at least going downstairs."

After dressing Miriam in warm clothing despite her protests, Marla fingered her thin hair. "You could use a soft perm, honey. Next time I come, we'll spruce you up. A couple of weeks later, we'll add a tint of color. It'll make you look ten years younger! Don't you ever visit with friends?"

Miriam gazed at her as though she were loony. "What friends? They're all gone. I'm just waiting to join them."

"No, you're not. You have spirit, Miriam. I'm surprised you're stuck in this room so much of the time."

"I may have my hearing, but I don't see so well. My bones ache, and it's only going to get worse. Agnes says I have to preserve my strength."

"Nonsense. You shouldn't stop living until you're dead."

"Like Kimberly?" The old woman's shoulders slumped.

"I'm sorry, that was a thoughtless remark." Remembering she'd seen a wheelchair in the hallway, Marla retrieved it. "Let's go. You can tell me where Kim grew up. Was she raised in this house?"

After easing herself into the chair with Marla's help, Miriam slouched back. "No, Stella lived in Palm Beach while her husband was alive. After he died, she sold their house and moved back here. Kimberly was already grown. She had an apartment and worked in various jobs instead of going to college like I urged her. She wanted the easy way out."

"Like a rich husband?" Marla wheeled the old lady into the hallway and toward an elevator at one end.

Miriam grunted. "Kim was hoping to hold out until she was thirty, when she became eligible for a percentage of her trust fund. She found a way out, all right: it just wasn't the one she'd expected."

"Wasn't she happy with Stan? He must have provided the kind of life she wanted."

"Why, did you know him?"

Whoops. "Er, no, I just assumed he was a wealthy man."

They emerged on the first floor, and further explanation became unnecessary as a woman bustled forward. She was an attractive lady in her mid-fifties who wore her hair in a short, layered style with a reddish brown tint. Her slacks set in royal blue and black gave her matronly figure a sleek look.

"Stella, this is Marla Shore. She's filling in for Agnes," Miriam said.

"Nice to meet you." Stella's cocoa eyes flickered briefly in Marla's direction. "I'm on my way to the club," she said to her mother. "We're adding the finishing touches to our centerpieces for today's luncheon."

"Your girl isn't in the ground for a week yet, and you're on your way out the door! How can you be so heartless?"

Stella's eyes misted. "I sat shivah for three days. Kimberly would want me to continue my work."

"Work!" Miriam shrilled. "You're a grown woman, and you still play at arts and crafts. If you want to work, go help Morris at the company."

"I'm not interested in confining myself to an office," Stella said, enunciating each word.

"You don't have the brains!"

"And you don't understand what I like to do! You never have, and you never will!"

Marla shifted uncomfortably, feeling like an unseen observer to an old argument. Was this how servants were regarded, as inanimate pieces of furniture?

"Focusing on other things will take my mind off Kimberly," Stella went on, standing ramrod stiff. "Until that man is behind bars again, there's little else I can do!"

"Do you believe Kim's husband is guilty?" Marla blurted.

Stella glared at her. "Have you been listening to our conversation?"

No, I'm just a doorpost. "Miriam is getting agitated. I'm in charge of her health while I'm here."

"Then tend to your duties and keep out of our family affairs. Bye, Mother. I'll be back in time for dinner." Whirling on her heel, she marched out the door.

Marla noticed the butler, who swung the door wide for her, had stood by like a statue during their dialogue.

"Idiots, all of them," Miriam muttered.

"What's that?" Marla asked, wheeling Miriam toward the front door. She nodded at the butler as they breezed past. A car was just turning into the circular driveway. Marla wouldn't mind calling that shiny red Mercedes her own.

"There's Florence." Miriam leaned forward, waving.

"Would you like to walk over?" Marla assisted the old lady up from the chair and supported her as they staggered toward the elegantly dressed blonde who'd emerged from the car. Stella, midway to the garage, did an about-face and headed toward them.

"Well? Did Stanley give you the albums?" Stella asked her older sister. Seeing them side by side, Marla noted Florence was a couple inches taller and more svelte than her sibling. She wore an expensive ivory silk suit with matching heels. Pearl accessories completed her ensemble.

"No, he insisted on keeping them. I told you he wouldn't be agreeable." She turned a wary glance on Marla. "Who is this?"

"This is Miss Shore," Miriam said, leaning heavily on Marla's arm. "She's taking over for Agnes on Sundays."

"Mother, you shouldn't be outside. It's too cold for you."

"I felt she needed some fresh air," Marla cut in. "Maybe a trip to the mall would appeal to her. It would be less windy."

Both women looked horrified at the idea, making Marla wonder if either of them ever took their mother anywhere.

"How are we going to get those albums from Stan?" Stella asked her sister. "I'd hoped to start working on them tomorrow."

"Give it up, pie-face. Stan won't give us the time of day now that Kimberly is gone."

Miriam swayed. Marla threw an arm around her waist, but not before Stella shrieked, "She's falling!"

"I've got her," Marla said reassuringly, guiding Miriam to the wheelchair. Perhaps it was a mistake to push the old lady too soon. Her leg muscles must be weak from inactivity. Either that, or the conversation was disturbing her.

"I think Mrs. Pearl is upset by the recent tragedy," Marla said, hoping to gain information. "Losing a granddaughter is heartbreaking."

"Yeah? Mother wasn't so broken up when she screamed at Kimberly to leave the house and never to return," Stella snapped.

Florence sniffed. "That's because your daughter was so greedy. She couldn't wait for her share of Daddy's fortune. Not even Mother's allowance could satisfy her expensive tastes."

"She wanted a change from that neighborhood with all the *goyim*. You can't blame her for wanting to move up."

"Not at the expense of her marriage."

Marla tried to fathom the dynamics of their conversation. Florence seemed to be attacking Kimberly's values while Stella was defending them. Why was the elderly aunt coming down so hard on the dead girl? Did it have anything to do with Florence having been in love with Kim's father?

She wheeled Miriam away to a discrete distance, on a slight rise where the driveway curved toward a tree-lined avenue leading to the obscured entrance beyond the woods. It was far enough that she wouldn't appear to be eavesdropping yet could still hear their faint voices.

"Morons," Miriam muttered. "The poor thing is gone. Why won't they let her rest in peace?"

Marla didn't respond, too intent on listening. Her hands placed lightly on the wheelchair handlebars, she inclined her head.

"I don't know how I'm going to get those albums if Stanley won't cooperate," Stella said, wringing her hands. "I should have gone myself. Maybe he'd have listened to me."

"You tried at the funeral, and he ignored you," her sister sneered. "Can you blame him, when you came right out and accused him of murdering his wife?"

"He knew what Kim was planning! You, of all people, should understand how it would cause him to react the way he did."

"By killing her?" Florence said in an incredulous tone.

"Who else could have done it? You?"

"Don't be absurd."

"You always resented my daughter. I know how jealous you were that she wasn't your child."

"Stop it! You're screaming. I hate it when you get hysterical."

"Did you do it?"

"Hell, no." Florence shook her elegant head. "If you want to know, Kimberly was messing in things she didn't understand. She should have minded her own business." Leaning forward, she spoke in such a low voice that Marla couldn't catch what she was saying.

Damn, she needed to be closer! Frustrated, Marla took a few steps forward. Suddenly, she heard a shriek. Whipping around, she let a cry erupt from her lips at the sight that greeted her.

Miriam's wheelchair coasted down the hill at an increasingly perilous speed.

Bless my bones, I forgot to apply the brakes! Taking off at a run, she charged after the errant wheelchair.

"Help!" wailed Miriam.

"Oh my God!" screeched the sisters in unison.

"I'm coming!" Marla shouted, flying down the driveway.

The wheelchair hit a bump and came to a crashing halt on the grass about two feet from a tree. Miriam slid to the ground in a crumpled heap.

"Dear Lord, are you all right?" Moisture sprang into Marla's eyes as she crouched to help the old lady to her feet.

"Wait, she might have broken something!" cried Florence, brushing forward to assist her mother.

"Oh dear! Oh dear!" howled Stella. "Should we call an ambulance?"

The front door opened, and Raoul peered out. "Heavens, madam!" He rushed over to assist them.

Marla grasped Miriam by the arm. The old lady glared at her but appeared to be moving all parts. "I don't think she's damaged anything."

"How can you tell?" Stella snapped. "What kind of nurse are you? You're not even in uniform!"

Florence gave her sister a quelling glance. "Don't just stand there; give us a hand."

"I'm so sorry," Marla intoned as she settled the matriarch onto the padded seat while Raoul steadied the chair. "Are you hurt? Any hip pain?" She knew that elderly women had a propensity for breaking their bones due to osteoporosis. Her mother told her to drink milk often enough, not that she'd reached the age where she needed to be concerned with such things. Hopefully, Miriam didn't have any minute fractures on her wrists, either. "How did you break your fall?" she asked anxiously.

"I landed on my butt, dearie."

Marla felt the old woman's probing eyes on her face, and she hung her head. "I suppose you won't want me to return on Thursday."

"What's that? Find my glasses, will you?"

Marla retrieved them on the ground, cleaned them off on her suit jacket, and handed them over. She was aware that both sisters and the butler were staring at her with malevolence. Miriam's gaze focused sharply.

"I said, you probably don't want me to come back," Marla murmured, her face flushing hotly. Her heart finally slowed its racing tempo as she faced the consequences of her negligence.

"You're right, missy," Stella said. "I've never seen someone so incompetent. First you force my mother out into the cold morning air, and then you walk away from her without wedging her wheelchair. I don't know where Morris found you, but you can go back there! We'll find someone else to cover for Agnes's days off."

Florence compressed her lips in agreement. As though in silent compliance, the butler took charge of the wheelchair and steered Miriam toward the house.

A strange noise bubbled from the old woman's throat, and Marla's breath caught. Was the old lady choking? Had she been damaged in a manner no one had noticed, like a rib puncturing her lungs? The matriarch waved an imperious arm, signaling Raoul to turn her around. When Marla faced her, she widened her eyes in disbelief. Miriam's face wore a broad grin!

"Come on, dearie, don't listen to them," Miriam said, cackling with glee. "I haven't had this much excitement in ages. Nor have my daughters paid me so much attention. I can tell being with you is going to be as good as taking a tonic." She giggled. "Hee, hee. Maybe I'll call one of my cronies after all. I've got to share this with someone."

Inside the house, Marla took charge. She stopped for a moment to brush debris off Miriam's pants and to straighten her sweater. Then she wheeled the old lady into a sunny parlor as directed, ignoring the feeling that hostile eyes followed her every movement.

Chapter Six

"I can't believe I was such a klutz," Marla said to Nicole at work on Tuesday morning. "Miriam has more spirit than I expected. I thought for sure she'd fire me."

"From what you've said, it sounds as though her relatives weren't too pleased." Nicole regarded her kindly as they shared a stolen moment together in the storeroom to scarf down some chocolate almond croissants Marla had brought.

"I didn't win any friends, but at least I was able to learn some new facts in the case." She gulped a sip of hot coffee. "Miriam didn't get along with her granddaughter. The sisters don't get along with each other, and Stella wants some family albums that are in Stanley's possession. Florence said something about Kim messing in things she didn't understand."

"Meaning?" Nicole licked a crumb off her mouth, a simple gesture as refined as the rest of her. Wearing a long-skirted jumper dress, she carried her tall, lithe figure with feline grace.

"I don't have a clue," Marla replied, wiping her fingers on a napkin. "She planned to leave Stan, but I don't think that's what Florence meant."

Nicole's eyes widened. "Why would she leave him if he was her sugar daddy?"

"Gary Waterford said Stan didn't treat Kim right. He implied Stan might react violently if he knew her plans."

"Did Stan mention this to you?"

"Of course not. It might give him a motive, although I've never known Stan to act physically in anger. He has a temper, but he lets loose his tongue, not his hand."

"Huh. What does Detective Vail think?"

"I haven't spoken to him. I tried to reach him yesterday but got his machine. I left a voice message, and he hasn't called back." She heard the forlorn note in her voice but couldn't help it. Apparently, Dalton wasn't interested in hearing her news.

Nicole tossed out their empty paper plates. "What's your next move?"

Marla scanned the shelves for the tube of Framesi color she required for her next customer. Spotting the right shade, she brought it to the sink. She squeezed the coloring agent into a bowl, added developer, and mixed the solution with a stiff brush.

"I tracked down Lacey Mills, who was Kim's friend. Gary gave me her name, but I'm not supposed to mention that I met him. I'm buying her drinks after work at Pebbles. The restaurant bar shouldn't be crowded on a Tuesday."

"If you learn anything exciting, you can tell Detective Vail tomorrow night. I'll bet he's waiting until he sees you in person to compare notes. In the meantime, good luck with Lacey!"

When six-thirty rolled around, Marla found herself hanging at the restaurant bar watching for Kim's friend.

"Are you Marla Shore?" asked a twenty-something dyed blonde who wore her hair in an attractive layered cut. She flaunted her generous assets in a cashmere sweater and jeans that fit so snug they looked about to burst. "I'm Lacey."

Marla shook her hand, then indicated a pair of empty stools. They gave their drink orders before she got down to business. "I used to be married to Stanley Kaufman," she said bluntly. "I understand you were a friend of his late wife, Kim."

The girl's tawny eyes narrowed. "We were best buddies. I didn't notice you at her funeral."

"I'd only met her a few times. We weren't . . . on the friendliest of terms."

"So I gathered, from whenever she spoke about you."

An awkward silence passed, during which time the bartender supplied their drinks. Marla had ordered a bushwhacker, her favorite alcoholic beverage. The cool, coffee-flavored liquid slid down her throat while she fumbled for a new opening.

"Stan asked me to help him," she admitted finally.

"Why?"

"I owe him one for old time's sake. He thinks I can find Kim's killer. I've helped the police solve cases a couple times before."

Lacey arched an eyebrow. "Aren't you a hairdresser?"

Marla nodded. "I know a lot of people around town, and they talk to me. Like you're doing now. Can you tell me about Kim's relationship to Stan?"

Lacey jiggled her hips, adjusting her seat. Marla noticed several male patrons glancing their way with interest. "She planned to leave him."

"I know that, because Ga—" Marla swallowed. She'd been about to say Gary's name. "Gathered as much from what her aunt said," she continued lamely. Oh gosh, she probably shouldn't have mentioned Florence, either. Lacey would wonder where they'd met. "Was Stan aware of her plans?"

"Heck, no, unless she told him. I don't think she'd be so dumb."

"What went wrong?"

"Stan didn't understand her, but it was partially her fault. Kimberly didn't realize what he was really like until it was too late."

"At least she had you to confide in. You were a good friend to stick by her."

Lacey clenched her beer glass. "I knew where she was coming from and where she wanted to go. Stan tried to control her spending. That was a bad move to make."

Marla grabbed a few peanuts from a dish on the counter. "How so?" she said, munching.

Lacey gave her an appraising glance. "Why do you care so much what happened to Kim? She said you were a selfish bitch who wouldn't sell a piece of property he co-owned with you."

"I need the income from my share. Stan just wanted to sell it to buy a bigger house because Kimberly wasn't happy where they lived."

"It wasn't a good neighborhood for her."

"Tell me she was not spoiled by her wealthy background. I heard she couldn't wait for her trust fund, and that's why she married Stan. Do you think she would've been satisfied with anything less than a beachfront mansion?"

"Kim had aspirations. You don't understand, just like Stan didn't."

"So explain to me. If I could get an inkling about her life, it might help me figure out who had reason to harm her." *Besides Stan*, she thought to herself. Would he have reacted violently if Kim confessed she was leaving him? Did he even know she had been planning that? "You do want to see that justice is done, don't you? I mean, if you cared about Kim, you'll help me find who killed her."

"I might have done it myself if someone hadn't beaten me to it," Lacey muttered.

"What's that?" Marla leaned forward.

"Look, if I tell you what I know, you'll report to the cops that I had nothing to do with her murder, okay?"

Marla's brow wrinkled in puzzlement. "Are you saying things weren't all that rosy between you?"

"We were best friends, darlin'. We disagreed on certain issues, that's all." Her pointed glance told Marla she'd better stay on safer turf or their conversation would be over.

"Tell me about Kim. What did she do after finishing high school?"

Lacey brushed back a strand of wavy hair. "She made it through one semester at Broward Community College but didn't have the patience to stay in school. She got a job at a bank, eager to earn money, but Stella hadn't prepared her for real life. She didn't like waking up every morning to work at a mediocre job. Marriage became something Kim saw as a way out, but only if she snagged a rich man. When her grandmother stopped her allowance, Stan seemed like the answer to her dreams."

"Go on." Marla wondered about the hard edge in Lacey's tone. Had Stan been the source of contention between two friends?

Lacey's attention wandered to a couple of men who hovered nearby, casting suggestive glances their way. They appeared to be typical yuppies wearing business suits and uniform haircuts.

"At first, Kim was really happy," Lacey continued, redirecting her attention to Marla. "She liked staying home as a housewife. She redecorated their house, planned dinner parties, and played tennis twice a week. She'd just started a new hobby, tracing her genealogy. She was totally taken aback when Stan cracked down."

"I can imagine." Memories surfaced of her own dismay when Stan took control of her life. At first she'd welcomed his overprotective nature. She had needed someone to care for her after Tammy's tragic accident. But when her ego began to rise from the ashes, she realized Stan had restricted her activities to solely waiting on him.

"Kim said it was the last straw when he put limits on her shopping. She retaliated by racking up charges on their credit cards. Stan could be really nasty, and he took her car in for repairs and never brought it home."

"That was pretty drastic," Marla agreed.

Lacey lowered her voice. "She was afraid of him, Marla. He even checked their Caller ID to see who'd phoned her during the day. Desperation made Kim consider her future more seriously. Like her mother, she had a flair for design. I picked her up one day, and we went to the School of Arts and Design. She registered for classes. No matter how long it took, she was determined to leave Stan."

"How did she go to classes if she had no car?"

"Kim made a case for staying in shape. She said her figure would fill out if she skipped her tennis games. Stan believed her and returned her car. He thought she was going to the club when she went to class. The jerk kept bugging her, though, so Kim decided to walk out on him before he cut off her funds. Gary warned her to be careful."

"Gary?"

"Gary Waterford. He's . . . a mutual friend."

"I see. Why did he warn her?"

"He feared Stan's reaction. Stan is the type of man who regards his wife as a trophy. He wouldn't take kindly to Kim's abandonment when he felt he owned her."

"I left him. He didn't hurt me, not physically at least."

"But did he ever really give up on you?"

Marla lifted the bushwacker glass to her lips, her movements jerky. "He kept harassing me to sell our property and persisted in telling me how much I needed him."

"See? He would never have let Kimberly go free. She was the type of woman he'd always wanted."

Oh yeah? Better her than me!

"Hey, guys. Wanna buy us a round of drinks?" Lacey called, winking at the two men ogling them.

"I have to go," Marla said, handing Lacey a business card. "If you think of anything to add, please give me a call."

During the drive home, she contemplated the various relationships. Either Gary hadn't left off his relationship with Kim when she'd met Stan, or else they'd started seeing each other again after her marriage. Had Kim gotten in touch with Gary at some point, and if so, why hadn't he mentioned it to her?

Lacey claimed Gary was a mutual friend. Just how close were Lacey and the repair man? How intimate had he been with Kim after they'd resumed their acquaintance? Gary had implied Lacey would be jealous if she knew he'd spoken about Kim. Did that mean Lacey was interested in him? Could it be possible both women had set their hearts on the same man? If so, that could have fueled Lacey's resentment.

Kim's classmates might shed more light on her personal ambitions. Gripping the steering wheel, Marla turned north on Pine Island Road. When would she have time to see them? Most likely not until the weekend. After work tomorrow, she had to meet Dalton for her birthday dinner. Turning thirty-five meant climbing another rung on the ladder of life. At least she had that chance, she thought gratefully, saying a silent prayer for Kimberly.

Arriving at the salon the next morning at nine, Marla stopped short inside the entrance. Coal black fabric draped the walls, and silver and black balloons floated from the ceiling.

"Surprise!" rang out her staff members, all of whom had dressed appropriately for the occasion in mournful attire.

"What is this?" she cried, laughter bubbling in her throat and mingling with tears.

"Happy Birthday, Marla!" Nicole, grinning broadly, presented her with a wooden walking stick. The curved handle held a horn with a squeeze ball, a magnifying glass that was supposed to be a rearview mirror, a rabbit's foot, and a sign: CONGRATULATIONS, YOU'RE OVER THE HILL.

"Hey, guys, I'm only thirty-five," Marla wailed.

"Arnie's bringing bagels," Nicole said, wearing a black cape from last year's Halloween costume. "We purposely didn't schedule any appointments until ten, not that you noticed."

"I guess my mind has been elsewhere." She greeted her other staff members, overwhelmed when they showered her with gifts. Her smile quivered when Arnie pushed through the door carrying a huge tray of bagels and pastries.

"Breakfast is on me!" He kissed Marla on the cheek before setting down his load on the coffee table. "I'll be right back. I have something for you." He rushed out, returning moments later to thrust a gift bag in her face. "Here, you'll enjoy this. Jillian sends her regards."

"What? Dalton and I are meeting you tonight. Why—?"

"Work calls. See ya." Arnie backed out, a wide grin on his mustached countenance.

She glanced inside the bag, delighted to see a bottle of Kendall-Jackson chardonnay, a package of Starbucks ground coffee, and a box of marzipan candies shaped like fruits. Yum, her favorite treats!

"Here's something from all of us," said Nicole.

Marla opened the envelope. It was a gift certificate for The Pelican Watch, a multilevel waterfront restaurant known for its prime seafood, intimate seating arrangements, and spectacular view of the Intracoastal. On the top floor was a dancing and dessert room popular with the singles crowd. Marla had dined at the restaurant a couple times with Stan, but it was no longer in her budget.

"This says it's good for their Valentine's Day special," she noted, confused. "That's tonight."

Nicole beamed at her. "Dalton made a reservation for the two of you. You've had a change of plans."

"But we were supposed to meet Arnie and Jill. Does this mean—?"

"You got it, girlfriend. A romantic dinner for two."

Oh joy. "Did my mother put you up to this?"

Giorgio piped in from across the room. "We thought of it all on our own. That detective is hot for you. Somebody had to make a move to put you in the mood."

Marla should have felt indignant, but as she greeted her first client and proceeded through the day's schedule, all she could think about was being alone with Vail. When a couple of deliveries arrived, her excitement increased. One was a huge bouquet of two dozen red roses in a crystal vase. The note read, *Happy birthday. See you tonight. Yours, Dalton.*

Those simple words fired her hormones until she couldn't wait to run home and prepare. Tally's thoughtful gift made her wonder how many of her friends had conspired regarding tonight's plans: she gasped with pleasure when she saw the short black and silver lace cocktail dress by Amazone. Its low-cut sweetheart neckline was sure to provide a generous view of her cleavage. *For this evening,* her friend's note said. *Some risks are worth taking. Love, Tally.*

Oh God. Why did she feel like she was being manipulated? *Because you are,* Marla told herself. Not that she was angry with her friends. She'd needed this kick in the pants to decide where things were going with Vail. But why now, when he was in the middle of a case involving Stan?

Why ever? She confronted her feelings during the drive home. *Let's face it, Marla, you've been avoiding the issue. It's easier seeing him on a casual basis without any real commitment on your part, but he wants more from you. How much more are you willing to give?*

She hadn't wanted to become involved with another man after Stan. Her road to independence had been long and hard, and she valued her freedom. How delightful to come home after work and grab whatever she wanted to eat without worrying about fixing elaborate meals for another. Yet hadn't she told Vail she wanted to cook for him and Brianna one night? Didn't the thought of serving him her favorite brisket dish and herbed garlic potatoes bring her pleasure? Yes, because she wanted to bring *him* pleasure, she realized with surprise. Her heart went out to the lonely man and his daughter who had no woman to care for them. Perhaps this was the difference between Vail and Stan. She'd needed Stan, whereas the reverse was true with Vail. He needed her, and that made her heart rate accelerate.

Damn, she hadn't wanted children, either. Yet she was becoming increasingly fond of Brianna since she'd started driving the girl to dance class. When she shed her bratty manner, the preteen could be downright vulnerable. Marla was supposed to help plan her thirteenth birthday, and she'd been neglecting this duty. Was it her way of avoiding the issue with Vail as well?

Knowing she'd have to come up with some answers by tonight made her a nervous wreck while she showered and dressed. Diamond stud earrings perfectly complemented her attire. She put them in before fixing her hair in what she called seductress style, using a curling iron to create soft twists that framed her face. Her hand shook when she applied Plum Brandy lipstick by Clinique. Sliding her stockinged feet into black leather heels, she squirted herself with Obsession, then pronounced herself ready.

The doorbell rang, and she glanced at the clock. It was only 7:15! He was early, but it didn't matter. She snatched up her purse and flung open the front door.

Stan faced her, a smug look on his face. He'd dressed in a suit, and his hair was slicked back in its usual suave style. "Happy birthday!" he called, thrusting out a gift-wrapped package.

Marla's heart sank. "I'm expecting company. This isn't a good time."

He shouldered his way inside. "Did you think I would forget? You're being kind enough to help me, so it's entirely appropriate for me to think of you in return."

"Why? You're haven't remembered my birthday since our divorce."

"I'd like to hear how you made out with Miriam. Did you get the job?"

"So that's why you came. I should have known." She glanced anxiously down the street, hoping Vail wouldn't arrive before Stan left. "Yes, I got the job and started on Sunday. I don't think her family likes me, though. I'm not terribly competent as a nurse."

Stan looked down his long nose at her. "That doesn't matter. What did you learn?"

Marla sighed. She wasn't going to get rid of him so easily. "Can I call you tomorrow? I'm going out on a date. Detective Vail is on his way to pick me up."

"Don't let your feelings for him get in the way of our plans," Stan warned, putting his gift down on a decorative table in the foyer. "I'll be really angry if you screw up. Really angry."

"Listen, I'm doing you a favor. Be careful how you talk to me."

Stan's expression darkened. "No, I'm doing you a favor by selling you my half of our property at a cheap rate. So tow the line, or you'll be sorry. Now tell me what happened when you went to my in-law's house."

She fumed with impatience. "Get lost, Stan. I don't want you here when Dalton arrives."

"Why not? Afraid he might think we're getting back together?" He sauntered closer. "What's so bad about that idea? We always were good in bed."

Her gut clenched as she heard a car's engine rumbling near. "You have to go now." She didn't want to be caught in another compromising situation.

"All right, we'll pursue this next time." His tone conveyed reassurance that his hard eyes didn't match. "I'm counting on you, Marla. I realize Vail would like to pin this on me. I need you to play ball in my court, not his."

"Take a hike, Stan. I'll talk to you later."

"Tell me one thing. Did Stella or Florence mention anything about family albums in my possession?"

"Yes, why?"

"Kim seemed to find something fascinating in one of them, and she became very secretive about it. I'm wondering what the relatives know that I don't. I won't return the albums yet, just in case. If you're a good girl, I may let you take a peek."

He had the audacity to kiss her before turning away.

Disturbed by the emotions his visit had conjured, Marla watched him leave. Curse the man. He still had the power to rile her.

Her palms sweaty, she watched Vail approach along her walkway. She gave him a tremulous smile, hoping her distress didn't show. How much had he seen of her encounter with Stan?

"What was Kaufman doing here?" Dalton demanded when he reached her doorstep. He appeared dashingly handsome in a slate gray suit that mirrored the smoky tint of his eyes.

"He wanted the results of my interview with the Pearls."

"Is that all? I saw him kiss you."

"There's nothing between us, Dalton. You don't have to worry." When he gazed at her searchingly, she looped her arm through his. "I think it's cute when you're jealous."

"I am not jealous."

"Good, because you're the one I want to be with tonight, not him. Thanks for the beautiful roses, by the way. They were a wonderful surprise."

"I ordered the flowers sent to the salon when Nicole called to tell me about the gift certificate and mentioned your staff would be throwing a party. Arnie and Jill didn't mind postponing our dinner together."

"Everyone has been in on this conspiracy!"

"You don't know the half of it," he murmured, a sly smile tilting his lips.

Chapter
Seven

"How long have you known about our change in plans? Arnie didn't mention anything to me," Marla said to Vail during the drive to the restaurant.

"Nicole notified me last week."

Marla noticed his secretive grin. "So this was her idea, to get us alone together?" She still couldn't shake the nagging feeling that her mother had had a hand in their scheme.

His smile broadened. "Nicole had a little help. Why look a gift horse in the mouth? Relax, sweetcakes. It's just you and me tonight."

That's what worried her the most. A meal together would be fun, even romantic. But what would happen afterward?

Butterflies swirled in her stomach as they entered the restaurant and were seated in a quiet alcove. Furnishings included etched glass partitions, Tiffany lamps, potted plants, and polished wood. Vases of bright red carnations provided a splash of color on white-clothed tables, while soft melodies playing in the background seduced the senses.

It was a rare occasion when they were alone together in an intimate setting, Marla realized. She fidgeted while Dalton ordered a bottle of pinot noir. Maybe what really frightened her was what she *wanted* to happen after dinner. She took a sip of the rich ruby wine after their waiter uncorked the bottle. Good stuff. Maybe it would give her a jolt of courage.

"Don't drink it too quickly," Vail admonished, wagging a finger. "You need to stay awake."

Dear Lord, the man could read her mind! Her skin heated as his hand snaked across the table to grasp hers.

"You look great in that dress."

"Thanks."

"You'd look better out of it."

"I don't know, Dalton. That would be a serious step for us."

"Yes, it would."

She glanced away. "I just wonder where it would lead."

"I thought you liked to take risks."

"That depends. There's more involved here. Brianna, for instance."

"I'm aware how my daughter can get on your nerves," he said wryly, "but she's mellowed toward you, ever since you saved her life in the sports club. I'd even venture to say she likes you."

"That isn't the issue. I'm not eager for a relationship including a child."

His lips compressed. "That's just an excuse. You're already taking Brianna to dance class. From what she tells me, you're also offering motherly advice. I suspect you care for her more than you're willing to admit. Anyway, this discussion is about you and me. You're afraid to get stuck with a bad apple again, aren't you?"

Darn right. She bit her lip, nodding. Put into a pinhole, she feared making another mistake. She already had two strikes against her: first Stan and then David. Ma said things happened in threes.

"I know you're a good man, Dalton, and you respect my career. But sometimes you come across as too demanding."

"That's because I want you to be safe."

"You can't protect me from the world."

"I realize that, and I also feel you're diverging again from the real issue here. You've hooked up before with guys who won your family's approval, but they were losers. It's tough for you to take a chance on someone different."

He leaned forward. "Let me tell you what I've rarely mentioned to anyone else. After Pam's death, I didn't think I could handle being with another woman. Not only did I miss my wife terribly, but I was concerned that if I cared too deeply about someone else, I might lose her as well. But then I met you, and the future suddenly didn't seem so bleak and lonely anymore. Think about how it makes me feel when you place yourself in the path of danger chasing after murder suspects. Getting closer to you is a risk for me, too, but it's one I'm willing to take."

"I hadn't thought about it from your viewpoint."

"So where do we go from here? I don't want to scare you off."

She took a drink of water. "I-I guess we'll just let things unfold as they're meant to."

"Good. Now that we've established how much you want me, I have something for you." He leaned back when the waiter brought their menus. After they'd given their orders, he reached inside his jacket pocket.

Marla held her breath. Not a ring, please don't let it be a ring. She didn't want to be forced into any decisions she'd regret later.

"Here," Vail said, "it's a photograph Kaufman found in his wife's room. This man called on Kimberly a couple of weeks ago, but she wasn't home. Kaufman answered the door. He recognized the same guy in this photo."

Dalton was showing her a picture found in Stan's house? Marla gaped at him. All right, so it wasn't a ring. But did he have to present a murder clue in the middle of a romantic dinner? That's what happens when you date a detective.

Pasting a placid expression on her face, she studied the photograph. An elderly woman smiled proudly beside a tall gray-haired gentleman. The man, who looked to be in his fifties, had a distinguished face and squared shoulders that gave him an authoritative air. Marla peered more closely at his deep-set brown eyes that looked somewhat familiar.

"Who is he?" she asked.

"I haven't a clue. He wasn't at the funeral, or I'd have nailed him there."

"Did Stan let you examine the Pearl family albums?"

Vail's gaze clouded. "I wasn't aware he had them."

"Stella is anxious to retrieve the books. Stan hinted that Kim had become fascinated by something in one of the volumes. I suppose I'll have to pay him a visit to see what it is. Do you think this photo fell from one?"

"It's possible."

"Stan had no idea what the man wanted with his wife?"

"Nope. Oh, the man left a message since Kim wasn't home. She should contact Uncle Jerry."

"Uncle Jerry? Who's that? Morris doesn't have a brother."

"Maybe he and Kim were on friendly terms," he suggested in a dry tone.

"This man is old enough to be her father!"

"Could be she found herself another sugar daddy."

"I don't believe it. Lacey would have said something." She related her conversation with Kim's best friend.

"I'll visit Lacey and show her this photograph. I brought it with me when I canvassed the neighborhood. One of the folks mentioned seeing this man around before when Stan wasn't home."

"Did anyone see or hear anything the morning Kim was killed?" Marla asked.

"No, but a couple of neighbors acted strangely when they spoke about the victim. When you see Stan next, ask him about the Addison and the Shpritz couples." His brows drew together. "I'll come along when you see him. You may not know the right questions to ask."

"Excuse me? I've been doing quite well on my own, thanks." A smile curved her lips. "You just don't want me to be alone with Stan. Don't worry, I can handle him."

"I'm more worried about how he handles you." His glowering expression left no doubt in her mind what concerned him.

They spent the rest of the meal exchanging small talk. Several times, Vail glanced at his watch, making Marla wonder why. Did he have to return to the station tonight? Sometimes he worked late shifts, but he would have said something earlier. Or was he worried about Brianna being home alone? Once you had a kid, freedom flew out the door. Just how much was she willing to sacrifice to be with Dalton Vail?

"It's time," he announced smugly after he'd paid the bill. "Let's check out the rest of this place. It was someone's house before being converted into a restaurant." He led her upstairs. "Each room is decorated differently."

"Look at that fireplace." She pointed. "Rather ornate, isn't it?"

He stopped in front of a closed double door. "This used to be the library. You go in first."

"Are we allowed?"

"Sure."

Imagining a room with dusty old books, Marla pushed open the door. Bright lights flashed in her face, and she heard the click of camera shutters.

"Surprise!" a chorus of voices shouted.

"Oh, no!" Marla covered her face with her hands.

"Hey, girlfriend, loosen up. This is *your* party."

Marla dropped her arms and smiled. "Nicole, I can't believe you didn't give away a hint at work today."

"I thought having a little surprise for you at the salon would allay any suspicions."

"How clever. Arnie and Jill, you rascals, letting me think you'd backed out of our date. And, Tally, no wonder you didn't ask me out to lunch today!"

Glancing at the sea of faces smiling at her, she whirled on Vail. "You knew about this all through dinner?"

His broad grin gave his answer. "You bet. The only reason I agreed to play along was because they let me have a couple hours alone with you."

"You're getting as deceitful as your suspects." Marla turned to greet her friends and accept a bounty of gifts. A clothed table held glasses of champagne and plates of chocolate raspberry torte along with a bouquet of Mylar balloons.

"This is too much!" she exclaimed, her voice shaking with emotion. She addressed one of the guests. "Lance, how good of you to come."

"I wouldn't miss it," said the computer guru. "Don't let your cop friend see this," he whispered, handing her a gift bag.

Marla peeked inside the wrapping. "SonicEarz. What is it?" Lance usually presented her with electronic gizmos.

"Earphones for when you want to snoop on people from a distance." His owlish face brightened at her delighted reaction.

She laughed. "Isn't that illegal?" Thank goodness Vail was helping himself to a piece of cake.

Tally gave her a Denise Austen dance video to play at home. "Gosh, the dress was enough," Marla said, smoothing her hand down the silken fabric.

"You enjoyed the Dancercize class at Perfect Fit Sports Club, and we're not members anymore. I thought you'd like this tape to use at home."

"Great, it'll help me stay in shape."

"Open mine next." Vail retrieved a foil-wrapped package from a table. He must have dropped it off at the restaurant earlier, Marla surmised. "I'm sorry Brianna couldn't be here," he said, "but she has an exam tomorrow."

"That's okay." Marla wondered if that was the true reason for his daughter's absence. Tearing open the gift wrap, she uttered a cry of disbelief. "A cellular phone! Dalton, you shouldn't have. This is expensive!"

"It's the only way I can have peace of mind where you're concerned," he said somberly. "I need to be able to reach you."

Jill presented her with a large ribboned box. Marla was delighted to discover a collection of cosmetics inside. "For your disguises," the blond actress said, hanging on Arnie's arm.

"I may need some lessons!" Marla joked. She put the package

down on a table set aside for gifts before greeting her other friends.

A commotion at the door caught her attention. A tall dark-haired man entered, his face brightening when he spotted her. He was accompanied by a lithe woman with hair the color of golden oak.

"Hey, sis!" her brother called.

"Michael and Charlene! I can't believe you came down from Boca Raton!"

"Wouldn't miss your birthday. Where's Ma?"

"I don't know. Is she coming?" Marla hugged them both. Charlene handed her a large gift bag, and she'd just added it to her loot and made introductions when Vail announced her mother's arrival.

Anita marched into the room, followed by a portly fellow in his late sixties judging from his sparse hair and lined face. The man covered up his bald spot pretty well, considering he didn't have much left to work with. Crinkles beside his eyes showed he smiled often. Marla pursed her lips, regarding his lime green pants and canary jacket. Another condo commando tired of wearing conservative suits throughout his working life.

Anita kissed her children. "I've been meaning to introduce you both to Roger. Roger Gold, this is my daughter, Marla."

Roger grabbed Marla's hand, beaming at her with a row of evenly capped teeth. "Delighted to meet you," he said, pumping her hand vigorously. "Anita has told me so much about her talented daughter. I see she understated your looks."

"You're too kind," Marla murmured. Why hadn't Ma mentioned this guy before? Come to think of it, Anita had left cryptic messages that she had something to relate, but Marla had been too preoccupied to follow up. So *this* is what she'd had up her sleeve. Marla eyed the man warily, cautious about anyone who gave effusive compliments.

"This is my son, Michael, and his wife, Charlene," Anita said. "How are the kids? Did you leave them with a sitter?" She cornered them to talk about her grandchildren.

"Let's get something to eat," Roger suggested, signaling for

Marla to accompany him to the dessert table. "Hey, where are those cream puffs I ordered? Waiter!"

"You made the arrangements?" Marla asked.

"Sure, doll. *Az der mogen iz laidik iz der moi'ech oich laidik.* You know what that means?

"No."

"When the stomach is empty, so is the brain. I'll loan you my book of Yiddish proverbs by Fred Kogos. It's in there. You know, feed the stomach and fuel the brain."

He turned his attention to the sweets and dug right in, stuffing a huge piece of torte in his mouth. "Anita told me all about you." Smacking his lips, he winked. "I know you have the hots for that cop."

"Really?"

He lowered his voice. "Doesn't bother me that he isn't Jewish. Your mom, though, she's still fishing for someone else to catch your eye. Heed my warning. Now where the devil are my cream puffs? This waiter doesn't deserve a big tip."

Marla didn't care for the way her mother hustled over at his summons. "The pastry chef is bringing the rest of the desserts," she told him. "This party was my idea," she explained to Marla. "Did you suspect anything?"

"Not a clue! Thanks, I love you." She hugged Anita and then stepped back, hailed by her other friends.

The older couple left shortly thereafter, ostensibly to avoid driving home late at night. Marla noticed her mother's glow and prayed that was the only reason they'd gone so early. Or maybe it was because Roger had consumed too many sweets. His skin had looked rather pale.

"I can't understand what Ma sees in him," she confided to her brother.

"He has a lot of energy," Michael suggested, grinning.

"He's a *fresser.* Did you see how many slices of cake he stuffed down? I'll make a date with Ma and ask her about him."

"She seems happy, Marla. In my book, that's what counts."

*   *   *

"I can't believe how everyone fooled me," she said to Vail during the drive home. Weariness settled into her bones as she sank back into the seat cushion.

"You've been preoccupied," he said in a teasing tone.

She considered her recent schedule. "I guess so. I don't have any free time coming up, either. I want to see Stan about those albums, talk to his neighbors, meet Kim's classmates, and I still have to take care of Miriam!"

"What happened during your interview on Sunday?"

"I never told you, did I?" She gave him an accusing glance. "You didn't return my phone calls."

"I didn't dare speak to you before tonight, or I might have given away the surprise."

Marla described her adventures as a nurse's aide. "I'll try to find out who this Uncle Jerry person is, although I have to be careful what I say when I'm at Miriam's place. If I reveal my intimate knowledge of Stan's affairs, I'll blow my cover." She patted her purse. "You can reach me on my cell phone if you need me. That was a really thoughtful gift."

He pulled up to the curb in front of her townhouse and shut off the ignition. Street lamps lent a soft glow to the night, but they didn't compare to the gleam in his eyes when he turned the full power of his gaze on her.

"I know how you can express your gratitude."

"I can't imagine what you mean." She smiled coyly. "Come inside, I have a Valentine's Day gift for you. Watch out for Spooks." After the poodle greeted them, she offered Vail a cup of coffee.

"I had enough at the restaurant. Let's sit on the couch."

Uh-oh. Dangerous place, a couch. She retrieved the wrapped box she'd forgotten to bring earlier and handed it to him. Her heart hammering, she sank down on the sofa. It delighted her to see the pleased reaction on his face as he examined the package.

"What is it?"

"You'll see."

He tore it open like a child, making her wonder when was the last time he'd received a genuine gift, other than from Brianna. "It's a beautiful pen." He turned the silver instrument around to examine it.

"You take notes so often. I thought you could use this."

"It's great." He placed it on the cocktail table before turning to her. "I'll thank you first." Putting his arms around her, he drew her close.

Pressed against his solid length, she felt her limbs liquify. His spice cologne sent her pulse thrumming.

His thumb stroked her cheek. "Your skin is so soft, just like your heart. Being with you takes me away from all the ugliness I face every day."

"Oh, Dalton." She saw the need in his eyes, and yearning overwhelmed her. Reaching up, she pulled his head down and kissed him.

"I've waited a long time for this," he murmured against her ear when they came up for air.

"Well, don't stop now!"

His hands slid down her body as he drew her in for a deeper kiss. "I won't be able to leave if we go any further."

"Mmm," she murmured. "I don't want you to go."

He sucked in a ragged breath. "Are you sure?"

"Yes."

With a groan, he slipped the dress straps off her shoulders. His mouth found her bared flesh, and Marla's senses reeled. She was just about to suggest they move to more comfortable accommodations when a cell phone rang.

"Is that mine?" she asked, springing backward.

"No, it's this one." He pulled it off his belt. "Vail here." A pause, during which time he picked his tie off the sofa. "Brie, is that you? Anything wrong?" He glanced guiltily at Marla. "No, the party is over. I'm at Marla's. Yes, I'm coming right home. You should be in bed already. No, I'm not doing anything I'll regret, and wash out your mouth for thinking that way. Don't wait up for me."

He disconnected, a sheepish grin on his face. "Gotta go. Next time, I'll make sure she sleeps over her friend's house."

Disappointment washed over her, followed by relief as she saw him to the door and waved good-night. *Another reason why not to get involved with a man who has children*, she thought while locking up. Too many interruptions!

Interruptions were something she couldn't afford right now. Three weeks remained before Stan's deadline. She needed to devote herself to finding Kim's killer before an innocent man went to prison for a crime he didn't commit.

Chapter
Eight

Thursday morning Marla was swamped at work. She barely had time to gulp down breakfast, let alone get anything extra done. A break came when her two o'clock appointment canceled. *Yes!* she almost shouted aloud. No one else had been scheduled during the two-hour block, so she was free until four.

She phoned Stan at his office. He agreed to meet her at his house but only for an hour. That was fine with her; she'd spend the rest of the time checking out his neighbors. Next Marla dialed the number for the School of Arts and Design. Claiming she'd been referred by her recently departed friend Kimberly Kaufman to their interior design program, she made an appointment for the next morning. How convenient that her first customer wasn't scheduled until eleven.

Not wanting to get stuck on the phone, she called a few numbers she'd jotted down earlier. She'd promised Vail to help plan his daughter's thirteenth birthday and had been negligent of her duty. Last night reminded her of the obligation.

"What do you mean, it's sixty-five dollars per person for a three-course chicken dinner?" she cried to a caterer on the other end of the line. "That's absurd. What? I don't care if that's what they pay at bar mitzvahs. This doesn't have to be so fancy." She slammed down the receiver. Better to find a restaurant with a private room. The catering places charged too much. She'd never imagined planning a teen party could be so demanding.

Eager to move ahead with her investigation, she snatched up her purse and was heading for the salon exit when she noticed a hearse pull up in front. *Oh God, what's that doing here?*

Ignoring the NO PARKING sign, the vehicle's driver shut off the engine and emerged. It was a woman dressed in a leather corset contraption and skin-tight black leather pants that fit into heeled boots. She wore a shawl, her only concession to the cool February weather. Heavy mascara fringed tawny eyes.

"I'm here about the ad," the woman stated, barely moving her raisin-painted lips.

Marla hesitated. "What ad?"

"For a colorist."

"Oh." *If your clothes are an example, you need to use a color chart yourself, pal.* "I'm Marla Shore, the owner. Can you give me an idea of your experience?"

The woman rattled off impressive credentials and showed her license. "I came by yesterday but you were having some sort of celebration. Loved the rags. I could tell you were my kind of people."

"My staff were celebrating my birthday. They wore their old Halloween costumes as a joke."

"Radical. So when can I start working here? I have to give my current place notice that I'm leaving."

"We're still interviewing prospective staff. If you leave your contact info, I'll get back to you."

The woman leaned closer, giving Marla a whiff of alcoholic breath. "You'd like what I do on the side, darlin'. Maybe you'd want to try it."

"What's that?"

"I'm a dominatrix. Lots of men get turned on when I whip them. You wanna come for a session? I'll bet you'd be good at it."

Bless my bones, what a winner. "No, thanks. I'm on my way out. I'll call you if I have further questions." Why did she get all the weirdos? Is this what graduated from beauty school these days?

She was late when she reached Stan's house. It was only the second time she'd been there, having come once before to retrieve the ceramic soup tureen given them as a wedding gift by one of her aunts. With seven bedrooms, four baths, a vaulted ceiling living room, fully equipped kitchen, and wood-decked pool area, the house seemed overwhelmingly huge to Marla. It hadn't been good enough for Kimberly, who'd wanted a location on the Intracoastal.

Facing Stan inside the marble-tiled foyer, she regarded her ex-spouse with wary eyes. He looked dapper in a three-piece wool suit, his black hair slicked off a wide forehead. Instead of his usual supercilious grin, however, his face wore a sad smile. *Don't let him get to you*, she warned herself.

"Thanks for meeting me here," she said. "I'd like to see those albums you mentioned."

"They're in the family room. Follow me." On the way, he checked his watch. "I can't stay long. I have a three-thirty appointment."

"That's fine. Detective Vail showed me the photograph you found in Kim's bedroom." Marla trailed him down a hallway to a family room brightly decorated in southwestern motif. Sofas upholstered in chili and turquoise accents, a handwoven wool rug with a Pueblo scene, Native American framed art, and mauve sandpainted vase lamps highlighted the room. *It's certainly different than the classic mahogany furniture you favored when we were married.* Marrying Kimberly must have cost him plenty.

Stan sank heavily onto a couch. "I think that picture fell from one of these albums," he said, pointing to several books scattered on a pine table.

"Which one was Kim most interested in?" She thumbed through an album showing Kim as a baby. The edges were brown, and many of the photos had become dislodged from the sticky backing.

"Try the red book," Stan suggested. "Stella wants to redo them, something about acid- and lignin-free paper. I won't let her have them until the investigation is complete. Florence keeps nagging me."

"Maybe there is something here that Kim's family doesn't want you to see." Putting the first book down, she picked up the red one.

It weighed heavily on her thighs as she opened the volume. Inside, younger versions of Morris, Stella, and Florence smiled from photographs capturing their carefree swimming pool days. Miriam posed proudly beside her husband Harris in a tropical setting beside a lake.

Flipping through the pages, Marla stopped when she came to a blank space fitting the dimensions of the photo Vail had shown her. "Look," she cried triumphantly.

"What is it?"

"This must be where that picture fell from. Who's this woman next to Harris? It's not Miriam." She reversed the book so Stan could see. The photo showed Harris with his arm around a slender, flame-haired girl. A later grouping showed the woman, having aged, smiling sadly at the camera next to a young boy who bore a strong resemblance to the man Kim called Uncle Jerry. It appeared as though there might have been someone else on the other side of her, but the picture had been cropped.

Stan shrugged. His gesture moved her glance to his shoulders, where she noticed flecks of dandruff. "I don't know who the redhead is, although she does look somewhat familiar."

"Wasn't Kim working on her genealogy?"

"You're right. She bought one of those computer programs to research her family tree."

"Can you access the program? Or maybe she left notes."

"I'll check into it when I have time."

"Will you please stop rapping your fingers on that table? The sound is annoying."

He threw her an irritated look. "You're here to help me, not to criticize."

"I can't concentrate when you insist on making noises."

"You never used to be this way when we were married. Never." His brows drew together in a disapproving scowl.

"I was afraid to open my mouth for fear you'd put me down."

"You needed my guidance, just as you need it now. Let me offer you a tidbit of information. I heard Carolyn Sutton is planning to open a salon in the same shopping strip at the other end from yours."

Tossing the albums on the table, Marla leapt up. "You're lying! Carolyn can't afford to open a business in Palm Haven. The last time I visited her salon, it was Deadsville. Who'd buy that place in such a seedy neighborhood? And, if she's been hurting for business, how can she afford to change locations?"

"Maybe she has financial support," Stan said with a wink.

"You wouldn't! I knew you were behind her attempt to undermine my lease before, but this is going too far."

"I didn't say it was me, did I? As usual, you're jumping to nasty conclusions." He rose slowly. "If you need legal advice, I'm available."

"Over my dead body."

"That could be arranged," he said slyly.

"What the hell does that mean?"

"Well, your cop friend believes I killed Kimberly. What's another wife out of the way?"

"Ha! You'd have nothing to gain."

He advanced toward her. "Oh no? What about our jointly owned property? We still have right of survivorship."

"That isn't funny, Stan. By the way, where are those signed papers you were supposed to give me?"

"They're on my desk in the study." He halted directly in front of her, looming like a menacing cloud.

Marla had an insane impulse to back away. What if he truly had killed his wife? Perhaps all this had been a ruse to get her alone. "Vail knows I'm here," she blurted.

He lifted a hand toward her, and she flinched. But he cupped her chin, raising her face so she peered into his stormy eyes. "I'm disappointed in you, babe. You've lost faith in me. Lost faith. I wasn't really threatening you. I just wanted to see how you'd react. Your lack of trust distresses me. Have you forgotten how much I've helped you in the past?"

"The past is over. I don't need your help now."

He dropped his hand. "But I need yours. It isn't easy for me, you know. Asking for help."

Especially from me. "I want those papers, Stan."

"I'll get them." He trudged off, his gait unlike the man's usual purposeful stride.

Marla followed, feeling emptiness echo through the house. She halted abruptly when Stan stopped in the kitchen. "I should have offered you a drink. I didn't think . . . Kimberly always took care of guests."

"I don't want anything, thanks." She shifted her feet impatiently, eager to move on.

"What will I do, Marla?" He whirled around, lines of consternation creasing his face.

"You'll survive, one day at a time. Just like I did, after Tammy's death."

"I've never realized how devastating it is to lose someone you love." His voice cracked. "I'm not sure how to go on. She's everywhere I look in this house. I can still smell her scent in the bathroom, feel her lying next to me in our bed. I wake up in the morning expecting to find her in the kitchen, making my breakfast. This house is too big without her."

Marla's throat tightened. "We'll focus on finding her killer. That should give you enough reason to get up every day."

"I suppose."

Before she stopped to think, Marla kissed him on the cheek. "I promised to help you, and I will. I always keep my word."

Stan's pain-filled gaze met hers. "I loved Kimberly, but I never stopped caring about you, Marla. We were a good team. A good team. You're the one who threw me aside like a sack of dirt after all I'd done for you."

How easy it had been to lean on him in times of trouble. He'd paid the bills, fielded her phone calls, kept all the ugliness and aggravation of life away from her. *Just like Vail wants to do,* Marla's inner voice cried. Was she doomed to repeat her mistakes by being attracted to strong, controlling men?

She shook her head. "Lust is all we had between us. You never

really respected me. Instead of boosting my self-esteem, you kept putting me down. You liked my being dependent on you."

"Not anymore. I wouldn't have asked for your help proving my innocence if I didn't believe you capable."

"Sorry, but your crack about Carolyn Sutton shows me you still think I'm susceptible to your charms." She lifted her chin. "Where are those papers you have for me? It's getting late."

"That's all you care about, isn't it? Remember, I'll only go through with the deal if you find Kimberly's killer before I go to court. Just don't desert me like *she* was about to do."

"What does that mean?"

His eyes glittered. "You think I don't know? I'm not stupid. My wife got what she wanted, only not exactly in the manner she'd hoped." He shook his head. "After all I did for her. We could have worked things out, if she hadn't ticked off someone enough to murder her. Help me find who did it, babe, and I promise I won't bother you again."

She retreated to the foyer while he obtained the documents. Her gaze inadvertently lowered to the marble floor where a vague stain showed. "You've cleaned up the place quite well," she told him upon his return. "Is this where—?"

"Yes." His glance met hers, then slid away. He handed her the papers, which she stuffed into her purse.

"You came down those stairs to find Kimberly lying here?" She didn't mean to be cruel. It was important to get the facts straight. Maybe he'd remember something that he hadn't told Vail.

"You got it."

"Did the cops ever find a murder weapon?"

"Not to my knowledge."

"It wasn't . . . still in her, was it?"

"No." A muscle in his jaw twitched.

"I suppose they searched outside your house."

"I suppose. I didn't really get into details of the investigation."

Again she was struck by his unfamiliar attitude. Normally, Stan was a vulture for information. This case had hit too close to home, and he was too upset to act in his accustomed manner. To her per-

sonal discomfort, this vulnerability appealed to her much more than his arrogance.

"Detective Vail mentioned a couple of your neighbors, the Addisons and Shpritzes," she said. "How well did you and Kim know them?"

"We played tennis with Cliff and Elise Addison. Kim said she was going to tell Elise about that sports club she'd joined. As for the Shpritzes, we used to go out with Adam and Jessica."

"Used to?"

He dashed a hand through his hair. "My group is involved in a malpractice suit against Adam, who's a dentist. I'm not involved, but he doesn't understand why I can't intervene. We haven't gotten together in months." His eyes narrowed. "Hey, you don't suppose he . . . thought of a way to get back at me?"

"By killing Kimberly? Don't be absurd. Besides, you told me Kim's family has the best motive."

"I forgot to ask what you learned when you went there on Sunday." He rubbed a hand over his face. "I'm not thinking straight these days."

Marla resisted an impulse to touch him. "Miriam is delightful, although the nurse treats her like an invalid. Her two daughters don't get along, as you said. I met Morris briefly but not the rest of his family. I presume they live in the other house on the property. Oh, thanks for your birthday gift," she added in a cynical tone. "I can always use a first-aid book and a pair of bandage scissors. They'll help with my disguise."

He smirked. "I figured you'd like them."

"So who is Kim's Uncle Jerry? A relative on her father's side?"

Stan's eyebrows shot up. "I almost forgot about him. Hang on a minute."

Marla examined the foyer while he raced upstairs. *How amazing, you could never tell someone had died here.* A shiver wormed up her spine.

"Here you go," Stan said upon returning. "I found this piece of paper tucked into a pocket of Kim's slacks. Look at the man's name scribbled on it: Jeremiah Dooley. I'll bet that's who this Uncle Jerry

character is, although I don't recall any relation by that name on either side of Kimberly's family. I've started to go through her things. Thought I'd offer stuff to her relatives before calling the donation truck. Say, does your child-drowning-prevention coalition do pickups?"

"No, we don't." She took the note, which included a phone number, and stuck it in her purse.

"I meant to give you the bottle of Obsession from Kimberly's dresser. It's your favorite scent, if I recall." He frowned. "Maybe the housekeeper misplaced it. I don't seem to be able to find a lot of things, lately."

"I don't want anything that you bought for Kimberly, thanks. I'm taking care of Miriam again tonight. I'll let you know if I learn anything important."

He gave a crooked smile. "I knew I could count on you, babe." Opening the front door, he followed her outside and pulled out his car keys. "Time is running short. I hope you get some answers soon. I'd hate to withdraw my offer to sell you that property, especially when we've reached a new understanding."

I wouldn't go that far. She smiled brightly. "Since we're so close, I hope you won't mind if I make a suggestion. You need to change shampoos. Your scalp is too dry, and you have dandruff. It shows on your jacket."

After he left, Marla glanced at her watch. An hour remained until her next customer. She'd knock on a couple of doors and see if any neighbors were home.

She lucked out a few doors down where she found a mailbox emblazoned with the Addisons' name. A woman answered the door. Wary jade eyes regarded her from an oval face framed by honey brown curls. A full head shorter than Marla, she wore a jogging suit. Her healthy complexion and lean frame showed her to be in top form.

"I'm Marla Shore, a friend of Stanley Kaufman," Marla began, handing the lady her business card. "He asked me to check out some information regarding his wife. I understand you were tennis partners."

The woman's gaze chilled. "That's right."

Marla adjusted the shoulder strap on her purse. "I'm wondering if you have any idea who might have wanted to harm Kimberly."

"Who wouldn't?"

It would be nice if you asked me inside, pal. "I sense a bit of hostility in your reply."

"Would you wonder why your husband gave another man's wife a set of concert tickets to a show at the National Car Rental Center? Do you know how much those cost? My name is Elise, by the way. Cliff is my husband. Say, you're not an undercover cop, are you?"

Marla laughed. "Nope. I presume you already spoke to the authorities. It appears no one in the neighborhood saw anything unusual the morning Kim was murdered."

Elise's face scrunched. "I didn't notice anything, but then I was working already at my computer."

"Oh?"

"I write e-mail newsletters for online companies."

"I see. Are you an early morning jogger? You look like you keep really fit."

"I only run four times a week. That morning wasn't one of my days."

"How often did you play tennis with Kimberly?"

"Often enough to notice the side glances Cliff gave her. We partnered with our husbands." She cleared her throat. "Cliff thinks I didn't know, but you can tell when your man's attention wanders."

"Excuse me?"

Her face paled. "I shouldn't have said that. I have to go now." She started closing the door.

"Wait! Did Kim ever mention an uncle named Jeremiah?"

Elise hesitated. "She talked about her Uncle Jerry, if that's who you mean. He has a Porsche; I saw it parked in front of her house once. It's a real beaut. Beats me where he gets the money when his ministry finances missionary work in impoverished countries."

"Is that what Kim told you?"

"Yep."

"Is he a priest?"

"I don't think so. Kim didn't tell me much about his visits, but I could tell she was excited about seeing him."

"Stan doesn't know anything about him. As far as he knows, neither does the rest of her family."

Elise shrugged. "That's not my business."

"Did she confide her plans to you?"

"What, to leave Stan? As though I couldn't guess what was on her mind!" She pointed a finger at Marla. "Don't tell the cops this, but I'm glad she's dead. Cliff has been spooked by the whole thing. I think he'll straighten out now that that vamp doesn't have her clutches in him anymore."

Marla kept her expression bland. "Well, thanks for your information. If you remember anything else, please call me. Can you tell me where the Shpritz family lives?"

"Jessica's house is number seven six oh six, one block south."

Mrs. Shpritz reminded Marla of a willow tree with her long limbs, graceful movements, and enveloping kindness. After studying Marla's business card, she gestured for her to enter.

"I don't know if you're aware of it," Jessica said after offering Marla a seat, "but Stan and Adam had a falling out. Stan's legal group is representing a malpractice case against my husband. Adam thinks Stan should intervene. You have no idea how upset we are about this lawsuit." She patted her swollen belly. "In my condition, I shouldn't have extra aggravation."

"I agree." Seated at a kitchen table, Marla watched Jessica remove a batch of chocolate-chip cookies from the oven. "Do you have any ideas about who killed Kimberly?"

"I can't say." Placing the cookie sheet on a rack, Jessica proceeded to remove her oven mitts.

Can't say, or won't? "Had you spoken to Kim recently?"

"We kept in touch. I felt she could have done more to influence Stan. I got annoyed when she wouldn't bring up the subject to him, but Kim had her own problems." Jessica rinsed out two coffee mugs, filled them from a freshly brewed pot, and handed one to Marla. "Cream and sugar?"

"Yes, please." Jessica must be a paragon of housekeeping, she thought, surreptitiously taking in the spotless countertops, gleaming tile floor, and array of appliances with surfaces that shone like mirrors. *Wanna come do my house next?*

Jessica sat opposite her. "Kim was very unhappy, in case you didn't know. How did you say you knew the Kaufmans?"

Marla jerked upright. "I was Stan's first wife. In my profession, I come into contact with lots of people. I've helped the police solve cases before. That's why Stan came to me."

"I think he knew." Jessica lowered her voice to a whisper. "She was seeing some older guy. You know, the rich man who drives a Porsche."

"So you saw it, too. Elise mentioned his car."

Jessica stiffened. "You talked to *her?*"

"Yes, why?"

"Here, have a cookie. Elise must be upset. Now she'll have to find a new tennis partner."

The phone rang, and Jessica picked up the receiver. Marla caught the deep tones of a male voice on the other end.

Her face reddening, Jessica glanced at Marla. "I can't talk now. I have company. She's a friend of Stan's. . . . Yes, you know I'll be there. Adam thinks I'm going to a bridge game. See you later, snookems." Hanging up, she grinned at Marla. "Where were we?" Her smile was a bit too bright.

"You were telling me about the rich man who visited Kim. I understand his name is Jeremiah Dooley. Kim called him Uncle Jerry, but Stan doesn't know anything about him."

"If you believe he was her uncle, I'll sell you a piece of land in the Everglades. Kim told me she planned to leave Stan, and this Uncle Jerry was her ticket out the door."

Chapter
Nine

"I'm on my way to Miriam's house," Marla told Vail after dialing his number on her cell phone. Traffic wasn't bad heading east on Broward Boulevard at 5:45 P.M., while long lines snaked in the opposite lanes. The sun had begun its daily descent, darkening the eastern horizon while awing visitors on the Gulf Coast. Marla hoped the snowbirds appreciated their balmy winter evenings, especially since the temperature had hit seventy.

"What happened with Stan?" Vail's gruff voice demanded.

She'd reached him at his office and imagined him at his desk in his work shirt and tie. A wave of longing shot through her. She'd rather spend the evening sparring verbally with Vail than fawning over Miriam.

No, that wasn't true. She looked forward to bringing some cheer to the old lady.

"Stan showed me the Pearl family albums. I found a space where your photograph belonged. The man in the picture is Jeremiah Dooley. A woman is with him in another photo, but Stan couldn't identify her."

"Good work." His smooth tone held warm approval.

"I mentioned him to the neighbors. They said Jerry drives a Porsche and runs some type of ministry. I have a phone number, but my purse is in the backseat."

"Tell me about the neighbors."

She steered with her free hand, watching the street signs as she crossed Federal Highway. "Elise Addison suspected that her husband Cliff was interested in Kim. She didn't shed any tears over Kim's death. Jessica Shpritz, on the other hand, believed Uncle Jerry was Kim's ticket to freedom. She implied they weren't blood relatives, either. So according to the neighbors, Kim was fooling around with either Cliff or this Jeremiah guy."

"I've got news for you; they're both wrong. Kim was fooling around all right, but with her former flame, Gary Waterford."

"I'd wondered about them." She veered left to a banyan-lined street in an older section of Fort Lauderdale. Flowering hibiscus and bougainvillea added splashes of crimson and pink. "Gary lied about not seeing Kim since her marriage to Stan. Their mutual friend Lacey clued me in. She gave me the impression that Gary is her territory, but maybe I'm wrong."

"What else did Stan tell you today?"

"He misses Kimberly. I actually felt sorry for him."

"Is that all you felt for Kaufman?"

"Dalton, you're not still jealous, are you? I told you there's nothing to worry about. Why don't I prove it to you by having you and Brianna come for dinner like I promised? We can talk about her birthday party. Do you have plans for tomorrow evening? I get off work at six, so you could come around seven. I'll whip up something special."

"You've got a date. Oh, there's something else—"

"I gotta go. Here's the road to their compound. Call me tomorrow."

She put the cell phone in her purse before emerging from the car in front of the Pearl mansion. A cloyingly sweet fragrance filled the air. She stretched her limbs, feeling strange wearing a white nurse's outfit. She'd chosen a tunic top and matching pants at the uniform store. On her feet, she wore a pair of sturdy New Balance walking shoes.

Juggling her sack of supplies and her purse, she trudged up the steps to the front door. Raoul swung it open before she rang the bell.

"You're late," Morris said, greeting her in the mirrored foyer. He tapped his foot impatiently. "Agnes left a half hour ago. Stella is keeping Miriam company upstairs."

"Sorry, I was coming from—" She stopped herself, having almost said *from my salon.* "From West Broward," she amended. "Traffic was heavy. I'll leave earlier next week."

"See that you do." He eyed her canvas bag suspiciously. "What's making that bulge?"

"I brought a few supplies." Curling iron, hair spray, brush, teasing comb, shears—all the essentials. Plus, she'd brought snacks and reading material in case Miriam fell asleep. "When do you expect Agnes to return?"

"Around ten." He paused, scrutinizing her. "Elizabeth spoke very highly of you."

"Who?" Turning, Marla headed for the stairs. Her foot had reached the fourth rung when Morris replied.

"Elizabeth Marsh, the woman you care for during the week. I called her when I checked your references."

"Oh!" Startled, Marla tripped on a fold in the carpet. Tottering backward, she lunged for the banister as her purse and canvas bag sailed through the air. Breath rushed from her lungs, but she managed to grab the rail and haul herself upright.

"Sorry," she mumbled, shaken. Her face reddened at the contemptuous look he gave her. *Why am I such a klutz whenever I come here?*

"You're not hurt, are you?" he asked without an ounce of genuine concern.

"I'm fine, thanks."

Her purse contents had spilled onto the marble tile. Before she could retrieve her things, Morris stooped to gather the makeup items, daily planner, pens, breath mints, and travel brochures for Tahiti she kept in her handbag. Not that she'd ever get there, but it was fun to daydream. Her throat tightened when she noticed Morris holding the paper with Jeremiah Dooley's name. His eyes narrowed imperceptibly before he stuffed the item into her purse along with the rest of her belongings.

"Elizabeth said to tell you hello," he continued, regarding her with a stony expression.

"Thank you." So he'd checked with Tally's mother to see if Marla really worked there. Thank goodness Tally had briefed her mom who was currently in town. "I'll go see Miriam now."

After retrieving her bags, she proceeded upstairs and breezed into Miriam's room.

Stella, who'd been sitting in a bedside chair, rose at her entrance. "It's about time! I have to get ready for dinner. At least *we're* conscientious about watching the clock. Morris has a fit if any of us hold up the cook. What was all that ruckus in the hallway?"

Marla felt like a schoolgirl confronting her teacher. "I tripped on the stairs."

"Figures. Hereafter, I won't wait around for you. You'd better be on time when you come next week. Mother needs help with her meal. See to it."

Marla turned her attention to Miriam. "Why are you in bed and wearing a nightgown already? It's just after six. And what is that awful stuff you're eating? It looks like baby food."

"Nice to see you again, dearie. This is my usual dinner. Can't chew well, you know."

"Nonsense, you can do better than this. No wonder you're so thin. Why don't you join the family downstairs?"

"I'm too weak."

"I'll help you get up. Does Agnes feed you in bed every night?" she asked, appalled.

"Of course she does. Agnes knows what's best for me."

"What time do your children gather for dinner?"

"Seven-thirty." Miriam's sad eyes regarded her from behind a pair of round eyeglasses. "I haven't made it down there in ages."

Marla cast a quick glance at Miriam's disheveled gray hair. "How about if we give it a try? If you get too tired, I'll bring you back to your room. Let's get you dressed, and then I'll fix your hair."

"I don't know. Agnes said I may be getting sick. I've been cough-ing ever since Sunday when you took me outside."

"You sound fine. What you need is some decent food and a change of scenery. I insist."

"You're a stubborn girl, aren't you? My teeth are in a cup in the bathroom. You'll have to clean them."

The things I do to gather information. How could she broach the topic of Jeremiah Dooley? Maybe by asking about Kim's relatives on her father's side. But how to get started?

In the lavatory, Marla discovered a set of false teeth soaking in a glass. She brushed them with toothpaste and rinsed them under cold water.

"Here," she said to Miriam, handing her the bridge.

"You'd better check my temperature before going to all this trou-ble," Miriam advised after fitting in her teeth. "You wouldn't want me getting worse sick by going downstairs."

"It can't do you any good to stay in bed all day," Marla muttered. She noticed the disapproving look on Miriam's face. "Oh, very well. Where's the thermometer?"

"Look in the bathroom, top right drawer."

Marla hadn't seen an old-fashioned mercury thermometer in years, but then she rarely took her own temperature. "Open your mouth," she ordered the old lady when she returned.

"Don't you know anything? That's a rectal thermometer."

Marla's nerveless fingers nearly dropped the instrument on the floor. "Excuse me?"

"You have to shake it down first. Look at the silver bar to get a reading."

Marla shook the thermometer then peered at the instrument, but for the life of her, she couldn't figure it out.

"Where's the lubricant?" The old lady gave Marla an exasperated look.

"Huh?"

"You need to put some K-Y Jelly on first. You'll find it in that same drawer."

"Oh, right."

While Marla scurried to comply, she heard Miriam mumble, "If that gal is a trained nurse's aide, then I'm twenty years old."

Back in the bedroom once again, Marla squeezed the petroleum jelly around the thermometer's tip. *Uh oh, I should have brought a tissue*, she thought when it dribbled onto the bed linens. *This is worse than that bikini wax I did in my first job as a beautician.* She'd never forget the customer who'd demanded that particular wax job, and Marla had vowed never to repeat the experience. *This holds a close second*, she thought, perspiration beading her brow.

"Look, I can't do this," she confessed. "There has to be an oral thermometer in the house. They make those digital ones now."

"Oh, forget it, dearie. I wouldn't be getting so riled if I was sick. It makes me wonder, though, where you received your education."

Marla straightened, squaring her shoulders. "I learned on the job. What I do doesn't require formal nurse's training. I've had plenty of experience caring for elderly ladies." *That's it, girl, the truth is always best.* "We'll get you dressed, then I'll do your hair," she added in a firm tone. She'd spiff the old lady so that she'd look good, and that in turn would make her feel better. It was amazing what proper grooming could do for a person's sense of well-being.

After helping Miriam change into a royal blue slacks outfit, she transferred her patient to a wheelchair and rolled her into the bathroom.

Within fifteen minutes, she'd curled, teased, and sprayed the old lady's coiffure. "You need some color on your cheeks," she added, applying some cosmetics found in a drawer. They were dried from disuse; she'd have to take the old lady shopping to buy a new supply.

Satisfied with the results, she turned Miriam to face the mirror. Pride swelled as a look of stunned surprise spread on Miriam's face.

"I can't believe it! You've made me look years younger."

"You'll look even better after I give you a perm on Sunday. Let's go down to dinner. You don't want to be late."

"Hmph! I must say you're a better hairdresser than you are a nurse, dearie."

Don't I know!

The surprise Miriam had exhibited at her new appearance was nothing compared to the shocked glances in the dining room. Six family members, seated around a rectangular dining table covered with a lace cloth, gaped at the matriarch.

"Mother! What are you doing out of bed?" Stella shrieked.

Morris, at the head of the table, shot to his feet. "You aren't well enough to join us."

"What happened to your hair?" Florence chimed in.

"Sit down, all of you. Kathleen," Miriam addressed the maid, "set an extra two places for us."

"Aye, madam."

Marla hadn't expected to be seated at the family dinner table. Swallowing hard, she took a place next to a woman seated on Morris's left. Across from them sat them a couple of teenage boys. The old lady introduced everyone. Barbara, Morris's wife, gave her a friendly smile. It was a much warmer welcome than the frosty glares she got from the two sisters.

"Mother, are you sure you're up to this?" Morris asked, concern etching his features. "Agnes said you were ill."

The old lady raised her eyebrows, darkened with the help of a cosmetic pencil. "Do I look sick?"

"You look wonderful," Stella gushed. "I love your hair that way, and you must be feeling good enough to put on makeup."

"Marla deserves the credit. I was feeling low before she came, but now I'm much better."

"You'll be stronger after a real meal," Marla inserted.

Their gazes swung to her in silent scrutiny, and she flushed. Wearing a white uniform made her self-conscious, especially when the others had dressed for dinner. Stella wore a satiny jacket dress that slenderized her stout figure. Its leaf green color enhanced her auburn layered hair and fair complexion. Not to be outdone, Florence had encased her tall, svelte shape in a silk sheath tiger print. It matched her dyed blond hair swept into a French twist. While her sister wore a sparsity of cosmetics, Florence had applied enough foundation to cover every wrinkle. At least Barbara wore a less pretentious pants set, Marla thought, instinctively liking the woman.

During the soup course, she chatted amiably with Morris's wife, careful not to reveal too much about her own background.

"They own coffee plantations in Costa Rica and South America," Barbara explained in response to Marla's question about the family business.

"Harris's father bought the plantations in eighteen-ninety," Miriam announced proudly, listening in on Marla's other side. "I reviewed the accounts yesterday with Agnes, and I noticed severely reduced profits. Morris, you didn't tell me we were having a problem."

Her son straightened his tie. "Prices are higher due to frost damage in Brazil. Our warehouse inventories are one third of last year's level."

"What are you doing about it?" the matriarch demanded, pinning him with her penetrating gaze.

"Not much we can do. The frost damaged nearly half of the country's three billion coffee trees. Our prices have gone up almost two dollars a pound since this time last year."

"Soon your product will match the cost of gourmet shade-grown coffee," Barbara commented. "Didn't I tell you to invest in some of those farms?"

"What's that, dearie?"

Barbara addressed her mother-in-law. "I belong to a bird conservation group. We're concerned about migratory birds who seek refuge for the winter in tropical tree canopies. More than one hundred and fifty species of songbirds nest in those trees, and the coffee plants that grow beneath them mature in the shady habitat. Unfortunately, the rain forests are being razed, so coffee growers can produce higher-yield crops sustained with pesticides and fertilizers."

"That's a shame," Marla mumbled. She appreciated the value of healthy trees to earth's ecology.

"Supplies are too limited to offer a single brew based on shade-grown plants," Morris countered. "We're having enough inventory problems with the frost damage. It's more cost-efficient to produce larger yields using modern technology. Our methods are becoming more widespread throughout the industry."

"I disagree." Barbara's tone indicated this was an ongoing argument. "Some of the finest coffee in the world is grown on thousands of low-tech farms where the cherries ripen in the shade without help from chemicals."

"Cherries?" Marla asked, confused.

"That's the name for the red fruit," Barbara explained. "When the cherries mature more slowly, their natural sugars increase. It makes a better-tasting coffee. You can buy these products now if you look for the songbird labels."

Marla was more interested in the financial problems plaguing Morris's company. Would Kimberly's share of their inheritance infuse needed capital into a floundering enterprise?

"Florence is helping plan our fund-raiser," Barbara said, beaming at her sister-in-law. "Stella, would you like to do the centerpieces?"

"Your money comes from *our* plantations, girls," Miriam snapped. "You should be supporting your brother."

"Sure, I'll help you," Stella replied, ignoring her mother.

"Was your daughter involved in this bird group as well?" Marla asked.

Stella gave a startled look as though she only just realized Marla was present. "She didn't care a whit for the family business or for volunteer work. Like me, Kim had a flair for design, but then she got bitten by the genealogy bug."

"Researching family trees is a popular pastime." Marla noticed an exchange of glances between Morris and Florence.

"Yes, and that's one of the reasons why I want our family albums back," Stella said. "I'm hoping to continue Kim's work, but I have to preserve the albums first. The photos need to be transferred to acid- and lignin-free pages. That lousy husband of hers won't give them to us." She clasped her hands and moisture tinged her lashes.

Marla busied herself cutting the old lady's steak into tiny pieces. "I'm so sorry. Miriam told me what happened to your daughter.

Perhaps her husband feels the albums are important to the police. I imagine he's anxious to find her killer."

"The cops should have kept him in jail! He wasn't the right man for her," Stella said, her words ending in a sob. "My poor baby."

"What a tragedy for someone so young," Marla commiserated. "Her funeral must have been well attended."

Stella sniffed. "Not really, just her friends and us."

"Oh? She didn't have any relatives on her father's side?"

"None who could come: an elderly aunt in a nursing home and a cousin in California whom she'd never met."

"Her father didn't have any brothers?"

Morris's coffee cup clattered into its saucer, sloshing the dark liquid onto his shirt.

"Marla, perhaps you'd be kind enough to help my mother with her asparagus? She's having trouble slicing it." He eyed the others. "Let's dispense with discussing business at the dinner table, shall we? Boys, let's hear from you," he said to his sons, who ate silently with bored expressions.

The rest of the evening wasn't nearly so stimulating as Marla prepared Miriam for bed and waited for the nurse to return. Agnes stalked in at five minutes past ten.

"I heard all about you," the heavyset woman said in a grating tone. They stood in the hallway so as not to disturb Miriam who'd fallen asleep. "If you hope to take my place by insinuating yourself into this family, you're mistaken, young lady. Miriam needs me to look after her properly. Now that you've exhausted her, it'll be the worse for me tomorrow when I have to return her to health."

"There's nothing wrong with her." Marla clutched her bags in one hand. "Miriam perked up this evening after I fixed her hair and put some makeup on her face. She was delighted to join the family. It isn't right to treat her like an invalid."

"She's eighty-five years old. The woman is frail and doesn't do well being exposed to the elements."

"Miriam is strong-willed and not as fragile as you think. She's sharp and alert for someone her age, especially if she can still review the family's financial accounts."

"What do you know about that?" Agnes stepped closer.

"She'd mentioned that she went over the books with you and found some decreased profits from the business. Morris explained about the lower inventory in their warehouses related to frost damage, and how that led to higher prices for their coffee."

Agnes's shoulders hunched. "You had no business listening in on a family discussion. It's not your place."

"My place is wherever Miriam wants me," Marla retorted. "But don't worry. I already work for another lady full time. I don't want your job."

As she walked toward the staircase, she felt Agnes's eyes on her back as though they were torches. She'd reached the foyer, almost joyful with relief, when Florence appeared around the corner. Raoul was noticeably absent from his post at the door.

"Oh, here you are," Kim's aunt said, approaching with the slinkiness of a cat. She cast a furtive glance over her shoulder, then lowered her voice. "I wanted to mention one thing before you left. My niece was murdered. It can be dangerous to ask too many questions, if you know what I mean."

Chapter Ten

Marla had little time to contemplate Florence's words of warning on Friday morning. Her ten o'clock appointment at the School of Arts and Design preoccupied her mind. When she arrived at the massive pink-facade building on Hollywood Boulevard, her hopes rose that this visit would produce something of value. So far, she hadn't any strong leads regarding Kimberly's killer. Everyone who knew Kim seemed to have something to hide.

A directory led her to the admissions office on an upper level. After giving her name to a receptionist, she took a seat and nervously thumbed through an *Entertainment Weekly* magazine. Five minutes later a man wearing a black suit and a friendly smile approached.

"Miss Shore? I'm John Crawford, one of the admission counselors. Please follow me to my office."

As soon as they were alone, Marla offered her rehearsed speech. "I was referred here by Kimberly Kaufman. I know you share in my sorrow about what happened to her. I'm interested in your interior design program, but this is an upsetting time for me. I'm a close friend of the family," she added in what she hoped was a convincing tone.

"We were stunned to hear the news of Kimberly's death. She was well liked by her peers." The admissions counselor opened a packet on his desk and picked up a pen. His brown eyes regarded her curiously. "What made you interested in interior design, Marla? I presume you're in some other field right now."

"I'm a hairdresser, but I don't like the long hours of standing on my feet. Creatively, I'd rather work with colors and design."

"Our program is very intensive, but you don't need any prior experience. Have you taken any college courses?"

Noticing his pen poised to write, Marla moistened her lips. She didn't have time for a lengthy interview. "Before we fill out any forms, is it possible for me to peek at some of the classes Kim attended and talk to her friends? She spoke so highly of your school, but I'm not sure about the level of commitment I can make right now. I'll have to work part time."

He nodded sympathetically. "Our average student is twenty-seven years old. Many are making career changes. They do quite well because they're already experienced in the working world."

His expression sobered, reminding Marla of a former math teacher who'd spent numerous afternoons tutoring her on the complexities of college algebra. "We expect you to attend classes regularly, including summers," he said in a didactic tone. "Here's a schedule of the sessions."

She took the paper, anxious to move on. She'd learn nothing if they were stuck in this office for the entire hour.

"As you'll notice, there's a track of general college courses. These can be waived if you've already satisfied the requirements. Our curriculum takes three years if you attend full time. You'll graduate with a bachelor's degree." He shuffled papers. "According to this schedule, Kim would've been in textiles class now. Would you like to check it out? I'll introduce you to her friends."

"That's great. Thanks."

Marla was dazzled by an array of fabrics and home decorating materials in the textiles classroom. A sea of faces greeted her as they entered. Students sat on stools around large rectangular tables on which were displayed numerous samples.

Mr. Crawford spoke quietly to the teacher, then motioned for Marla to come forward. "This is Sue Burns," he said, indicating the teacher. "She'll seat you with Kim's friends. You can join the class to get a feel for what it's like here."

This was more than she'd hoped for. She gave him a warm smile and shook his hand. "Thanks so much. I really appreciate your kindness. I'll get back to you on my application," she said before turning to the instructor.

A few moments later, she was seated beside Rocco Morales and Christine Kent, supposedly Kim's bosom buddies. A surreptitious glance at her watch made her heart flutter. She'd better hurry if she wanted to be back at the salon in time for her client.

When the teacher freed them to work on assigned group projects, Marla turned to the duo. "I understand Kim was excited about her classes," she remarked to Christine, a round-faced brunette who wore her hair in a ponytail. A splatter of freckles decorated her complexion like spots on a Dalmatian. Marla thought they were rather cute, but from the girl's application of cover-up, it appeared she didn't share Marla's opinion.

"How did you know her?" Rocco interrupted. Despite his macho name, he was a spindly creature. Too tall for his musculature, he looked like a tree that would blow down in a stiff wind. In contrast, Christine was stout as a shrub.

"I'm a friend of the family."

"I didn't see you at the funeral," he said, his natural squint becoming more pronounced.

"I was working. Wasn't it awful how she died?" Marla shook her head in pretended sympathy. "I couldn't believe it when I heard the news."

"Yeah, what a bummer." Rocco exchanged a glance with Christine.

Marla felt she needed to prove her acquaintance with Kim. "It's a shame she won't be able to carry out her plans now."

"Oh God," Christine burst out, "and with her being, you know, it was such a struggle."

"Her being what?"

Christine's jade eyes widened. "If she didn't tell you, it's not for me to say."

"Gary had plenty to say on the subject," Rocco snapped. "Remember his snide comments the last time we all went out together?" He picked up a swatch of thin cotton material. Rubbing it between his fingers, he gave a grunt of disapproval and tossed it aside.

"Gary Waterford?" Marla said.

"You know him?" Christine raised an eyebrow.

"I spoke to him about Kim."

"Gary didn't say anything about us, did he?"

"No, but he mentioned Kim's friend Lacey."

Rocco laughed. "That guy likes to walk a tightrope."

"Look who's talking," Christine countered, twisting a brocade fabric sample. "Until they find out who killed Kimberly, we're all under scrutiny."

"You said you're a friend of the family. Which family?" Rocco demanded.

Marla didn't think Stan would be the correct choice. "Kim's grandmother, Miriam." That much was true, at least. "Have the cops talked to you about Kim?" she asked, tucking a loose strand of chestnut hair behind her ear.

"They've questioned us," Christine admitted.

"We had nothing much to contribute," Rocco said, staring pointedly at her.

Electricity crackled between the pair, but Marla couldn't discern the cause. "The sooner this case is closed, the quicker we can get back to our normal lives," she said soothingly. "We all want justice for Kim. Do you have any idea who might have wanted to harm her?"

Marla's cell phone rang before she had a chance to hear their answer. Wincing at the noise, she pulled it out of her bag and pushed the TALK button.

"Marla, where are you?" Nicole's voice said. "I thought you'd be back at the salon by now."

"Why, is my next customer there already?" she answered in a hushed tone. "I still have twenty minutes."

"Betsy canceled. I don't know what's happening, but you have a lot of no-shows lately. You lost that highlights yesterday. This morning your first appointment wasn't until eleven, and now this."

A frown of worry creased Marla's brow. "I see your point, but I'll deal with it later. I'm in the middle of something important. See you soon." She hung up, putting the cell phone back in her purse. Darn, now she'd lost Rocco and Christine's attention. They were occupied on their project, and the class was nearly over.

"Can I treat you to an early lunch? It has to be quick. I'm expected back at work." She handed them each a business card.

"I thought you were applying for school here," Christine said, stuffing her books into a backpack along with Marla's card. Other students had already left the classroom.

"I'm a hairdresser, but I've always been interested in design. I didn't know Kim that well, but she inspired me to check out this school." She paused. "Her grandmother is anxious to learn the truth about what happened to her."

"I don't know why," Christine said, giving her a curious glance. "Miriam cut her off. She's the whole reason Kim felt trapped."

Rocco trailed behind as they strolled into the hallway. It would have been easier to talk to Christine alone, because the girl genuinely seemed to care about Kim. Marla wasn't sure about Rocco, but she sensed self-interest motivated him. He shadowed them like a Secret Service guard, silent and observant.

In a cafeteria, Marla paid for their food, aware that she didn't have time to linger. After eating a few bites of her tuna sandwich, she focused on Christine's last words.

"What did you mean about Miriam cutting off Kimberly?"

"The old lady wouldn't part with any of her husband's money, even though Kim was entitled to an allowance. Kim said her grandmother insisted she prove her worth, so she didn't turn out like her useless mother. She had to wait until she reached thirty to access her trust fund," Christine explained.

"How did that make her feel trapped?" Marla queried.

"Kim's mother didn't prepare her for the working world. It wasn't her fault if she led a pampered life. That's why she married Stan."

Rocco took a gulp of his Coke. His prominent Adam's apple

bobbed up and down when he swallowed. "Kaufman is a jerk. He didn't know how to handle her, man."

"She told us about the nasty things he did to her," Christine confided, her gaze darkening. "If I were married to a loser like him, I'd sure make a quick exit!"

"Is that what Kim tried to do?" Marla asked. Not so hungry, she pushed away her tray.

"Going to this school was her hope for the future," Christine said. "She got fired up about the program. Finally, she'd found something suited to her talent. When they lived in Palm Beach, her mother kept redecorating their house, and Kim helped her choose fabrics and such. She'd just never thought of the possibilities for a career in design before, plus she lacked the patience." Her expression soured. "Now that she'd finally set goals, Kim feared Stan would discover her ruse. She couldn't lie to him forever. If he learned about her plans, he would have been furious."

"Plans to pursue a career, or her intent to leave him?"

"Both. My guess is, Stan found out about Gary Waterford."

"You're forgetting something," Rocco interrupted. "Kim told us she'd be getting some money soon, and it would be enough to let her get a place of her own. It would come from the same source that paid her tuition."

"Why did you mention Gary?" Marla said. "Did he loan her money?"

"Are you kidding?" Rocco lifted his eyebrows. "Gary was looking forward to using her trust fund. I think that's the only reason he let her play up to him. Lacey is more his type."

"You don't know that," Christine retorted. "Kim told me she and Gary were getting back together. I think Stan found out, and he killed Kim so she wouldn't leave him for another man. In his eyes, she belonged to him. If he learned—"

"Maybe Lacey is the one we should consider," Marla interceded before she lost her train of thought. "How serious is she about Gary? She could have been jealous over his attention to Kim."

"I think you're both wrong about Gary. He's hot for Lacey." Rocco folded his arms across his chest.

"Maybe the two of them conspired to get Kim's money," Marla suggested. "Is Gary in debt?"

Rocco snorted. "He's always in debt."

"Gary would have had to leave Kim in order to be with Lacey, so that doesn't make sense," Christine contributed.

"Murder doesn't have to make sense," Marla reminded her. "What about this extra source of income you'd mentioned? If it wasn't coming from Gary, what was Kim talking about?"

Christine gave her a sly look. "I didn't tell this to the police, but Kim mentioned the name of Stan's previous wife."

Marla stiffened. "Who?"

"Leah Kaufman. It's possible Kim worked out an arrangement with her."

"What do you mean? I saw Leah recently, and it looked as though she could use extra income herself. She has two children to support."

"Sorry," Christine said, rising. "Regarding Kimberly, there are some secrets we can't reveal. She kept our confidences, so the least we can do is return the favor."

At her gesture, Rocco shoved to his feet. They left the cafeteria arm in arm, smug smiles on their faces.

Marla had just thrown out her trash and turned toward the exit when a hand clamped on her shoulder.

"I'm sorry, I couldn't help overhearing part of your conversation," said an Asian student balancing a stack of books. "I liked Kim, so I'll help you. Kim said something to me after she'd been to Rocco's apartment: *I could get him kicked out of school.* But she'd promised to keep quiet, because the reverse was also true. They were protecting each other. I was afraid for her, because Rocco acts weird sometimes. He's not someone I would trust."

Marla didn't have time to think about her conversation at the school until later. Finishing work at the salon, dashing home to start meal preparations, and answering phone calls kept her occupied until Vail and Brianna showed up for dinner.

"Hi, Brie," she said, hugging the girl, who wore jeans and a Banana Republic sweater along with a sullen expression on her face.

Long braids trailed down her back, making Brianna appear younger than her twelve years.

Vail grinned his greeting, handing her a bottle of chilled chardonnay. His clothing bore an L.L. Bean look: blue cotton pinpoint oxford shirt, Norwegian crewneck sweater in charcoal to match his hair, and black wool gabardine trousers. When he brushed past her, she got a whiff of spice cologne that set her pulse thrumming.

She engaged her guests in small talk during the salad course. When they were on the lasagna, she broached the subject that bothered her.

"What do you think Rocco and Christine were hiding?" she asked, after relating the gist of their conversation. "Whatever it is can get them kicked out of school. They knew something about Kimberly that might have gotten her in trouble, too."

"When you saw Stan, did he mention anything about Gary Waterford?" Vail asked between bites. His casual tone belied the keen interest in his eyes.

"No, why? Do you think he knew Gary and Kim were seeing each other?"

"Possibly."

"Do you think this is the secret Christine meant?"

"Kim's personal love life wouldn't get her thrown out of school. If Stan learned she wasn't spending time at the athletic club, however, he might have interfered."

"How? By notifying the school she didn't have his approval to attend? So what?"

"Where did she get the money for tuition?" Brianna cut in.

"Good question." Vail beamed proudly at his daughter.

Marla studied the girl thoughtfully. "Perhaps that's how Stan would have ended her ambitions. If he knew where she got the resources . . ." She let her voice trail off, wondering how Kimberly had paid for her college costs. If Miriam wasn't giving her an allowance, than her only source of income was Stan. Unless someone else was helping Kim, willingly or not. Could she have resorted to blackmail?

"Marla, you said you'd plan my birthday party," Brianna said, licking a dribble of tomato sauce from her mouth. "Are you sure you have time? I mean, between work and all, you're so busy. It's enough that you still drive me to dance class when Daddy works late."

Marla smiled gently. "It's something I want to do, honey. I don't have much experience with this sort of thing, though. The places I checked are way too much money." She rattled off the names of the caterers.

"This is a thirteenth birthday party, not a bar mitzvah," Vail reminded her, chewing a piece of garlic bread. His bemused glance created havoc with her hormones.

"Bat mitzvah," she corrected. "I don't know who else to call."

"Heck, Marla, don't you know anything about kids?" Brianna rolled her eyes as though her patience was being sorely tested.

"Suppose you tell me what to do."

"Look in the Yellow Pages. You're not trying very hard." Her accusing glance made Marla swallow guiltily.

"I thought you wanted a big splash. Aren't you being invited to a lot of fancy parties?"

"My friends' parents can spend all their money on expensive affairs. I don't have to compete."

"You're right. I'll work on it this weekend." The deeper she got involved with Vail, the more obligations she took on with his daughter. Marla had enough responsibilities already, but she felt bad for the girl, whose mother had passed away. Brianna needed a guiding female hand, not that Marla was applying for the role. It just seemed to drift in her direction, and she'd never been able to say no to someone in need.

She switched to a more comfortable topic. "Did you look up that phone number I gave you for Jeremiah Dooley?" she asked Vail, after refilling his wineglass.

He nodded, his smoky gaze searing through her defenses. When he looked at her that way, it was difficult to deny him anything. "It connects to the Ministry of Hope in Tarpon Springs," he said. "A tape recording mentions Dooley's Sunday morning television show. Channel thirty-nine at eight o'clock. He's some kind of televangelist."

"How do you suppose Kim met him?" A bite of lasagna slid down her throat, its tangy tomato flavor lingering on her tongue.

"Beats me. I need to talk to this fellow. I left a message, so I hope he calls back. Otherwise, I thought I'd take a drive up on Monday. Want to come?"

"That's a long ride for one day. Isn't it five hours each way?"

"She's right, Daddy," Brianna said, innocent brown eyes regarding him. "Marla has enough to do. You should go by yourself, or else let me skip school, and I'll go with you."

He chuckled. "I don't think so, muffin."

"I'd be happy to come along," Marla quickly inserted. "Will Carmen stay with Brianna after school until we get home?"

"I don't need a baby-sitter," the girl whined.

"I'll ask the housekeeper," Vail said to her. "I won't leave you alone for that long. We'd be getting back very late."

Brianna gave Marla a resentful glare. "You didn't tell *her* about the murder weapon. How come you can tell me these things, but you won't let me come along?"

Marla put down her fork. "What's this?"

Vail used a napkin to wipe his mouth, but it didn't erase the grimace of annoyance on his face. "I was going to mention it."

"Oh yeah? When?" she retorted. "Spill it, Detective."

"We found a dagger, or actually a letter opener, buried in Kaufman's backyard. Tests have proved conclusively that it was the murder weapon. Stan's name is etched on the blade."

Chapter
Eleven

"Finding the murder weapon in Stan's yard doesn't mean anything," Marla said, stiffening. "The killer must have dropped it there."

"Uh-huh." Vail, finished with his meal, pushed his empty plate to the side.

She glanced at his implacable expression. "If Stan murdered his wife, do you think he'd leave the knife in such an obvious place?"

"The front door was unlocked. Maybe he killed her, opened the door, ran outside and around to the back of his house. He wasn't thinking straight, just wanted to get rid of the letter opener with its damning inscription."

"Oh, and then he returned inside the house to call the police? Stan wouldn't be so stupid. Did you tell him you'd found the weapon?"

"Not yet, and you won't tell him either."

They glared at each other, while Marla's heart pounded in her chest until another thought surfaced. "Christine mentioned Leah's name during our conversation. She said Kim might have worked out an arrangement with Leah. What do you suppose this meant?"

"Are you implicating Leah?"

"I'm not implicating anyone! Unlike you, I have an open mind. I don't believe Stan killed his wife."

"You're biased in his favor."

"And you're jealous!" Marla shoved to her feet. Ignoring the smirk on Brianna's face, she collected their dishes.

In the kitchen, she rinsed the plates. Footfalls sounded behind her, and she felt Vail's hands on her waist. Her breath hitched as his body heat radiated toward her.

"Sorry," he said in a soft, low voice that aroused her senses.

Clutching a dish in her hand, she resisted the urge to turn into his embrace. They still had too many barriers between them despite their shared confidences.

"You know I don't want you to get hurt," he murmured, his hot breath near her ear. The scent of wine mingled with his masculine essence to batter down her resolve.

"Dalton, do you really believe Stan is guilty?" She placed the plate into a dish drainer and then wiped her hands on a towel. Slowly, she turned to face him. His arms encircled her, drawing her close. Through her cranberry sweater and short black skirt, she felt every point of contact between them.

"He's the most logical suspect, but I'm looking into all possibilities. Circumstantial evidence isn't enough; it has to be conclusive."

"I know you want Stan to be the culprit."

"Only so he'll stop bothering you." His intense gaze stole her breath. "You've had a lot of grief from him in the past. It's time to turn the page on that chapter in your life."

"Same as for you and Brianna? You have your own sorrows that need healing."

He lowered his head until his lips hovered above hers. "We can help each other."

A few inches more and their mouths would meet. Marla tilted her head, wanting nothing more than to be pulled into his arms.

"Hey, isn't it time for dessert?" Brianna demanded, trouncing into the room.

Marla jerked back, but Vail didn't let go of her. His eyes flamed with desire. "Brianna, you're going to have to get used to this," he said. "Marla and I like each other."

"So I see," Brianna said, her voice full of disgust.

Marla disentangled herself, turning to the preteen. "I care about your father, honey, and about you, too. I'm not trying to steal your father's attention, or . . . or subvert your mother's memory. I'd like to be part of your lives . . . I think."

"Well, you're not very helpful about my birthday," Brianna whined, but some of the sullenness left her expression.

Marla blinked. Was that a hint of grudging respect she detected? "I promise I'll work on it this weekend," she said.

"We'll have more opportunities to discuss things on Monday," Vail added, his suggestive gaze making her wonder what other activities he had in mind.

I don't know how much talking we'll do, Marla thought to herself. A whole day together without distractions. Just thinking about it made a delicious shiver run up her spine. Still, they had a long drive either way to Tarpon Springs. *Not much you can do with a console between your car seats.*

"I made a lemon meringue pie for dessert," she announced. "Oh, wait till you hear what my mother said about Roger. He's Ma's new boyfriend," she explained to Brianna.

Once they'd settled in the dining room, she told him about her earlier conversation. "Roger bought tickets to the Miami City Ballet so he can escort Ma to the next performance. By coincidence, he also likes to play bridge and feast on Thai food. Don't you think it's strange how they have so many interests in common?" she asked Vail.

"Why do you consider it strange?" queried Brianna, giving her a frank stare. "Just because you and Daddy have nothing you do together?"

"We talk about murder suspects." Vail winked at Marla.

"You know what I mean." Brianna played with her fork, pushing pieces of pie around on her plate. "We used to take walks in the park with Mom, and we'd have contests on who could identify the most palms. And how about action films? Have you ever taken Marla to see one? You and Mom studied the newspaper listings together."

"I didn't know you liked those things," Marla said quietly, feeling like an intruder.

"There's a lot you don't know about me," he replied, his eyes sparking with an unmistakable invitation.

"I'm just curious how Roger waltzed into my mother's life, likes the same things she does, and Ma falls for him like a schoolgirl. No offense, Brianna." Her face reddened.

"You're probably reading too much into things," said Vail. "Why don't you invite them both over one evening so you can get to know the guy?"

"I don't have any free time!"

She contemplated her words Sunday morning on her way to the Pearl residence. Saturday she'd been too busy with work and book-keeping to spare any thoughts beyond her salon. Today would be taken up with Miriam all day, and tomorrow she and Vail would have their excursion. What Marla needed was to divide herself into three people: one to manage the salon and work with her clients, a double role in itself that was difficult enough to handle; one to chase after suspects; and one to relax and enjoy life. This last goal seemed to be the most elusive, and if she got involved with Brianna, she could kiss freedom out the door. What was it she'd said to Vail? *I'd like to be part of your lives.* Her face blanched as she recalled her exact words.

Don't think about that now. You've got important things ahead of you today.

Marla arrived at the mansion early enough to catch Agnes before she left. "We have to talk," she said to the nurse in the downstairs hallway where Agnes donned a sweater prior to leaving. Smoothing down her starched white uniform, Marla plopped a hand on her hip.

Agnes, her hair pulled into a severe bun, scowled at her. "You've given Miriam ideas that aren't good for her. Going outside in the cold weather, joining the family for dinner. She gets worn out from these efforts, and then I have to work doubly hard to keep her well. I've recommended to Madam and her son to dismiss you."

"You treat the old lady like an invalid, so it's no wonder she tires easily," Marla retorted. "With you as her caretaker, she's cooped up in her room all day. If anything isn't healthy, it's confinement and limiting Miriam's social contacts!"

"Who are you to talk about health, missy? I'd like to see your credentials."

"Morris accepted my references. I don't have to show you anything," Marla said, lifting her chin.

"If the old lady hadn't taken a liking to you, you'd be gone by now."

"But I'm not, am I? Miriam enjoys my company, which is probably more than she can say for yours."

Agnes's expression, which already looked as though she'd swallowed a prune pit, became more taut. "If I didn't have to leave . . ."

"What is this pressing personal business, Agnes? How come you haven't needed to take Sundays off on a regular basis before? Why now?"

"I always had a day off each week."

"But not so urgently, from what Miriam told me. Do you have a sick relative who needs care? Or are you meeting someone of whom Miriam would disapprove?" Marla asked.

A flash of anxiety clouded Agnes's blue eyes. "I don't believe it's your concern. See that you take good care of Miriam today. I don't want any harm to come to her under your ministrations."

The nurse's words set off alarm bells, and Marla hastened upstairs, but the old lady slept peacefully in her bed. Time to get her up and out.

"Why do you put up with Agnes?" Marla said, rousing the matriarch, who snuggled under the covers.

Miriam groaned in protest, but she allowed Marla to plump her pillows. "She takes good care of me, but Agnes doesn't think you do. She wants me to get rid of you."

"So she told me. Where does she go on her days off?"

"Agnes keeps a small apartment in Hollywood Beach. I believe she checks on things there and visits her sister in a convalescent home. The sister needed eye surgery and isn't doing so well." She pointed a regal finger toward the bathroom. "Call Kathleen for my breakfast and then get my pills. What's in that suitcase you're holding? Are you moving in, dearie?"

Marla laughed. "I brought a few beauty supplies. We'll use them after you're fed and bathed."

Shoving herself into a sitting position, Miriam grimaced. "Oh, my bones ache. I should stay in bed today."

"Nonsense, it's too nice outside." Marla scuttled into the lavatory to retrieve the medication bottles.

"Morning, ma'am," Kathleen said about ten minutes later. Entering with a breakfast tray, she set it on the bedside table. "I made Madam's gruel just the way she likes it," the maid told Marla.

Marla glanced at the bowl. "Yuck, what is that glop? Where are the eggs and toast? This is food for a baby!"

"Agnes says I have to eat Cream of Rice since my stomach was upset after dinner Thursday night," Miriam interjected, although she didn't appear too enthused.

Marla compressed her lips, unwilling to go against too many of Agnes's dictates. Maybe the old lady had suffered a bout of diarrhea as a result of changing her diet. She didn't want to clean up after her if that were the case.

Kathleen smiled sympathetically at Marla, who in turn took an admiring glance at the middle-aged woman's auburn hair. Those silver streaks added dimension, like the lilt in her voice. "I'll see that Cook leaves you something more substantial for lunch, ma'am. If you don't need me until later, I'll be going to church. The minister promised us a fiery sermon, bless him."

Marla raised an eyebrow. "Have either of you heard of the Ministry of Hope or its leader, Jeremiah Dooley?"

Miriam, who'd lifted a spoonful of cereal, froze for the pace of two heartbeats and then resumed her motion. Kathleen uttered a choking cough.

"Never heard of them," the maid said, her face flushed. Her skirt swished as she turned and left.

"Marla, I need my teeth," commanded Miriam, effectively dismissing the subject.

She wasn't about to be swayed from her course. After she brought the old woman her teeth, Marla switched on the television to Jeremiah Dooley's show. The distinguished-looking, gray-haired man exuded charisma like a messiah as he exhorted his audience to listen to the Lord.

"You've heard His words. You read them in the Bible," he said, gesturing. "Y'all must do good in the eyes of our Lord if you expect to enter the pearly gates of Heaven. Surely, what could be more generous than helping those poor unfortunates who are too downtrodden to help themselves?"

Marla heard a gasp and whirled around. Miriam's face had turned a ghastly hue. "Turn that off," she croaked.

"In a minute." Marla returned her attention to the television.

Jeremiah pointed to a map of the southern Americas displayed on a wall behind his pulpit. "Our missionaries in Costa Rica and Brazil bring hope to the people. We provide food for the multitude with our fish farms. Yields finance our operations so we can offer sustenance to those who embrace the Lord. I know you want to contribute. Your hearts are open to do God's bidding. We'll accept your offering . . ."

Her mouth curved down in disgust, Marla shut the TV off. "Those shows are all alike. What do you think, Miriam? Do you believe people really fall for his spiel?"

"Why did you take a job with this family?" The old lady had recovered her composure enough to fix her with a piercing glare.

Marla swallowed. "I, uh, heard about the opening and needed to earn extra money."

Miriam pointed to her Louis Vitton handbag. "You don't look as though you're hurting."

"That was a gift." *You'd better change the subject fast, girl.* "If you're finished eating, let's move into the bathroom. We have a lot to do this morning. I'm going to make you look years younger!"

"It's amazing," Miriam admitted two hours later as she studied her reflection in the vanity mirror. Her gray hair, which had been blunt-cut and dull, now fluffed in soft waves around her face, which

Marla had enhanced with makeup. "You're very talented, dearie. Where did you learn to do hair like this? You use a pair of shears like a professional."

No kidding. "A friend who's a hairdresser taught me." She wouldn't call Cutter Corrigan a friend, necessarily. He'd been her best teacher at cosmetology school, but now he ran Heavenly Hair Salon on Las Olas. Marla hadn't spoken to him in years.

Someone knocked on the bedroom door. "Mother, are you there?" shrilled Stella's voice.

"We're in the bathroom," Miriam answered. "Come on in."

Stella sauntered into view. "Oh my God, what is this mess?" Her gaze widened in shock as she surveyed the cut hairs on the lavatory floor surrounding Miriam's wheelchair.

"I'll clean up later," Marla said. "Doesn't Miriam look great?" Winding the cord around her blow-dryer, she started to pack away the supplies that cluttered the small counter space.

"What's that smell?" Stella wrinkled her nose.

"Perm solution. Miriam's hair was too flat. I gave her some lift along with a body wave." She licked her lips in anticipation. "Next weekend, we'll turn you into a blonde," she addressed Miriam.

Stella gasped in horror. "These fumes are too strong for her, and you're planning to put more chemicals on her hair?"

Marla gave her a sardonic glance. "I see you're not averse to coloring your hair."

"I'm not frail and in poor health."

"Having heart failure doesn't mean I'm dead yet, dearie," announced Miriam, eyes gleaming. "What did you want to see me for anyway?"

"I can't find my cameo. I haven't worn it in years, but it would go perfectly with this blouse. I'm on my way to a floral art design class in Davie," she explained.

"Why don't you take bookkeeping instead? That would be more useful than those silly crafts. Then you could help Morris with the business."

"I hate math, and besides, you do the accounts."

"I won't be around forever, and my mind isn't as sharp as it used to be."

"Agnes helps you. She's good with figures. Maybe Morris will hire her after you don't need her anymore."

"Ha! Wishing me dead already!"

Stella's face puckered, and her eyes clouded with pain. "I don't think so. One death in the family is enough."

Miriam half-rose from her chair. "I'm so sorry, child. Forgive me. This has been difficult on all of us. We don't need to bicker with each other."

"Let's go downstairs," Marla suggested to break the silence that followed. "We'll go out later after it warms up."

"If you find my cameo, let me know, will you?" Stella said, her shoulders sagging as though she were drained. "I must be losing it. Can't seem to find lots of stuff these days. Last week I lost my best pen."

You look like you lost more than that, Marla thought sympathetically. Maybe Kimberly's loss was just now beginning to sink in.

Morris arrived while Marla was pouring a cup of tea for his mother in the parlor. "Everything all right?" he said in his gruff manner.

"We're just fine," Miriam answered, looking spry in a turquoise pants outfit. She grinned at him, her false teeth giving her an even smile. Marla had transferred her from the wheelchair into a high armchair.

"What happened to your hair?" Morris said. "You look different."

"Marla spruced me up. She wants to take me to the mall this afternoon."

"What?" He couldn't have looked more astonished if he'd swallowed a live grouper.

"It's not that cold out today," Marla explained. "I'll bundle her up, and we'll park in one of the garages at Galleria. Just in case, I'll take some of her medicines along. Miriam is sturdier than you think."

"We're going shopping for cosmetics," Miriam said in a childishly eager voice.

Her tone made Marla think of Brianna. Had anyone taken the girl under her wing in regard to makeup and other feminine advice? She didn't know if Brie would accept her guidance, but next time they were together, she'd offer it.

"Will you join us for dinner later?" Morris asked his mother.

"If I feel well enough, sonny."

"I enjoyed our discussion on coffee growing when I was here last Thursday," Marla said, mentally refocusing. His plantations were in Costa Rica and Brazil, same places as Jeremiah Dooley's missions. Maybe she could learn more about the family business. "Are the coffee cherries edible?" she asked with a naive smile.

Morris leaned his elbow on the fireplace mantel. "They're not really cherries in the sense that you mean."

"How so? Does coffee grow on trees, or is it a plant?"

A hint of amusement seeped into his eyes. "Let me start at the beginning. The three most cultivated types of beans are arabica, robusta, and liberica. Arabica beans taste better because they grow at higher elevations. They account for nearly seventy percent of the world's coffee production."

"I remember reading somewhere that they come from Africa."

"That's true, the first arabica coffee plant was discovered in Ethiopia. However, Africa and the Far East account for only forty percent of the market share. Columbia, Brazil, and Central American countries produce the rest."

His cadence of speech increased, as though she'd wound up a toy that needed to spend its energy. "We plant the beans in moist, fertile soil. Seeds germinate six to eight weeks later. At this stage, healthy seedlings are transplanted to nurseries." He gestured animatedly. "When the nursery plants reach two feet high, we remove them to our plantation. Here it takes up to five years for the tree to mature. It can grow as tall as twenty feet high, but usually we prune them to under twelve feet."

"What does the tree look like?"

"It has glossy evergreen leaves and blooms with fragrant white flowers."

"The tree bears fruit?" Marla refilled the old lady's teacup from a silver service set on a cocktail table.

Morris nodded. "After blossoms appear, it takes six to nine months more for the trees to produce the rich red berries that we call coffee cherries. The size of the cherries depends on the amount of water received during the sprouting process, so plenty of rainfall is desirable. Ripened cherries are handpicked. Harvesting can take as long six months, so unripe cherries have a chance to be picked later in the season after they mature."

"Where does the coffee bean come from?" Marla glanced at her patient. Miriam seemed content to watch her son, pride glowing on her face.

"In the center of the cherries are two seeds. These are the green coffee beans," he explained. "Each bean is covered by a thin parchment skin. The pulping process removes pulp and debris, then the beans are fermented using either a wet or dry technique. The wet fermentation process gives the beans more acidity, while the dry method gives them more body."

"Which one do you use?"

"We wash the beans. The drying method is too dependent on the weather, and you get more debris."

"So what happens next?"

"A huller removes the silver skin and parchment and polishes the beans. They're sorted and graded by standards set for coffee roasters, with Grade One being the best quality. The higher the altitude where they're grown, the hardier and better the coffee bean. Lastly, the beans are roasted."

"Did you tell her about the poisons you put on the plants?" demanded Florence from the entry.

Chapter
Twelve

Morris's mouth curved downward as he regarded his sister. "Pesticides are necessary to control insects."

Florence sashayed into the room, her slim figure looking svelte in a pastel pink suit enhanced by enough jewelry to open a store. "If you grew the plants in their naturally shaded habitat, nature would take care of the bugs. You wouldn't need chemicals, plus you'd preserve the tree canopy where migratory birds nest. Good morning, Mother. Hello, Marla," she added in a condescending tone.

"I remember Barbara said you're helping with a fund-raiser," Marla said.

"Yes, I believe it's for a worthy cause." She patted her hair, swept into a classical French twist. "Did you know birds are losing their habitats to high-tech farms at an alarming rate? Without their shade canopy, coffee plants exposed to the sun need more fertilizer. Those high-tech farms lack natural predators that control insects, making pesticides necessary. There's more erosion, toxic runoff, and loss of trees. Our organization promotes shade-grown coffee production which preserves the forests."

"You're not considering the practical applications," Morris protested. "Our methods produce higher yields. Besides, you should support your own plantations. That's where our money comes from!"

"Blame your wife for involving me. Barbara says our company could just as well invest in traditional coffee farms."

"We don't have enough capital to invest right now!"

"That's your problem. Mother, I just wanted to see how you felt this morning. I have to meet Elise Addison at the country club. She's putting together a cookbook that we'll sell at the fashion show."

"Elise? You mean Stan's neighbor?" Marla blurted. When all eyes turned to her, she realized her mistake. "I mean, Kimberly used to play tennis with her. We're, uh, acquainted."

"Really?" Florence crooned. "I'll ask her about you."

Bless my bones, now you've done it. Quick, change the subject. "Have you noticed your mother's new hairdo?"

Florence's eyes widened in surprise as she swung her gaze to the matriarch. "Why, Mother, I thought you looked different! I love it. What have you done?"

The old lady waved a finger. "Marla fixed me up. Next week, she's promised to dye my hair. I'll tell Agnes to take some lessons from her!"

Marla gulped. *That's just what Agnes needs to hear.*

"I don't know how much longer I'll be able to play my part," Marla told Vail the next day during their drive to Tarpon Springs. "Someone in Miriam's household will tag me, and I'll be fired. I hope they don't summon you to arrest me."

"Why would they do that?" He gave her a bemused glance.

"For taking the job under false pretenses, or invading their privacy." Nervous laughter hid her anxiety. "I had such a good time with Miriam yesterday, wheeling her around Galleria Mall. We bought a few things at Burdines and ate lunch at Vie de France. Miriam encountered one of her friends. I'm afraid she'll hate me when she discovers our game."

"You really like the old lady, don't you?"

"I do." Marla folded her hands in her lap. "She's sharpminded, retains a sense of humor, and has interesting stories to tell when anyone bothers to listen. It's such a shame her family doesn't treat her better."

They sped past the Miccosukee Service Plaza on Alligator Alley, heading west toward Naples before veering north on I-75. Evergreens mixed with sable palms and cypress trees in the flat landscape bordering the highway. Winter was the best season for spotting wildlife in the Everglades, especially birds. Besides the usual graceful egrets and white ibis, she caught sight of an anhinga and a great blue heron feeding by a slough.

After searching in vain for alligators sunning on logs, she shifted her gaze to study the fluffy clouds overhead. Where else could you enjoy an infinite blue sky with a three-hundred-sixty-degree view? A sense of primeval peace pervaded the place, from its eastern fringes hedged by sawgrass, on through the Big Cypress National Preserve.

"Have you thought about how we're going to present ourselves at the Ministry of Hope?" she asked. "Will you mention that you're investigating a murder? Do we even know Jeremiah Dooley will be there?"

A devilish grin transformed Vail's craggy face. Marla's toes curled with warmth. Seated beside him in his car, she was acutely aware of his presence and his sideways glances in her direction. Her heightened senses detected every movement he made and recorded every expression on his face.

"When I phoned them, I said we'd watched Dooley's show on television and were considering a major contribution," Vail replied. "I said we hoped to tour their facility and meet personally with the minister before writing a check. After I mentioned the word *donation*, doors opened."

Marla chuckled. "Well, I hope I look the part of someone rich enough. I wore pants because I knew we'd be sitting in the car most of the day." She'd brought along a rust-colored blazer to go with her silk eggshell blouse and black slacks. Gold button earrings and a Rado watch were her only accessories.

"Oh, I almost forgot." Struggling against his seat belt, Vail reached inside his trousers pocket and withdrew a small object that he handed to her. "Here, you'll need this."

Marla fingered the black velvet box. Her jaw dropped when she opened the hinged lid and saw the ring inside. A brilliant purple stone was surrounded by two tiny diamonds in a gold setting. "What's this?" Her voice held a tremor.

"I told them we were engaged. Put it on your left finger."

Too stunned to protest, Marla slid the unexpected gift on her ring finger. It fit perfectly. *Don't get too excited*, she told herself. This must be a loaner, part of her disguise.

"You can keep it," he said casually. "Consider it another Valentine's Day gift."

"Amethyst is my birthstone," she murmured, "but I can't accept this, Dalton." Her words died on her lips as she regarded his smoldering gaze.

"I want you to have it, regardless of how things turn out between us." His hand snaked over to cover her thigh. "You know how I'd like them to turn out, or should I say turn on."

Speaking of turn-ons, the weight of his hand on her thigh did strange things to her body. Her imagination took flight, and she imagined his touch creeping northward. When he began lazy circles with his index finger, her breathing quickened.

"Stop that," she said, swatting him away. A lock of hair fell in her face, and she pushed it behind her ear.

"Why? You like it when I touch you, and Brianna isn't here to interfere this time."

Marla moistened her lips, acutely aware of how handsome he was in his customary charcoal suit. Stretched against his broad shoulders, the jacket made him look like a football star. His coal black hair, parted on the side, revealed silvery highlights in the sunshine streaming through their windows.

"I'd rather talk about the case," she said, effectively changing the subject. "Florence mentioned she knew Elise Addison. They're working together on a fund-raiser benefiting some bird society. What I find interesting is that their goals conflict with the Pearl family business."

"How so?" Gripping the steering wheel, he reverted to his businesslike demeanor. Up ahead was the tollbooth situated before the highway turned north toward Fort Myers.

"Morris's wife, Barbara, promotes shade-grown coffee. She got Florence interested, and now they're dragging Stella into the loop to do centerpieces. In traditional farms, tall shade trees protect the smaller coffee plants from the sun, provide mulch, and harbor natural predators that control insects. At large plantations, many of these trees are being cut down in order to increase production. Barbara's group supports organically grown coffee because it preserves the tropical forests; the tree canopy serves as a refuge for migratory songbirds. Morris, on the other hand, could care less. He's converted his plantations to high-tech farms that abuse the environment."

Vail's face folded into a puzzled frown. "What does this have to do with Kimberly?"

"Morris's plantations are located in the same countries as Jeremiah Dooley's ministry operations. That may or may not be a coincidence."

"Was the deceased involved in this conservation cause?"

"No. According to Stella, Kim's most recent hobby was genealogy. I wonder if Stan found anything in her files." She chewed on her lower lip, oblivious to the scenery whizzing by.

"Where do you want to stop for lunch?" Vail said after an interlude of silence.

"I'd rather wait until we're in Tarpon Springs. Tally mentioned some good restaurants there. I hope you like Greek food."

"I'll eat anything." He cast a suggestive glance in her direction, and she got the distinct feeling he was talking about something other than a meal. Her gaze fell to his chiseled mouth, and she remembered how his lips tasted pressed to hers. Her thoughts roamed to the other night at her townhouse. What would have happened if Brianna hadn't interrupted with a phone call?

Stop it, Marla. You're getting distracted.

His grin broadened as though he knew what she was thinking. Her cheeks warmed under his scrutiny. *Think fast, say something else.*

"I should visit Elise again and sound her out regarding the Pearls. Do you think Kimberly knew about her connection with Florence?"

"Possibly."

"I got the distinct impression Elise thought her husband Cliff was having an affair with Kim. Do you think Elise shared her suspicions with Florence? Maybe that's why Florence said Kim was messing in things she didn't understand."

Vail raised a bushy eyebrow. "Kim had been fooling around with someone," he conceded. "Did Stan find out and kill her in a rage?"

Marla zeroed in on his mention of Stan. "Here we go, back to my dear ex again. Why don't you consider other possibilities? Lacey, for example. Kim's classmates said she'd fixed her sights on Gary. Lacey could have killed Kim in a jealous fit."

"How would she have obtained Stan's letter opener?"

"That's for you to figure out." Her stomach rumbled, and she pulled a bag of cheese crackers from her purse. They still had three more hours to go before reaching their destination, and she'd never last that long before lunch. "Want some?"

"Sure." He held out his open palm.

"I brought an extra water bottle if you're thirsty," she offered. "Oh, I have something else for you to investigate. Miriam's nurse, Agnes, keeps the old lady confined in her room. Maybe I'm paranoid, but I sense she has more than a professional interest in keeping Miriam dependent on her. On her days off, Agnes visits her sister in a convalescent home. At least, that's what she told Miriam. I'd like to know if this is the real *megillah*. Can you find out?"

Vail's face creased into a smile as he cast a tender look her way. "You act like Miriam is related to you."

"I hate how Agnes smothers her spirit. Aside from a mild case of heart failure, she's in good health. There's no reason for her to be stuck in bed when she could be meeting friends and getting out more."

"Maybe her family members have their own reasons why they want her secluded." Vail reached for the spare water bottle, unscrewed the cap, and took a long swallow.

She stared at him. "Such as hiding the company's losses? Miriam hasn't given up her hold over the family finances; she checks the accounts with Agnes's help."

"Morris can't be happy about his mother's supervision. She must think he's incompetent."

"Maybe Kimberly found out their company was losing money and threatened to tell her grandmother. Morris killed her before she could rat on him."

He snorted in disbelief. "Did Kim care that much about the family business?"

"Not really," Marla said, remembering her conversation with Stella.

"I thought you said Miriam mentioned declining profits."

"That's right. Morris explained that inventories were lower because of frost damage." She paused. "I wonder if that's a valid excuse. If supplies for a commodity are lower, wouldn't prices skyrocket?"

"Are you implying Morris may be covering up for a financial loss?"

"Who knows? He might be afraid his mother will fire him if she still holds the legal strings."

"Fire her own son? Doubtful."

"Maybe Barbara decided to get Kim out of the way. Would she kill for Morris to keep his job?"

"You just said she doesn't approve of his methods of coffee production."

"She'd have to support him if she wants his income." Her argument sounded weak even to her own ears. Barbara hadn't struck her as being greedy. Florence, on the other hand, would be concerned with keeping her social position. Was that enough motive for murder?

"Look, there's an outlet mall. Too bad we don't have time to stop."

"I'd rather take you shopping when there isn't another case hanging over my head," Vail stated in a morose tone.

"We don't get too much time together, do we? I mean, when there are no murders to discuss, no children. Just the two of us." She hoped he didn't take her comment about children the wrong way. Marla didn't mean to dismiss Brianna, but she'd like to have Vail to herself. Today they were alone, but again she used the crutch of suspects to put distance between them. What would happen when their relationship didn't revolve around his work?

After crossing Tampa Bay on the Sunshine Skyway, they headed north on Route 19 into Tarpon Springs.

"Our appointment isn't until four o'clock," Vail said when they arrived at their destination, "so we have some free time. Let's have lunch, and then I thought we'd ask folks around town about Dooley's ministry."

They drove past the historical district and followed signs to the Sponge Docks. Dodecanese Boulevard bustled with activity. Crowds milled along the sidewalks, while people gawked at gift shops, Greek restaurants, and fishing boats bobbing on the water. Marla's legs ached to take a stroll. Vail pulled into a two-dollar parking lot.

"Any recommendations for lunch?" he asked after they'd emerged into the strong afternoon sun.

"I've heard of Pappas." She pointed down the road to an impressive structure. The Louis Pappas Riverside Restaurant stood as a landmark at the end of the street. "But let's go to Hellas. It's right here and looks lively."

White lights studded a bright, spacious interior. They were led to a ceramic tiled table that sported a bottle of olive oil as a decoration. They sat on wood-frame and blue-vinyl chairs. A mural of what looked like the Parthenon highlighted one wall. Potted plants and faux Grecian statuettes added to the cheerful atmosphere. Aromas from an adjacent bakery made Marla's mouth water.

They ordered Greek salads, which came with a slab of feta cheese and a loaf of crusty bread. Afraid the portions might be too large, they shared a combo platter that included generous servings of moussaka, pastitsio, gyro, dolmades-stuffed grape leaves, and tzatziki sauce. More than enough for both of them, the meal came with roasted potatoes, peas, and a watermelon wedge. The Greek house white wine, served in a regular glass, was the color of apple juice. It tasted mild with little body and probably less alcohol. In the background, dishes rattled, people chattered, and Greek music played.

Marla fought an overwhelming urge to take a nap when they had finished. She felt more stuffed than a grape leaf and a couple of pounds heavier. Vail insisted on paying the bill, and she didn't argue. This was one time she was glad to be treated.

"Now what? We still have an hour," she said when they left the restaurant.

"Let's ask some of the shop owners if they know Jeremiah Dooley. Many of the families who settled here were Greeks; I wonder how he picked this location to establish his ministry. Was he from this area, or did he migrate here? What was his connection to Kimberly Kaufman?"

They began at the end of the street where *Jaws* music blared from the Coral Sea Aquarium opposite Captain Duran's Seafood Gallery. The first block held a clothes boutique, ice cream parlor, Birkenstock store, flag shop, and museum store. After several inquiries, they had gained no further information about Jeremiah. They passed the Fudge Factory and came to a fishing pier. Picturesque vessels rocked on the current. Marla breathed in the salty scent of fresh sea air.

"Where next?" she said, eyeing a collection of natural sponges, olive oil soap, bird feeders made of coconuts, and jungle starfish outside a souvenir shop.

Vail shaded his face from the sun. "We'll ask that guy." He indicated a man selling tickets for the Saint Nicholas Boat Line, a live sponge-fishing demonstration.

After an exchange of pleasantries, Vail got to the point. "I'm looking for a friend who lives in the area. His name is Jeremiah Dooley."

The huckster glanced at Marla. "Dooley, eh? Name sounds familiar. A better person to ask would be Aleko, our diver. He's been in town goin' on twenty years."

"Where can we find him?"

"Why, you'll have to buy tickets for the boat ride, folks. Five dollars each." He beamed a gap-toothed smile.

"Do we have time?" Marla asked, sniffing. Her glance fell on a display of sponges. They emitted a strong briny odor.

Vail grimaced, glancing at his watch. "Maybe we should ask some of the shop proprietors."

"Boat ride boards in five minutes," said the salesman. "See, she's comin' in now. You'll be back in less than an hour."

"Oh heck, why not?" Vail said, pulling out his wallet. "It's a nice day for a cruise, right?" Grinning at her, he winked.

"Do you give a triple-A discount?" Marla asked, ever mindful of bargains.

"Sure do. You get a dollar off each ticket. Here you go."

Marla felt amazingly carefree as they watched the orange, gray, and white boat slide into the dock, where it spit out a crowd of tourists.

When they were allowed on board, Marla found a seat on a white slatted bench lining one side. The diver, wearing a bulky diving suit and blue knit cap, marched to the aft deck accompanied by a tour guide. As the engine kicked in and the boat cruised along the bay waters, the tour director related a brief history of the sponge-diving industry in Tarpon Springs. Sponges were retrieved by hooking until a Greek fisherman introduced the technique of diving in 1905. Many Greeks had immigrated to the area to work in the thriving industry.

"Several types of sponges have commercial value," the man said. "The first grade is the wool sponge, which lasts from four to five years. It's good for bathing because it holds a lot of water. Second grade is a yellow sponge. Third grade is a wire sponge, which is abrasive. Fourth grade is a grass or vase sponge that is often used as a shoe-polish applicator or to start off flower seeds in. The fifth grade is the finger sponge, which has decorative value."

He held up samples of each one and passed them around the group. Then he pointed to the diver, whose suit and equipment weighed numerous pounds. "The helmets are made by hand and can last up to forty years with daily use," the guide explained.

Marla studied the diver, a handsome fellow with a mustache and ruddy face. As they glided past Marker Forty-Seven, he tied a nylon cord around his suit and donned his helmet. Standing at the boat's edge, he jumped into the murky green water. He held a hook in one hand to detach sponges and a netted basket in his other hand. Waving, he sank beneath the surface. Bubbles rose to indicate his location.

He remained in the water about fifteen minutes, his tethered hose steadily moving outward from the boat. They weren't very far from shore, because Marla could easily see the sandy beach and mangroves several hundred feet away. Seagulls circled lazily overhead. Sunlight warmed her skin, and she savored the fresh, salty breeze. February in Florida . . . how delightful compared to the weather reports from up north!

When the diver returned, they passed around the sponge he had snagged. Dark slime covered its surface. Marla cringed as she touched the remains of animal matter. It felt like wet fungus.

"Normally the sponges are laid out on deck for two or three days to process," the tour guide said. "They're covered with burlap and kept wet until the animal dies. The remains are scraped off and the sponges rinsed. Anyone want to get your photo taken with the diver? Come on up."

Now was their chance, although neither she nor Vail had a camera. Vail nodded at her, and she waited while a man took a picture of his sons flanking the diver. When they moved off, she approached him. After offering a few compliments about his technique, she got to the point.

"I'm trying to locate a friend, Jeremiah Dooley. You've lived here a long time. Do you know him?"

The man's mustache quivered as his face lit up. "That's Colleen's son! Sure I know him."

"Colleen?"

"The Irish gal who married Piotr Sebastian. Their son runs a fish farm on the outskirts of town. He didn't want to do no diving like his daddy. If you ask me, it wasn't in his genes."

"How so?"

The diver leaned closer, and she smelled onions on his breath. His dark eyes gleamed with wicked delight. "I heard tell that the boy wasn't his, if you know what I mean. You go speak to Lorraine Parker at the Historical Society. She knows every soul in town. If anyone can give you the scoop on the Sebastians, she'll be the one."

Chapter
Thirteen

The Historical Society office was located on Tarpon Avenue in a converted train depot. Inside the entrance, Marla gazed in fascination at a rolltop wooden desk with pigeonholes, bentwood desk chair, cast-iron potbellied stove pipe, dental chair and microscope from 1900, and an exhibit of arrowheads from Safford Mound, an Indian burial site near the Anclote River.

"Nice stuff," Vail commented, a flicker of pain behind his slate gray eyes.

This place brought back memories for him, Marla surmised with a surge of sympathy. She'd been to his house a couple of times, and it looked as though he hadn't rearranged anything since his wife died. Unlike Pam, who had collected antiques, Marla preferred contemporary furnishings.

Her musing broke off as an attractive brunette strode into the room from a back office. "Hi, I'm Lorraine Parker, the curator," she said with a friendly smile. "How may I help you?"

"We need information about Jeremiah Dooley," Vail spoke up, showing his badge.

Lorraine smoothed down her shirtwaist dress. "I've never met him personally, although I've watched his television show a few times. He follows his own church, if you get my drift. Jeremiah should be in his fifties now if I'm figuring right."

"I noticed a lot of Greek religious ornaments in the souvenir shop windows at the Sponge Docks," Marla said. "It appears he didn't follow his parent's Greek Orthodox religion."

"His mother was Irish Catholic." Lorraine stood in front of a framed photo collage depicting a winter water carnival in 1923. "Colleen wanted him to keep her last name. That's part of what led to the gossip, but it was also his early birth and full-term weight. Jeremiah didn't have Piotr's dark coloring, either."

"You mean the child wasn't his?"

"Not that he let on. Piotr hinted that the rumors were jealous ramblings started by Harriet Stanton, daughter of a town magnate. She's the one you should interview. Harriet set her sights on hand-some Piotr, and everyone in town thought they'd tie the knot. Then Piotr vacationed in Fort Lauderdale and came back with a bride. No one could have been more shocked than his family! Piotr's parents never forgave him for their disappointment."

"How did the townspeople treat Jeremiah?" Marla asked. If people disliked his mother, they might have taken it out on the poor child.

"Colleen worked hard to earn the respect of Piotr's friends. They welcomed Jeremiah even though she raised him as a strict Catholic. Evidently, he decided religion was his calling, although he seems to have created his own sect."

Her snide tone pricked Marla's ears. "You think he should have followed in his father's footsteps and become a sponge diver?"

"He lives by the sea but grows fish in landlocked ponds. I'm not familiar with his missionary aims, but he supports some operations in Latin countries. You'd think he would focus his efforts here, where people need his help."

"Is he an ordained minister?"

"I'm not sure."

"Is he married?" Vail interrupted. He'd been studying a photo display of street scenes from the 1890s.

"Divorced, no children. Both parents are deceased."

"So the familial line ends with him, if he even carries it from his father. Where can we find Harriet?"

"She lives in Spring Bayou. Piotr would have been wealthy if he'd married her. Her family descended from the original settlers. Are you familiar with our early history?"

"Not much," Marla admitted, hoping the woman wouldn't keep them long. They could visit Harriet before their appointment at Ministry of Hope. She didn't look forward to the five-hour drive home. Groaning inwardly, she mentally reviewed her work schedule for the next day. Between sleuthing, styling, and managing the salon, she had no free time. This had to stop. After Stan got off the hook, she'd think about cutting back her hours.

"We didn't start out as the sponge capital of the world," the curator said, her eyes radiating enthusiasm for her topic. "One of the first settlers was A. W. Ormond who, along with his daughter Mary, built a cabin near Spring Bayou in 1876. Mary married a fellow named Joshua Boyer. Impressed by the tarpon that swam in the bayou, she proposed a name for the place.

"Next came Hamilton Disston, a wealthy manufacturer from the north who purchased four million acres of Florida land for twenty-five cents an acre. Along with his business associate, Anson Safford, he set up a land company to develop Tarpon Springs. Visitors arrived by steamer until the railroad came in 1887. That's the year Tarpon Springs became incorporated. It turned into a popular winter resort, with millionaires building Victorian mansions around Spring Bayou. We call that area of town the Golden Crescent."

"When did the Greeks arrive?" Marla asked.

Lorraine pointed to a pamphlet display on a small table. "Our sponge industry was started by John Cheyney, who worked for the leading landholding company in Tarpon Springs. Cheyney realized seasonal tourism didn't provide a stable annual income. Inspired by the industry in Key West, he established a sponge company here and hired a Greek, John Cocoris, as a sponge buyer.

"Cocoris proposed that the Greek method of diving was much more productive than the hook boats currently in use. He sent for his brothers, and then others from the Dodecanese Islands followed. In 1905, hundreds of Greek sponge fishermen came with their rubberized diving suits and copper helmets. A booming industry resulted as boat builders and suppliers arrived. With their families, a close-knit Greek community developed. Over the generations, the Greeks have been integrated into American culture."

"So Harriet is a descendant of one of those millionaires from the north?"

"Correct." Lorraine wrote down the woman's address. "Take Tarpon Avenue to the end, and park in the lot at Craig Park. You can walk to her house from there. Harriet will be able to tell you more about Piotr's family. Sadly, after being rejected, she never married."

As directed, Vail drove down Tarpon Avenue, which ended at Spring Boulevard. Turning left, they passed Banana Street before entering a parking lot next to a bayou that looked like a huge lake.

"Let's use that path." Vail indicated a concrete walkway winding around the water's edge.

Dead leaves crunched underfoot as Marla kept pace with his long stride. A chilly breeze blew off the murky brown water, bringing with it a briny odor. Wishing she'd worn a jacket, she hugged her arms as she watched a stingray swim by in the water, chasing a school of fish. In the distance, a couple of boys fished off a jetty. A crescent of mansions faced the bayou, some fully restored, others needing work. Squirrels scampered across grassy lawns toward oak trees hanging with Spanish moss.

On North Spring Boulevard, they climbed to the road and crossed the street. Continuing on the sidewalk, they passed a house built in 1885. Restored in 1976, it had a gated driveway with a NO TRESPASS-ING sign. Farther along, Marla paused in front of a delightful pink house with white gingerbread trim, a hexagon turret, and a wrap-around porch. It reminded her of a candy cane. A gazebo stood on the front lawn.

"Is this Harriet's place?" she asked.

Vail referred to the paper Lorraine had given them. "Nope. Move on, we don't have time to linger."

Nor was it the three-story house with the myriad angles and gabled windows that made Marla eager to explore. Harriet's address was at an austere brown and white manor with an abundance of chimneys and fan windows, highlighted by a columned porch and a center turret. Despite the sunshine casting a soft afternoon glow on its facade, Marla shivered. The house reminded her of the Haunted Mansion at Walt Disney World. An unkempt lawn did little to assuage the overall effect.

"Can I help you?" asked the woman who opened the door at their summons. Her strong, assertive voice went along with a pair of piercing blue eyes.

Vail flashed his badge. "We'd like some information about Jeremiah Dooley, if you don't mind. This is my fiancée, Marla Shore."

Harriet glanced speculatively from Vail to Marla. "I only have a few minutes. I'm on my way to a meeting for the Garden Committee."

"We won't take much of your time," Vail reassured her.

As they followed the older woman inside, Marla tried to reconcile her expectations with Harriet Stanton's surprisingly young appearance. If she was within Piotr's age range, she should be in her eighties. But the lady who led them didn't look a day over sixty. Nor did she look like a spurned spinster. Her dyed blond hair, too light for her coloring, was teased into a bouffant style as though she'd just come from the salon. She walked with an erect, proud posture. Her flowered silk blouse hung a bit loose on her thin frame, but it tucked snugly into the waistband of a knee-length skirt.

"You have a beautiful house," Marla said, halting in a foyer with a wood parquet floor. A long hallway stretched ahead with archways leading to different rooms. From the unassuming exterior, she'd never have guessed the inside could be so impressive. Too bad they didn't have time for a tour.

Harriet gestured for them to take seats in the living room. "You're probably wondering why I live alone in a house with twelve rooms and five fireplaces. My father made his money in timber, and he used cypress and hard pine to build this place. It needs a lot of renovation, but that won't get done until my cousin inherits." She chuckled. "Poor Mortimer will have to wait awhile. His kids are more likely to inherit."

Vail balanced himself on the edge of an armchair. "Lorraine Parker said you were nearly engaged to Piotr Sebastian."

"That's right." Harriet's glance fell to the Oriental rug covering the floor. "Did she tell you I never married after the shock I received?"

"You must have been terribly hurt," Marla said kindly.

The woman's narrowed gaze swung to meet hers. "Piotr had promised we'd announce our engagement after he returned from a business trip to Fort Lauderdale. You can't imagine how I felt when he came back with a bride."

"I thought he was a diver," Vail commented.

"Piotr was a diver, but he also acted as a buyer for other interests. My family had hoped for better prospects for me, so they were thrilled when he returned with another woman. All I wanted was Piotr. A more dashing man you'd never meet."

"Did Piotr explain how he'd met the woman he married?" Marla asked.

"Colleen worked for a family with whom he had business dealings. You could tell she was Irish working class. We all thought it strange how she delivered a full-term baby eight months later."

"Did Jeremiah resemble his mama?" Marla persisted.

"Well, now that's the odd part. Jeremiah didn't have any of Piotr's dark Greek looks, nor did he have Colleen's red hair or fair complexion. His brown eyes and hair were a puzzle. The girl, she looked the spitting image of her mother."

"What girl?" Vail demanded. He cast Marla an impatient glance, nodding at his watch.

"The daughter, Katie. Didn't you know Jeremiah had a sister?"

"No, we didn't," Marla burst out. "Does she live in Tarpon Springs like her brother?"

Harriet's mouth dropped open. "Land sakes, gal, Jeremiah left these parts ages ago."

"How is that?" Vail said. "His Ministry of Hope is located on the outskirts of town. We have an appointment to meet him there."

Harriet regarded him with amusement. "That's his mission headquarters. He tapes his show elsewhere. The last I heard, he had a place down south. Miramar, maybe? No, it's in Margate."

Margate! That's just north of Fort Lauderdale, Marla thought. Meaning he hadn't been so far away from Kimberly after all. "Where does his sister Katie live?" she repeated.

"I haven't a notion, honey. I haven't seen her around town for quite some time."

Marla handed her a business card. "If you hear of Katie's whereabouts, can you call me?"

"Sure thing. Say, Jeremiah hasn't done anything wrong, has he?"

"Nope, we're just gathering information," Vail said with a disarming smile. He rose, signaling Marla to follow. "Thanks so much for your cooperation, Miss Stanton."

In the car, Marla voiced what had been on her mind during their silent walk to the parking lot. "Jeremiah doesn't live in Tarpon Springs but closer to home. He may have been around the morning of Kim's murder."

"That doesn't mean much. As far as he's concerned, all we have on him is an old photo from Kim's family album, plus neighborly gossip. That doesn't provide a clear connection between him and the deceased."

"Stan said Jeremiah called on Kim one day when she wasn't home," Marla reminded him as they headed for the main road.

"So what?"

"Kim's neighbor thought she might be fooling around with Jeremiah. He drives an expensive car. Someone paid her tuition at the design school and gave her reason to believe she'd have enough money to leave Stan."

"Hmm." He directed his gaze forward, not meeting her questioning glance. "Maybe the neighbor was right," he said after a short interval. "I tried to tell you the other day on the phone, but you cut me off."

She remembered their quick conversation in the car on her way to the Pearls' house on Thursday. He'd started to say something when she'd arrived at the house and hung up. She'd forgotten to ask him about it Friday when he came for dinner. "What is it?"

"We got the medical examiner's report." He paused. "Kimberly was pregnant."

"What!" It was a good thing she wasn't driving, or she would have swerved off the road. "Bless my bones, Dalton, Stan wouldn't have harmed her if Kimberly had been expecting their child. You can't possibly suspect him anymore!"

"What if he knew the child wasn't his?"

"Dammit, you're still trying to pin this on him."

"I am not. Be reasonable and consider the possibilities."

"You're the one who's not being reasonable! No matter what, you still come back to accusing Stan. Admit it, you're jealous."

His knuckles tightened on the steering wheel. "That's not fair. You don't have any faith in me."

"Ha! Look who's talking."

"I'm doing my job, examining all the angles, which is more than I can say for you. You're the one who's biased."

"Because I know Stan didn't do it!"

"You see!" he chortled triumphantly.

Angry words hovered on her tongue, but she bit them back, clenching her teeth. Staring out the side window, she forced herself to review the options. Would Stan have been happy if Kimberly bore his child when he already supported two children from his previous marriage? Maybe he'd flown into a rage when Kim told him they'd be adding a new family member. Grabbing his letter opener, he'd followed his wife downstairs.

No, she discarded that scenario.

Let's look at other possibilities. What if the child wasn't Stan's? That would give him an even greater motive to kill his wife in a fit of passion. But it gave others a motive as well. Kim's classmates said she intended to hook up with Gary after leaving Stan. Had Kim mentioned to her best friend Lacey that she was pregnant? Maybe Lacey, who lusted after Gary, had killed Kim in a jealous rage, believing the father to be Gary. Or maybe Gary himself had done the deed. From the state of his business, it didn't look as though he could support any added burdens. Then again, if he was misleading

Kim for her money and really intended to stick with Lacey, he might have gotten rid of Kim to save that relationship.

Gads, it was all so complicated. She ran a hand over her face, hating herself for her suspicions, resenting Vail for making her wish she could take back her angry words. Was he considering the same possibilities, or did he truly believe Stan to be guilty? Stubbornness kept her from discussing the issues with him. He'd accused her of being biased, but he was the one who kept pointing the finger at Stan. Besides, if he'd heard Kim was pregnant, why hadn't he told her sooner? She must be the only one who hadn't known!

Leah's enigmatic sentence popped into her brain: *She couldn't have chosen a more convenient time to die.* Of course! If Stan and Kim had offspring, then her children would no longer be his prime beneficiaries. Leah's remark implied she knew about Kim's pregnancy. Yet somehow, Marla couldn't think of Leah as a killer.

How about Elise Addison, who suspected her husband Cliff was cheating on her? If Kim had confided she was pregnant, Elise might have jumped to the conclusion her husband was the father. She might have offed Kim to get rid of the competition. On the other hand, Jessica Shpritz had implied that Jeremiah Dooley was Kim's paramour. The minister wouldn't want his reputation sullied. Had he bumped her off to silence her?

Kim was getting money from somewhere. Maybe she'd threatened Jeremiah with a paternity suit if he didn't cough up the dollars. He might have paid her tuition and promised a large enough payment to get her started on her own, away from Stan.

She looked forward to their discussion with Jeremiah Dooley. He might be twenty-plus years older than Kimberly, but that wouldn't matter to a gold digger. What had Jessica called him, a sugar daddy? Maybe Kimberly had found her golden ticket, but he'd torn it up in her face before she could collect the final prize.

Whatever else he was, Jeremiah Dooley might be their key to unlocking the mystery of who killed Kimberly Kaufman.

Chapter Fourteen

Ministry of Hope stood in the glaring afternoon sun like a concrete bunker in the middle of farm country. The Tarpon Springs headquarters for Jeremiah Dooley's organization consisted of a square tan building with a single door in front and a second level that led to a tiered structure of concrete tanks, metal walkways, pipes and hoses. Beyond stretched raised ponds interspersed with sandy trails in a patchwork pattern.

Marla shoved herself out of Vail's car with a groan of fatigue. Dust clogged her nostrils, adding more misery to the heaviness throbbing at her temples. "This visit had better be worth it," she said, wishing they were on their way home.

Vail, after stretching to his full height outside the car, tossed his jacket onto the backseat. "Let's check it out."

As they approached the front entrance, a sign directed visitors to a stairway in the back. They trudged over grass, brown and brittle from lack of rain, to an access area in the rear with gaping double doors. Against a wall leaned an assortment of fifty-pound aquaculture feed bags. Inside the garage-like entrance, rakes and other garden implements, a washer and dryer, different length hoses, and eel tanks met her bewildered gaze. Peering into one tank, she grimaced when a slimy black creature slithered to the surface.

"Hello there," said a gray-haired man wearing jeans and a green polo shirt. His casual outfit seemed incongruous for a gent with his dignified bearing, but he appeared at ease in the surroundings. Marla couldn't believe this was the same man she'd seen on television, where he'd ruled the pulpit with such fervor. She would never have pictured him on a fish farm.

They'd caught him in the middle of a conversation with two young men in shorts. "Finish with your measurements, and then get back to me," he told them before turning to his visitors. He spoke with a slight Southern accent that hadn't been noticeable on his TV show. "You must be Mr. Vail and his fiancée. I'm Reverend Dooley." His brown eyes glowed with a friendly welcome.

They shook hands, then Jeremiah led them up a steep flight of stairs to a makeshift office that held desks covered with papers, graphs, and posters; trash cans overflowing with empty soda cans; and tilapia fish tanks. Marla gazed in awe as several magnificent specimens swam into view. Wide and sturdy, with shiny scales, they made her mouth water for a seafood dinner.

"I understand y'all are interested in making a substantial donation to Ministry of Hope," Jeremiah said with a fatherly smile. "I can't tell you how much our congregants need your help. Our operations in Latin countries provide jobs for hundreds of workers, and food for more. Your contribution will help us carry forth the Lord's work."

"I'm not familiar with tilapia farming, but I imagine it must provide a good source of revenue," Marla murmured, smoothing her slacks. She must look rumpled after a day of travel. She'd left her blazer in the car, and the silk blouse stuck to her sweaty back.

"Indeed." Jeremiah gestured to the fish tanks. "Tilapia has been raised as far back as ancient Egypt. Legend tells us that tilapia was the fish our Lord multiplied to feed the masses. Since it comes from the Nile River, this is probably true. Tilapia is the most popular fish in freshwater aquaculture because it's so hardy and easy to breed."

"Really? What does that mean in terms of production values?" Marla persisted, attempting to gauge his organization's financial status.

"Just to give you an idea, annual yield in the United States approximates twenty million pounds," Jeremiah said, puncturing his remarks with gestures. "In Florida, fish farms produce over one million pounds per year. Let me add that tilapia are a tropical fish."

Marla cast a glance at Vail. While she'd kept Jeremiah occupied, he had sidled over to peer at a stack of papers on the minister's desk. She could tell he was more interested in the office accouterments than the fish tanks. *Okay, I can play this game, she told him silently.* "What happens with temperature variations?" she queried, plastering a look of rapt fascination on her face.

"Warm water increases their growth rate. Cold weather can kill them if the water temperature drops below fifty degrees."

"What are these different types?"

The reverend pointed to each tank in turn, speaking like a professor to a student. "This is blue tilapia, which is naturalized in Florida and inhabits the Everglades. That's white tilapia, and the other one is a hybrid of Nile tilapia. You can tell by its stripes. The hybrid is also more aggressive."

"I'm curious," Vail said from the opposite side of the room. "If you direct your activities from this location, where do you tape your television shows?"

Jeremiah puffed out his chest. "I live in Margate, and I do the shows from Miami. Regarding the missions, we have a manager who oversees our business operations, and an aquaculture specialist who supervises the farms. So I only come up here on special occasions, to meet folks like you or to make sure everything is running smoothly." His eyes narrowed, as though he'd just noticed Vail wasn't listening to his lecture. "You said you're from Palm Haven, but I didn't catch the name of your company."

Vail had a ready answer. "I'm in security, and Marla owns a chain of hair salons. Why don't you give the good reverend one of your business cards, sweetcakes?"

She returned his dazzling smile with a conspiratorial wink. Handing Jeremiah a card, she said, "This is for my anchor store. Come in sometime, and I'll give you a complementary cut." The minister's hair didn't have a single strand out of place. He must use a generous share of his pocket money on hair spray, she surmised.

Her glance took in his manicured fingernails. No wonder he didn't work on the farm; it might soil his hands. She hoped to kick up some dirt herself while they were here.

"My friend mentioned your show," Marla ventured. "Her name was Kimberly Kaufman. Maybe you read about her in the newspapers since you live near Fort Lauderdale. She was murdered a couple of weeks ago."

"How horrible," Jeremiah said, steepling his hands in a prayer position.

"Kim said she knew you personally."

Jeremiah glanced from Marla to Vail, who was engaged in casually picking off a fleck of lint from his pants. "We'd met a couple of times. Like yourself, Mrs. Kaufman was interested in donating to the cause. I always try to meet our benefactors in person."

"Did you attend her funeral?"

"No, I wasn't on intimate terms with the family. When I didn't hear from Mrs. Kaufman again, I just assumed she'd lost interest. I'm so sorry to hear she met such a dreadful end."

If you weren't intimate, why did she call you Uncle Jerry? "How did you meet each other? Did Kim contact you?"

"You seem mighty interested in my relations with your friend, Miz Shore."

Marla moistened her lips. "If it weren't for Kimberly, Dalton and I wouldn't have known about your work. We've always been concerned about world hunger, so we were thrilled to learn about your efforts. Breeding fish in ponds is an excellent means of providing food for thousands."

She'd hit upon the right subject to divert him. "You're absolutely right. Praise the Lord for his gift!" Jeremiah raised his arms. "He giveth us the means to produce a bounty of consumables. Who needs material wealth when we have food stocks? You can't eat money."

No, but you can buy a Porsche with it, pal. From the corner of her eye, she watched Vail shift a few papers on a file cabinet. "Do many people know about tilapia?" she said hastily to grab Jeremiah's attention. "It's not a common fish on the menu at restaurants."

He gave her a benevolent smile. "Look for it at the fish counters in your local grocery store. Tilapia is rapidly gaining consumer recognition. Besides being white, firm, and moist, it's mild in flavor, so it accepts sauces well. You can use it in recipes that specify other kinds of fish. Let's go outside, and I'll show you the rest."

Nodding agreeably, Marla hoped her companion noticed how well they were working together as a team. A moment's guilt flushed through her at their deception. Vail had arranged this meeting under false pretenses. It was bad enough that Marla had deceived the Pearl family in her role as nurse's aide. She dreaded the day Miriam would discover her ruse, especially since she'd become fond of the old lady. Maybe the reverend would give her a blessing and absolve her from sin.

Yeah, right. Believe that, and you can make hair sprout on a bald head with a prayer.

They emerged into the sunshine on a raised walkway. Marla was aware of Vail's presence directly behind her. When he placed a possessive hand on her shoulder, she folded into him, leaning against the solid length of his body. His arm curved around, encompassing her waist. A slight smile lifted the reverend's lips as he regarded the intimate gesture.

"We grow tilapia in outdoor tanks and ponds since our weather is fairly predictable," Jeremiah continued, squinting in the bright light. "Other farms may use greenhouses to control the climate, but we don't worry about that here. I mentioned that tilapia is a hardy fish. Since they have strong immune systems, they're more easily grown than other fish species which are prone to disease, plus they don't get as stressed by environmental changes. These factors make tilapia a highly marketable, protein-rich food source as well as a cash-generating crop, so it's perfect for our third-world missions."

"Don't you have sites in Costa Rica?" Marla asked.

He nodded. "Our farms use pure rainwater from the cloud forests. It flows by gravity through our farms at such a rate that the ponds exchange their water every twenty minutes."

"Is the fish sold there?"

"We harvest the fish six days a week. Some of it is distributed locally and the rest is flown to Miami each evening. From there, we deliver the fish to customers by truck or air."

"Kimberly's family owns coffee plantations in Costa Rica," Vail commented in a dry tone.

"Really? What a coincidence." Jeremiah gripped the black metal railing that lined the walkway.

"Are you acquainted with Morris Pearl?" Vail asked. "He's the family member who runs their business."

"Sorry, never heard of him."

"Where did you say you lived in Fort Lauderdale?"

"Margate." The reverend frowned at Vail. "I don't understand why you're asking these questions. I thought you wanted a tour of our facilities before making a contribution. Perhaps you're ready to conclude our business."

Marla felt Vail stiffen and stepped away from him. "How long does it take to grow one of the tilapia?" she asked in a ditzy tone, hoping to ease the sudden tension that had sprung up between the two men.

Jeremiah seemed happy to resume his didactic role. Plowing a hand through his styled hair, he said, "It takes six to twelve months for them to reach full size. We harvest them when they reach a pound and a half."

"How often do they reproduce?"

"Too often!" Jeremiah laughed, and the tenseness dissipated like a flock of egrets taking flight. "Tilapia are mouth breeders. Normally, the male digs a nest in the sand. By flashing his tail, he attracts the female, who lays eggs. He fertilizes them, then she picks them up in her mouth and holds them until they hatch, which takes a couple of weeks. She can carry up to one thousand babies, called fry, in her mouth. An average female hatches over three hundred fingerlings every month year-round. Considering this rate of reproduction, you see how overpopulation becomes a problem."

"How much do they sell for?" Vail asked bluntly.

"Tilapia bring up to two dollars per pound. We sell our crop wholesale to seafood brokers, fish markets, restaurants. It's a more valuable commodity than something like catfish."

"Why isn't the water clear?" Marla asked. The water in the concrete tanks was so deep and murky, she couldn't see any fish swimming inside.

Jeremiah pointed. "That greenish tint is due to algae that forms from sunlight penetrating to the bottom. Young fish feed on algae; tiny combs in their gills allow them to remove it from the water. They have efficient digestive systems and convert a greater proportion of their food into growth than many other fish species."

"They don't eat anything else?"

"Older specimens eat floating fish food. Come this way." He led them up a short flight of stairs and along a maze of elevated walkways, pipes and hoses, netting and buckets. They detoured around workers engaged in various tasks. All of them deferentially made way for the minister and his guests.

"Besides the algae, tannin and fish poop alter the clarity of the water." Jeremiah chuckled at Marla's grimace. "When we're ready to harvest, we put the fish into a tank of clear water to flush metabolites from their system. This purges toxins so no odor remains. That process takes two or three days. Because they don't feed on other fish, which might contain pollutants, tilapia are one of the cleanest varieties."

"According to what you're saying, tilapia are only as pure as their water supply," Vail cut in, draping his arm around Marla's shoulder.

"Good point." The reverend speared him with a keen glance. "Our water passes through a filtration process beginning with a biofilter system. After passing through particle settling and nitrogen conversion tanks, the water sifts through a micron particle filter to remove fine fragments. Then it's mixed with oxygen and pumped into the fish tanks."

Marla sought a way to bring up Kimberly again, but this didn't seem an appropriate time. Vail seemed content to play along with their ruse for now. His sharp gaze surveyed their surroundings, absorbing details.

"What is that guy doing?" Marla indicated a mustached young man working with a net.

"Manuel is censuring the tank, which means catching the fish and weighing them." Jeremiah waved to the fellow. "This tells us their chronology so we can project when to harvest them. We'll weigh a sample of twenty-five fish to get the average in a tank. Each tank holds eighty thousand gallons of water and produces around ten thousand pounds of tilapia. We drain the tanks to harvest them. Hey, Manuel, show them how to catch one."

The man flashed them a grin before tossing a weighted net into the water. Holding an attached rope, he pulled the net from one end of the tank to the other before gathering it up and over the railing. Fish spilled out, flopping on the concrete path, mouths gaping. After weighing one, he threw them all back in the tank.

"Fish water is rich in nitrogen and phosphorus," Jeremiah continued, "so we use it to grow crops. Green peppers, tomatoes, and lettuce are some of our produce; plus herbs such as basil, oregano, and spearmint. The yield is all natural, without pesticides or chemicals. We sell it to natural food stores. Y'all heard of hydroponics? Well, aquaponics is the official term for the combination of fish water and hydroponics. Come take a look."

Marla's ears picked up various sounds as they followed him: gushing water, trickling streams, a humming generator. She didn't smell much in the way of fish, which surprised her.

"Our hydroponics system consists of hydro-pipes, hydro-raceways, and ponds," Jeremiah said. "This is where hydro-pipes supply return water to nourish the plants. We place cuttings in small plastic trays or plastic-lined Styrofoam flats. See where their roots hang down through holes into the water? Water enters the system through one end and exits the other end."

Jeremiah broke a sprig of spearmint and held it out to her. She sniffed the heady fragrance. When he offered her some basil, she sighed with pleasure. Her herbs in the kitchen had never smelled this fresh!

At his signal, they moved toward the edge of the concrete structure. "We keep our people busy. Among other tasks, they weigh and feed fish, take water quality readings, and adjust water flow and aeration."

"Do you have a set schedule?" she asked, fishing for a question relevant to their purpose but unable to conceive one. She felt a flash of annoyance toward Vail. He'd given her the burden of carrying on the conversation. When was he going to play hard-hitter?

The minister grinned. "We catch fish on Tuesdays. On Wednesday and Thursday, we harvest vegetables. Fridays are fish sales when buyers come."

He led them off the structure and around the rear of the bunker. "This is our wetlands area where we grow cultures of pickerelweed, arrowhead, and red mangroves. Note the hydro-pipes that channel water from the fish tanks. The ponds are raised above ground and lined with plastic to prevent leaks."

They headed down a dirt path, kicking up dust. "Here is our raceway section for high-density production of tilapia, eels, and sturgeon."

"I noticed eel tanks in the building earlier," Vail said, scooping Marla's hand into his. She gave him a startled glance. Wasn't he overplaying his role? Not that she'd dare protest, since Jeremiah seemed taken in by their act. What she saw in Vail's eyes wasn't pretense, however. A coil of desire snaked its way through her body as she squeezed his hand in response.

"Eels are very popular for sushi," Jeremiah answered, beaming at them. "They sell for five to nine dollars per pound wholesale. Since birds like to eat them, we have to protect our outdoor tanks with netting. You'll find up to ten thousand eels in one tank. They grow into small, medium, or large sizes."

"How did you become so knowledgeable about all this?" Vail asked on their way back to the main building.

Yes, Dalton. Now that Jeremiah is off guard, slam him with the real questions. Marla avoided looking at him, afraid she'd smile and give away their game.

"I studied marine biology before receiving my calling. I think the good Lord meant it that way. He gave me the means to feed thousands and provide work for our less fortunate brethren."

"How did you arrive in Tarpon Springs? I thought mostly Greeks lived here."

"My father was Greek, not that it matters. People move here for different reasons."

"Your last name is Irish."

"It's my mother's name. She didn't change it on the birth certificate."

"Piotr didn't mind?"

Jeremiah stopped, his expression darkening. "How do you know his name? Have you been checking up on me?"

"Before I give money to anyone, I always investigate," Vail replied.

"You've asked enough questions." He led them inside his office. "You can make your check out to Ministry of Hope."

Gone is the smooth-talking representative of the Lord. Here is the true huckster in prime form. Marla wondered how Vail would get out of this one.

"I'll have to get back to you," Vail said. "You're doing some wonderful work here, but I'm not sure you need the extra funding. Your operations must produce plenty of income."

"Any funds we generate are funneled right back into our missions," Jeremiah said, facing them. "We work among the poor in third-world countries. Our aim is to feed and house our farm workers in addition to the missionaries and their families. It's never enough when you're doing the Lord's work."

Vail pulled out his wallet. But instead of offering the reverend a signed check, he showed him a photograph. "Recognize these people?"

The minister's face paled. "Where did you get this?"

"From Stan Kaufman, Kimberly's husband. He said you called on her one day, but she wasn't home. He recognized you in this photograph found in her room. Neighbors claimed they saw your car a couple of times in the neighborhood. They said Kim bragged about her rich Uncle Jerry. She was pregnant, Mr. Dooley. I suspect you were involved with Mrs. Kaufman in a manner your congregation would not condone. Were you the father of her child?"

Jeremiah's mouth gaped like a fish out of water. His skin turned the color of a white tilapia. "W-who are you?"

Vail ignored his inquiry. "Where were you on the morning of February fifth?"

"Get out. Both of you, leave n-now," Jeremiah sputtered.

"You paid for Kim to go to design school, didn't you?" Marla offered. "After she told you she was pregnant, you tried to buy her silence. It would be easy enough for her to pass the child off as Stan's. But Kim wanted to leave her husband. Did she threaten you? Is that why you killed her?"

The reverend clenched a pen in his hand. He stepped toward her, a menacing light in his mud brown eyes. "You'd better not spread these lies to anyone, or I'll scale you alive."

Chapter
Fifteen

"What did you make of Jeremiah's last remark?" Marla asked Vail on the way back to his car. "Was it a real threat?"

His slate gray eyes simmered under drawn brows. "I didn't care for the reverend's choice of words, but he may be more bluster than brawn. Those evangelist types tend to spout off. After we get home, I'll check on a few more things, then he'll be hearing from me again. Next time, I won't be offering money."

"Did you see the gold chain he wore under his shirt? He must give himself a generous salary, or else he imports more than fish from those third-world countries."

Vail's lips quirked into a half-smile. "His ministry makes enough money from tilapia. It's an easy cash crop. Plus his television show solicits contributions. The man has good business sense; you can't fault him for using his talents."

After he unlocked his car doors, Vail rolled up his shirt sleeves and opened the top buttons at his neck before sliding into the driver's seat. Marla caught a glimpse of springy chest hairs when she settled into the passenger side. Swallowing at her body's sudden rise in temperature, she reached for her seat belt. Just as well they were an arm's length from each other. She could feel the heat radiating from him where she sat.

"It's too much of a coincidence that his missions are located in the same countries as Morris's coffee plantations," she said once they were on the road. "Do you suppose there's a connection?"

"Anything is possible."

"Morris seemed to react when he saw my note with Jeremiah's name scribbled on it, and Miriam got upset when I turned on his TV show. Logic tells me they know something about this man."

Vail gave her a sardonic grin. "What else does logic tell you?"

"Suppose he was the source of Kim's financial windfall, allowing her to pay the tuition for school and fulfill her plans to leave Stan. She had to have some kind of hold over him."

"Such as?"

"If Jeremiah fathered their child, maybe Kim was blackmailing him."

They sat in silence for a while, until their car sped south on I-75. "I don't believe Jeremiah's story about how they met," Vail said finally. "Kim didn't call him because she wanted to make a contribution. She needed his money. So where else did they meet, and under what circumstances?"

"I'll bet Kim's family is involved in this somehow." She glanced at him. "Jeremiah might have been in Kim's vicinity the morning she was murdered. The only thing we need is a motive. If he was paying her off, there you have it."

"You're forgetting about the murder weapon. How would the reverend have obtained Stan's letter opener?"

"How would anyone have gotten it? Someone stole the thing!"

"Kaufman didn't report anything missing. Wouldn't he have noticed its absence before the murder?"

"He told me he couldn't find certain objects in his house," she said thoughtfully. "I wonder if he checked with his cleaning lady."

"You're still trying to lay the blame elsewhere. Kaufman has the strongest motive, especially if the baby wasn't his and Kim was about to leave him. The highest incidence of domestic homicide occurs when a wife is about to walk out."

"And you keep coming back to Stan, even when there's something highly suspicious about Jeremiah Dooley."

Vail compressed his lips, and Marla realized he must be frustrated by his lack of progress on the case.

"Why would Kimberly shack up with Dooley at all?" Vail said. "He's old enough to be her father."

"That's reason enough for lots of women who want a wealthy man to take care of them."

"So you think they met somewhere, and he hooked up with her because she was a good-looking chick? Despite the risk of disclosure to his constituency, he had an affair?"

"He's not the first prominent figure to have an illicit love affair." She appreciated that Vail was at least trying to understand her viewpoint. "As for Kim, he was her ticket to freedom. She traded sex for money."

"I'm glad you have it all figured out." He gave her a sly glance. "And what will you trade for sex?"

His words caused an instant reaction. Her pulse rate accelerated, and her skin flushed. "Uh, I don't think that's the topic up for discussion."

"Why not? All we ever talk about when we're together is some case I'm working on. Let's talk about us for a change."

"How can we have a relationship when we stand on opposite sides of the coin regarding Stan?"

"Let's put Kaufman aside for the moment. If this weren't an issue between us, would you?"

"Would I what?" she asked, knowing exactly what he meant.

"You know." His right hand slithered across the console to rest on her thigh.

She shifted, but his hand didn't budge. Heat migrated from where his palm touched her slacks. The sensation intensified when his fingers stroked her. She felt like a melted puddle of wax, pliable to his touch. "Stop that."

"Feels good, doesn't it?" His fingers inched northward.

"Ah-h-h." She fell into a blissful silence, allowing him to explore her body. Her mind emptied of all other thoughts except what he was doing to her.

"I think we should stop somewhere," he said, taking a ragged breath as he put both hands on the steering wheel.

"Huh?" Reality returned with a blast of air-conditioning. "We can't stay overnight. You have to get home to Brianna."

"That's not what I meant." He flashed her a devilish grin. "Although I'd like to take you up on the offer some other time. I mean, we should stop for dinner. I know a place in Punta Gorda. Fishermen's Village on the Peace River isn't far from the exit, and we'd have a choice of several restaurants."

"Oh, okay." *What did you think, that he was propositioning you? Admit it, girl, you're disappointed. You'd rather Dalton hunger for you than for food.*

"I should have you and Brianna over for dinner again," she said. "I'll invite my mother. There's no need for her to wait until the dance recital to meet your daughter."

"Sounds good to me. I'll return the favor. I can barbecue a mean steak on our grill."

Marla glanced out the side window. "I haven't heard from Ma lately. She must be involved with her new boyfriend."

"Good for her."

"Maybe you should check up on his background. People do that today, don't they? Hire someone to investigate their date's records."

"Only if they have reason to be suspicious. You're not giving the guy a chance. See what you think next time he comes around."

His words were prophetic, because Tuesday morning at work, who should walk into the salon but her mother and Roger himself. Accompanying them was a sandy-haired fellow with the most startling blue eyes.

"Marla!" Anita walked right up to her while she was teasing a client's hair. "You remember Roger? I want you to meet his son, Barry. He's an optometrist."

Marla, holding a comb in one hand, waved. "Nice to see you." Customers chattered in the background, competing with the whir of a blow-dryer and popular tunes from the radio.

Barry grinned, showing a row of even white teeth. "Congratulations on your thirty-fifth birthday. My father has been raving about you ever since your party. When he said you're a hairdresser, I coaxed him to introduce us." He touched his head of thick, curly hair. "Any advice? Humid weather makes it go in every direction."

Marla stepped toward him and fingered a few strands. "I'd recommend Vavoom by Matrix. It's a straightener without harsh lye like some earlier products. Like a perm, it needs to be applied, set, and neutralized. It'll leave your hair in much better condition than it is now." She smiled gently so he wouldn't take offense. "The process removes frizz and relaxes curl, but it won't turn your hair stick-straight. It'll make your hair easier to manage. If you'd like to make an appointment, please tell our receptionist."

"Hey, Marla," yelled Giorgio's customer from across the room. "My hair gets frizzy an hour after I walk out of here. What should I do? Would that work on me?"

Giorgio waved his curling iron. "You should have told me earlier, Elaine! Next time you come in, I'll use Str-8 by Rusk. It's a lotion that penetrates the cuticle of your hair, but it needs heat to react. I have to apply it to your wet hair before blow-drying. You don't need the straightener treatment. That's only for someone with really curly hair."

Finished styling her client's hair, Marla gave her a final spray of Rusk Shining. "See you next week, Alma," she said, removing the woman's cape.

"Are you free to join us for a cup of coffee?" Anita asked, her expression hopeful. She glowed with good health, aided by a tan that contrasted sharply with her layered white hair. Or maybe her inner glow came from being admired by a man again.

"Yes, doll, take a break," urged Roger, looming beside her mother. His bulbous nose gave him a quizzical expression.

Marla shook her head. "Sorry, my schedule is full today, and I have a prospective stylist waiting to be interviewed. We'll get together soon, I promise. I'd like to have you over for dinner when things calm down."

Roger clapped her on the shoulder. "Maybe you and my boy can work something out before then, eh?" He winked.

Marla raised an eyebrow. "I take it you're a rich Jewish professional who is straight, single, and unattached?" she said bluntly to Barry.

He gave her a smile totally without guile. "I don't know about the rich part, but I make a comfortable living. I'm constantly harangued by matchmaking mavens. They don't understand that I just haven't met the right person yet. It's not as though I haven't been looking."

"I don't want to raise false hopes. Did my mother tell you I'm dating a police detective?"

Anita jabbed a manicured finger in the air. "Oh, she's not serious about him. If she were, she'd . . ." Anita broke off, staring at Marla's left hand. Oh, yes. The amethyst ring Vail had given her.

Marla's cheeks colored. "We interviewed a suspect in his latest case yesterday. We, uh, went undercover and pretended we were engaged."

The look of shock on Anita's face was comical. "You did what?"

"I said we *pretended*, Ma. Dalton gave me this ring to make it seem real. He said I could keep it as a Valentine's Day gift."

Barry's blue eyes clouded with disappointment. "Oh, I guess you're taken then."

"Not really. I mean, we're seeing each other but we're not, you know, committed. Yet." She noticed her next client walking in the door. "Sorry, but I'm terribly busy. Barry, why don't you make an appointment, and we'll talk more then."

The rest of the day passed by in a blur. It was only when she was getting ready to leave that Marla got a call from Leah.

"I need to talk to you, Marla. I feel bad about something I said last time you were here," Leah explained on the telephone.

"I can stop by on my way home," Marla said. She wasn't in a hurry except to let Spooks out; Vail had resumed taking Brianna to dance class. Her evening agenda consisted of bookkeeping tasks. "I'll be there in about twenty minutes."

Nicole had promised to lock up, having the last appointment for the day. Marla halted by her station, interrupting the stylist in the middle of a haircut.

"I heard some disturbing news from Stan. He said Carolyn Sutton is moving her salon to this shopping strip. I'll call Mr. Thomson tomorrow to see if it's true. There's nothing in our lease that can prevent it, unfortunately. What bothers me is that Carolyn may be siphoning off my clients."

Nicole's eyes widened, and she paused with a pair of shears in her hand. "Is that where you think your recent no-shows are going?"

"Think about it." Marla gave a mirthless smirk. "Carolyn and I have been rivals ever since we once worked together. She's always resented my success. Moving her salon from Palm Haven proved to be a big setback, and she's been itching to return. All she has to do is offer free services and a lot of clients will switch to her place. If she's planning to move back here, it's one way she can hurt me."

"Knowing her, she'll find more. That's awful, Marla."

"Don't worry, honey," piped in Nicole's client, who'd been listening. "Customers who are loyal to you won't be going anywhere. And when this other hairdresser stops offering complementary sessions, she'll lose clients, too, who will come back to your salon."

"I hope you're right." Marla addressed Nicole. "I liked that stylist I interviewed earlier. She has an upbeat personality, dresses conservatively, and seems enthusiastic. I may call her back by the end of the week."

"That's great. Someone called about the shampoo assistant job. I told her to come in tomorrow." Nicole resumed cutting the blond woman's hair.

"Thanks. I'm on my way to visit Leah. She has something to tell me." Marla had filled Nicole in on recent events earlier that morning.

"Marla, if you find Kim's killer and the deal goes through with Stan, where are you going to come up with the funds to buy his half of the property? Or do you have that covered already?"

Marla shifted her handbag to her other shoulder. "I'll worry about that when it happens. My car lease is up for renewal next month, too."

"If you need help. . . ."

"Thanks, but I'll manage somehow."

Her thoughts turned to Leah on the drive to Coral Springs which took a half-hour due to rush-hour traffic. Last time she'd visited the woman, Leah had seemed weary beyond words. Marla wondered what happened in the interval for Leah to call her.

The tantalizing aroma of roast beef reached her nose when she approached the ranch-style house. Leah opened the door before she even rang the bell. The woman looked better than the last time they'd met. Her auburn hair fluffed in soft layers around her oval face. She'd applied a light foundation of makeup and wore a knit sweater over a pair of tight jeans.

"Stan came to see us," Leah said when they were seated in the living room. Her children were engaged in the family room watching television, so they had a quiet interlude. Leah hadn't wasted time offering Marla a drink, and she was just as glad. She wanted to hear what Leah had to say.

"I told Stan you wanted him to visit the kids," Marla replied. She leaned back in an armchair with worn upholstery. Toys littered a carpet that had seen better days.

"He's worried the police detective is going to pin Kim's murder on him. He said you and Detective Vail are dating each other, and he's afraid you'll be swayed by his opinion." Leah wrung her hands together. "If Stan goes to jail, what will happen to my child support?"

So that's why you called me. "I can't be sure what evidence the detective has against Stan, but he's a fair man. He'll look into other possible suspects. That's his job."

"I suppose he knows Kimberly was pregnant?"

"How did you find out? You didn't mention her pregnancy when I was here last."

Leah's charcoal eyes studied a splatter of blue finger paint on the wall. "Kimberly told me before she died." Her voice was so low, Marla had to lean forward to hear. "She came here hoping, I don't know, that I could give her money."

"Go on." She remembered Christine, Kim's classmate, had mentioned the possibility of Kim making a deal with Leah. Christine must have known Kim was pregnant.

"Kim knew my kids were Stan's beneficiaries unless he had children with her." Leah's voice cracked, and she swallowed. "The witch boasted that her baby wasn't his, but she wouldn't tell him so unless I paid her off. I laughed in her face. Me! Couldn't she see how I struggled to make ends meet? I realize this is a heartless thing to say, but her death was highly convenient because it left my children in the clear in terms of Stan's will."

"You realize that gives you a motive? Where were you the morning of her murder?"

"Getting my kids ready for school, then I left for work. Besides, Patti James saw me at the bus stop. I'm more afraid for Stan." Leah stopped, as though wrestling with emotion. Fear, mingled with confusion, crossed her face. "What if he did it, Marla? He would have been furious if Kim told him the child wasn't his. He'd already figured out she planned to leave him. You know how Stan likes to control things."

"Stan doesn't get physically violent," Marla responded, upset by Leah's lack of faith. "He gets angry and is quick to put you down, but his display of temper is mostly verbal."

"Who else do you think could have murdered her? She said the father wanted their child."

"Really?" That seemed unlikely, if it was Jeremiah Dooley. The minister would want to hush up his affair so as not to expose himself to his constituents.

"Kimberly said Gary was mostly worried about money. That's why she came to me."

"Huh?"

"She'd found a source to help her get away from Stan, but she needed more until her trust fund kicked in."

Marla waved a finger in the air. "Wait a minute. Can we backtrack here? What was that about Gary?"

Leah blinked. "Last time you were here, I told you about Gary Waterford. He was the guy Kim dated before meeting Stan."

"Yes, I've talked to him."

"It's pretty obvious, isn't it? Gary is the one who got Kim pregnant."

Chapter
Sixteen

Marla barely noticed her surroundings during the drive home. Heading south on Pine Island Road, she let her mind dive into autopilot while she mulled over Leah's parting words.

So Gary was the father of Kim's baby! That put a new spin on things. If Jeremiah wasn't giving Kim money because of her pregnancy, could he still have been the source of her tuition payments? It didn't seem likely they were having an affair, as Kim's neighbor had suggested. According to Leah, Kim was shacking up with Gary, her former boyfriend. That went along with what Kim's classmates had said. Certainly Kim's source of funds couldn't be Gary, who lacked enough money to put his shop in order. Why, then, had Jeremiah visited Kim, and which one of them had made the initial contact? And if the minister was paying her off, what hold did she have on him?

Vail had promised to look into Jeremiah's business practices, and she was content to let him handle that angle. They needed more answers, and fast. Her deadline was rapidly approaching. Less than two weeks to go, or Stan would revoke his agreement. Not that she'd arranged for financing to afford the lump-sum payment he required. That was another item on her list of things to do, including Brianna's birthday party.

The phone was ringing when Marla entered her house. Throwing her purse on the counter, she rushed to lift the kitchen phone. "Hello?"

"Is this Marla Shore?" rasped a familiar female voice.

"Yes, who is this?"

"It's Kathleen. You remember me, luv?" she said in a hushed tone.

Recognition dawned. "The Pearls' housekeeper." Alarm frissoned up her spine. "Is something wrong? Has Miriam . . . ?" Words gagged in her throat.

"I know who you are."

"Oh." This wasn't about the old lady then.

"There are things you should know. I can't speak here. You'll have to meet me." Her staccato sentences held a note of fear.

"I'll see you tomorrow night at the Pearls' house, won't I? I hope you won't tell them who I am until we have a chance to talk. I really do care about Miriam's welfare, you know."

"I won't be there. They've given me the evening off. Besides, it's too dangerous. He warned me to keep quiet, but I felt you should know."

Marla gripped the receiver tighter. "Know what? Who told you to keep quiet?"

Voices merged in the background. "I have to go," Kathleen muttered. "I'll be at the Shlock Mart on Thursday. Miriam likes the papayas from the produce section, and she sends me there once a month. It's part of my ordinary routine to go."

"You mean the flea market on East Sunrise Boulevard?"

"Aye, luv. Meet me by the circus at eleven-thirty. It'll be crowded, so hopefully no one will spot us."

"I'd rather meet you tonight. I could leave now."

"No, no! He'd see me! Wait until Thursday." *Click*.

Marla hung up, more confused than ever. What did Kathleen have to tell her that was so urgent, and who'd warned her? She'd used the male pronoun. Did she mean Morris?

Marla went about her evening duties half-heartedly. After shoveling down a quick turkey burger with french fries, doing the dishes, and leafing through her mail, she leashed Spooks for a walk. A leisurely stroll might help clear her mind.

Marla's eyes feasted on the colorful displays of flowers along the path, still visible despite the darkening sky: peach and tangerine impatiens, purple Hong Kong orchids, crimson penta, and burning-hot pink bougainvillea. Orange blossom perfume permeated the air. Balmy with ocean breezes, it was a night made for intrigue.

On her way back to the house, she ran into Goat outside. Her scrawny neighbor glanced up from where he was examining an anthill. He wore a sheepskin vest over a Hawaiian shirt with a beaver cap on his head. "Hey, Marla, what's doin'?"

"Working on another case." She allowed Spooks to sniff his ankles.

Goat scratched the poodle behind its ears, then he straightened. "Ugamaka, ugamaka, chugga, chugga, ush," he chanted, undulating his body. "*Vroom* went the car, shinier than a jar, doesn't belong around *hyar.*"

The pet groomer liked to talk in riddles. "What are you saying?" Marla asked.

A shriek emanated from inside his apartment, and he cringed. "Uh-oh, I think Junior may have met Mrs. Almo's parakeet. I forgot to close the cage, man."

Junior was his pet snake, which he'd alluded to in previous conversations. Marla had never been brave enough to set foot inside his place. "Wait, before you go. What car did you see?"

"An expensive sets of wheels." He scratched his sparse beard. "Foreign model."

"Half our neighbors have foreign cars. What's so unusual about that?" West Broward County qualified as a showroom for expensive automobiles. It would have to be something unusual indeed to catch Goat's attention. "Wait a minute, you don't mean a Porsche, do you?"

He stared at her blankly. "I dunno. Gotta go feed Junior, although I think she's already had her meal."

"Great, see you later." Leaving him to his pet snake, Marla turned away. Had the unknown driver been Jeremiah Dooley? He could have returned home yesterday, after she and Vail left Tarpon Springs. But why would he be interested in casing her territory?

She didn't have time to think about it, because as she neared her townhouse, a Mercedes pulled into the drive.

Oh joy. Just what I need. Why couldn't Dalton drop over instead of Stan? Vail had promised to call her, but she hadn't heard from him since he had taken her home last night.

Stan accosted her on the sidewalk. Her heart lurched when she took in his haggard appearance. It wasn't like him to unbutton his dress shirt, discard his jacket, and loosen his tie. His hair, normally greased off his forehead, hung in wet strands as though he'd just ridden down a waterfall. A moment's trepidation shook her, and she had half a mind to call after Goat. But Stan's hazel eyes glowed with excitement, not menace, as he grasped her arm.

"Wait till you hear what I found out!" he said in an urgent tone. Before he took another step, Spooks attached himself to Stan's leg. Cursing, Stan kicked and stamped, but the dog maintained his grip.

"Spooks, get off," Marla ordered. "What is it? Do you know who killed Kimberly?"

"Not yet, but this is important. Aren't you going to invite me inside?"

His earnestness overrode her caution. "All right. Come in, and I'll put Spooks in the backyard so he won't bother you."

When they were seated in her living room, she folded her hands patiently. "All right, what's your news?"

He perched on the edge of an armchair. "I searched through Kim's genealogy files. She'd taken a lot of notes, even checking birth records. That's where I discovered it."

"Go on."

His eyebrows lifted. "Jeremiah Dooley is the bastard son of Harris Pearl."

"What?"

"You heard me. It appears that wealthy coffee magnate Harris had an affair with their Irish maid, Colleen. Birth records list Harris as the father, not Piotr, whom she married before having the child. It's doubtful Harris even knew about her pregnancy."

Marla stared at him, thoughts tumbling in her head. Jeremiah . . . Uncle Jerry. This meant he truly was Kimberly's uncle! "Did you know Kimberly was attending school and studying interior design?" she asked Stan.

Stan lowered his gaze. "I-I believed Kim when she said she was going to the sports club. She lied to me, Marla. Lied to me. What did I do to her that she hated me so much?"

A surge of sympathy swelled to the surface. "I don't think she hated you, Stan. You tend to be too controlling. Limiting her friendships, curbing her credit cards. She wasn't accustomed to restrictions."

"But I gave her everything she'd wanted: a nice house, a generous allowance, security."

"It's not enough! You can't make a wife happy by constantly putting her down and telling her how much she needs you. That's where you went wrong with me. I needed to grow, but you held me down. It's obvious Kimberly reached the same point."

"She was too naive to know what she wanted. That's probably what got her killed."

Marla gave an exasperated sigh. No matter what, Stan still put the blame elsewhere. Three failed marriages, and he hadn't learned a single lesson.

"I think Kimberly was killed because she knew someone's secret," Marla said. "Take Jeremiah, for instance. Who else in the Pearl family knows about his existence? Judging from her reaction to his television show, I'd say Miriam is aware of their connection. Presumably, so is Morris, who recognized Jeremiah's name on the piece of paper you gave me. Let's not leave out Florence, who'd mentioned Kim was messing in things she didn't understand."

"So? If they already knew about Jeremiah, why would they care about Kimberly finding out?"

"I don't know, but let's look at the reverse situation. Maybe

Jeremiah is the one who doesn't want word to spread. After all, he's a popular televangelist. How would it affect contributions to his ministry if his constituents found out he was half Jewish?"

"It may not make any difference, except to him."

Marla related their interview with the preacher. "He lives around here, which puts him in the vicinity the morning of Kim's murder. Jeremiah didn't say anything to us about his relation to Kim." She crossed her legs. "I'll see what I can find out when I'm taking care of Miriam tomorrow night."

"Be careful. Obviously, Jeremiah Dooley is a touchy subject with them. And you never know . . . it might be dangerous for whatever reason to talk about him."

She noticed the creases on his forehead. "Are you actually concerned for me?"

"I never stopped being concerned. You didn't want me, remember?"

We've been down that path. "There's another possibility."

"Kim's pregnancy." Stan nodded glumly. "Leah told me about Gary. Detective Vail will believe I killed my wife because I suspected her child wasn't mine."

"That's not how I see it. Kim's friend Lacey had her sights set on Gary. Lacey could have been jealous enough to kill her rival. I'd like to talk to Gary again."

"You seem to have covered all the bases." He didn't sound pleased, but then, time was running out, and they hadn't discovered the killer yet. Too many people who'd known Kim had possible motives.

"You know, Elise Addison suspected her husband was having an affair with Kim," Marla said. "But if Kim was sleeping with Gary, then Elise got it all wrong. Maybe she bumped off Kimberly in a fit of misplaced rage."

"I can't conceive of Elise as a killer. Besides, I asked Cliff who he was seeing." He shot her a furtive glance. "Our other social partner, Jessica Shpritz, is pregnant. Her husband, Adam, was away on a business trip an appropriate number of months ago."

Marla's mouth gaped. "You mean Jessica Shpritz and Cliff Addison?"

"You've got it. I think Elise will catch on soon enough if she hasn't already. If you ask me, Cliff is a fool."

At least you never played around while we were married.

She rose and stretched. "Thanks for the information about Jeremiah. If you don't mind, I have things to do now."

As if to emphasize her point, her cell phone rang. Striding quickly into the kitchen, she snatched it from her purse. "Hello?"

"I hope I'm not interrupting your dinner," said Vail's gruff voice.

"I ate earlier, thanks. Stan is here. He found out that Jeremiah Dooley was Kimberly's half-uncle."

A moment of silence met her words. She didn't know if her statement was news to him, or if Dalton was annoyed about Stan's visit. "Explain," he ordered.

"Are you busy? Stan is just leaving. You could come over for coffee, and I'll bring you up to date."

"Good, I just dropped Brianna off at dance class, so it won't take me long to get there."

Stan didn't seem in any hurry to leave. When she returned to the living room, he was still ensconced on his chair, flipping through a *Quick Cooking* magazine. "You didn't offer *me* coffee," he said idly.

She thought of his big empty house, and for a moment was tempted to invite him to linger. "Sorry, but this interview is over. I'll call you in a few days and let you know what I've learned."

Tossing aside the magazine, he shoved his body out of his seat. Facing her, he displayed a wounded look. "I don't want to go to prison, Marla. Are you sure your feelings for that police detective aren't getting in the way?"

Marla took a few steps toward him, then halted. "I'm on your side, remember? You can rely on me. Bye, Stan."

As soon as she'd closed the door behind him, she rushed into her bedroom to prepare for Vail's visit. Her sweater and slacks would have to do, but she quickly brushed her hair and spritzed herself with perfume. She barely had time to turn on the coffeemaker before he arrived. Her pulse quickened as she took in his neatly styled hair parted to one side, freshly shaven jaw, body encased in knit shirt and jeans.

"Hi," he said, smiling in her doorway.

"Hi. Come on in."

"Don't I get a proper greeting?" he asked after she'd shut the door. Before Marla could protest, he swept her into his arms and lowered his head.

Whiffs of spice cologne drifted into her nostrils. His lips, insistent, forced hers to part as his tongue traced the outlines of her mouth. Heady sensations spiraled through her, weakening her knees. She slid her arms around his neck, pressing her body against his hard form. He reacted to her responsiveness by tightening his arms.

Realizing she risked losing her resolve, she reluctantly tore herself from his embrace.

"We don't have much time before you pick up Brianna," she said breathlessly. "I have things to tell you."

"I'd rather do this"—he kissed her again—"and this." He nuzzled her neck.

"Not now, Dalton." She brushed him off, hearing Spooks barking at the back door. "I have to let the dog in, and our coffee should be ready by now. Come into the kitchen."

Vail leveraged his large frame into a kitchen chair, stooping to pet the poodle while she poured two mugs of coffee. Spooks yapped a happy greeting until she threw him a biscuit. Grabbing the treat with his mouth, Spooks ran into the living room to chew in privacy.

"I've been checking into Jeremiah Dooley's fish farm business, tax records, and so forth."

"Isn't his ministry exempt?" She added cream and sugar to her beverage.

He took a sip of the steaming brew. "Yeah, and it appears to be a thriving enterprise. The only thing that bothers me is that his wholesalers pay more for his product than is the norm."

"You think he's giving kickbacks?"

Vail shrugged his broad shoulders. "Could be. His imports seem to be legit. At least, Customs hasn't found anything besides tilapia fish in his shipments."

"He's Morris Pearl's half-brother. Maybe this explains how they both ended up with properties in Costa Rica and Latin America. Harris might have deeded some of his land to Colleen."

"That's assuming Harris knew Colleen was pregnant. So the old man had a fling with their maid, did he? Here's another option: Miriam paid Colleen off to get rid of her."

"I'll ask her about it." It was time for a reckoning with the matriarch, but Marla didn't look forward to her making her confession. She'd miss cajoling the old lady out of her shell after her dismissal, the inevitable conclusion to her deceit.

"You know," she said, "Stan mentioned their neighbor Elise, who thought Kim might be fooling around with her husband. It turns out the husband has been shacking up with Jessica Shpritz. Elise was suspicious of the wrong person, but I wonder if she confided in Florence. They work together for a bird conservation group."

"You told me that already. What's your point?"

"Florence might have carried tales to the family about Kim's infidelity. Kim was cheating on Stan, albeit with Gary. But it could be a reason why Kim's mother is convinced of Stan's guilt."

What else did she have to tell Vail? Another item niggled at the back of her brain, but it wouldn't gel. It surfaced only after the detective left. Of course! She'd forgotten to tell him about her appointment with Kathleen at the Shlock Mart on Thursday. Oh, well. That was another day away.

Wednesday morning she left the house bright and early to make a stop on her way to work. She hoped to catch Gary Waterford at his shop when it opened. Marla needn't have worried; eight o'clock found his repair place door slightly ajar. After knocking lightly, she pushed open the door and entered. No one greeted her, but she heard voices coming from a back room.

"Look, Lacey, no one knows," Gary said. "So what if that cop came to see you again?"

"So what?" Lacey's voice rose to a hysterical pitch. "I told you not to trust Christine and Rocco. They must've ratted on us."

"It's no big news that we're together."

"No, but Christine knew you pretended to care about Kim when all you were after was her money. You didn't tell me she was pregnant! That detective all but accused me of knifing Kim out of jealousy."

Marla stepped closer, hoping to hear more, but her foot dislodged some screws scattered on the floor.

"Shit, someone's out there," Gary snapped. "It must be Irving. He's usually the first guy through the door. Hey, buddy, wanna take a chance on Galloping Gerlinda today?" he called, striding into the front room. Spotting Marla, his jaw dropped in astonishment.

She stepped over a length of discarded piping and peered at an open newspaper on the counter. It listed the one o'clock post time for Gulfstream Park.

"What are you doing here?" he demanded.

Lacey, following on his heels, hissed when she saw Marla. "You!"

"Yes, me. It's time for the two of you to come clean. Or would you rather talk to Detective Vail down at the police station?"

"I don't know nothin' about who killed Kimberly," Gary said, hunching his shoulders. He wore a sweatshirt over faded blue jeans with stylish holes at his knees.

"She was pregnant with your baby," Marla said quietly.

"How do you know?"

"Because she told Christine."

Lacey's pale face scrunched in dismay. Her blond hair hung in stringy clumps as though she'd just gotten out of bed, an image reinforced by her rumpled cotton blouse and jersey pants. "Gary, you were supposed to get her money and then dump her. You lied to me!"

"No, I didn't." He put his arm around her shoulders, but she shrugged him off. "I thought she was on the pill. She's the one who lied to me."

"How did you feel when Kimberly told you?" Marla asked Gary.

His expression darkened. "Annoyed as hell. I can't afford no child support. I told her to make like it was Stan's, but she wouldn't hear of it. *I'm leaving him as soon as I get enough money.* No way did Kim care if he found out, even after I'd warned her."

"Who paid Kim's tuition at design school?"

"Damned if I know. She said somethin' about a rich uncle." He pointed to the doorway where footsteps sounded behind Marla. "Ask him. Maybe he knows."

Marla swirled around, exchanging an amazed glance with Morris Pearl.

Chapter
Seventeen

"What are you doing here?" Marla said to Morris Pearl.

His eyes narrowed. "I might ask you the same thing."

Out of the corner of her eye, Marla noticed Gary slide the newspaper off the counter. "My guess is you're here to place a bet," she told Morris. "I never would have connected you to Gary Waterford."

Morris stepped forward, stopping a few paces from her. "Who are you?"

She fortified herself with a deep breath. "I'm helping Detective Vail with his investigation."

"Hey, man, don't you know?" Gary inserted. "Miz Shore used to be married to old Stanley."

Kim's uncle stared at her, aghast. "You tricked us!"

No kidding. "Stan heard you were looking for someone to care for Miriam on the nurse's day off. Since I'm experienced at taking care of elderly ladies, he suggested I apply for the job. Stan is worried he'll be falsely accused of murdering his wife."

"You've been snooping into our family business. You have no right!"

"Folks, can you take this outside?" Gary pleaded, glancing at the clock. No doubt he was afraid his early customers would walk in during their confrontation.

"I'm outta here," Lacey said, swaying her hips as she strode toward the door.

"Wait," Marla ordered. "What did Kim know about Rocco that could get him kicked out of school? Did she ever tell you?"

Lacey sneered as she stopped and turned. "You're not a detective. I don't have to answer your questions."

"Lieutenant Vail already suspects you of murdering Kim out of jealousy. Do you want him to interrogate you again? Or will you help us find Kim's killer? Maybe you fought over Gary, but she was your friend once. Tell me what you know, for the sake of justice."

A play of emotions crossed Lacey's face. "Only to get you off my back, understand? Rocco has this thing going on his computer. It's not exactly legal."

"Porno?" Marla grimaced. "Or is he a hacker?"

"He sells pictures. You fill it in."

Morris gestured. "Maybe that fellow killed Kim so she wouldn't give away his game."

Marla's glare silenced him. "I don't believe Rocco did it any more than I believe Lacey here is guilty." Kathleen wouldn't have sounded so urgent if she didn't fear someone closer to home. That made Kim's family the most likely suspects.

"What are you doing here, Morris?" she asked. "Planning to place some bets on the horse races? My guess is your sweet wife doesn't know you have a gambling habit. Is that why your business is losing profits? It isn't the cold weather causing damage to the crops. It's your gambling losses."

His face suffused with color. "Watch what you say, or I'll charge you with slander."

"Go ahead. It'll bring things out into the open."

He clenched his fists. "Why, you miserable *klipeh!* Don't come near our house. You're fired."

Her shoulders stiffened. "I may be an imposter as a nurse's aide, but I'm still hired to take care of Miriam, and I can do that job quite well. Your mother needs me. She's renewed her spirit since I spruced her up, and I promised to color her hair. I don't quit on a client until she looks her best. If Miriam wants to replace me, that's her call."

"I'll tell her who you are."

"Be my guest. I'd planned to tell her myself. I'll also inform her that I believe the truth about Kim's death lies close to the nest."

His gaze narrowed. "You'll be putting yourself in danger if you return."

"Is that a threat? Because if so, Gary is a witness."

The repair man raised his hands. "Hey, man, leave me outta this. I got enough problems."

"I don't need to hear this garbage, either," Morris retorted. Whirling around, he marched toward the exit.

"Maybe you'd like to explain to Detective Vail how Jeremiah Dooley is your half-brother," she blurted.

Kim's uncle halted and did a slow about-face. "Where did you hear that?"

"I have my sources."

"It's none of your business."

"I interviewed him at his fish farm. From what I understand, Jeremiah runs a successful ministry. He didn't mention that he was closely connected to Kim. I don't imagine he's eager for word to get out about his origins."

Morris's mouth compressed. "You know too much. It's not good for your health."

"From whose viewpoint, yours or his?"

A sly look stole over his features. "Keep snooping and you'll find out."

On her way to the Pearls' compound later that day, Marla reflected on his words. Morris wouldn't have made such overt threats if he were guilty, would he? Vail hadn't wanted her to go tonight, but Marla didn't want to disappoint Miriam, who would be looking foward to getting her hair colored. Besides, she owed it to the matriarch to come clean. It wouldn't be an easy interview, and Marla dreaded losing the old woman's regard, but integrity compelled her to face Miriam and explain.

Gaining entry was a problem she hadn't anticipated. Raoul shut the door in her face. Morris must have left orders to bar her entrance. Wondering if he'd show up for dinner, Marla decided to enlist the aid of his wife.

An expression of surprised delight lit Barbara's face when Marla knocked on their cottage door. "Marla, I'd forgotten it was Wednesday and you were due here. Will you and Miriam be joining us for dinner again?"

For a moment, Marla forgot her purpose. "You mean Agnes hasn't been bringing her to the dining room?"

"She says Mother is too frail, and the spicy food upsets her stomach. I believe Miriam really enjoyed being with us, though."

"I need your help. Raoul won't let me in."

"Why not?" Barbara removed the apron she wore and slung it over her arm. Tendrils of highlighted hair graced her weary face.

Marla sniffed the aroma of a baking cake. At least Morris's wife didn't rely totally on the family cook. "It's a long story," she said. "Your husband doesn't like me, and I'm afraid he gave orders to Raoul not to allow me entrance. But unless Miriam has someone to care for her, I'm not leaving her alone."

"Oh dear. I suppose one of us could fill in."

"Please, Barbara. I have to see Miriam."

A flicker of doubt crossed the woman's fair-complexioned face. "Let me ring her up. If Mom says it's all right, I'll help you. Wait here."

Barbara shut the door, leaving Marla shifting her feet on the doorstep. The baking-dough aroma mingled with the scent of a nearby Hong Kong orchid tree. It was a delightfully warm evening, and Marla glanced appreciatively at the Malaysian coconut palms, sea grapes, and gumbo limbo trees gracing the lawn. That spreading banyan tree must be decades old, she thought, admiring its hanging roots. Like the family living here, it had entrenched itself into the soil, forbidding any other plant life from encroaching on its territory. Was that how the Pearls felt about Jeremiah Dooley?

The door swung open, and Barbara faced her with a smile. "Mom said to let you right in. I've instructed Raoul. He shouldn't give you any further trouble."

The butler responded by opening the mansion door and standing aside while she passed, his nose turned up in disdain. If it weren't for the old lady whom she cared about, Marla would have been happy never to set foot in this place again.

She lugged her bag of beauty supplies along, hoping the matriarch wouldn't dismiss her right away. They both had a lot of explaining to do.

A greeting party met her at the second landing. Agnes, dressed in a severe black pants set, swept toward her with the swiftness of a storm cloud. Stella and Florence stood side by side, barring the entrance to Miriam's room. Their stern faces were disapproving.

"I knew you were an imposter," Agnes snapped. "You don't know the first thing about nursing. Miriam has insisted on going downstairs to the parlor every afternoon thanks to you! She'll break her hip, and it'll be your fault for interfering." The nurse pursed her thin lips.

"I'm glad she's more active," Marla stated firmly. "If she hurts herself, it's only because you've kept her confined to bed. The poor woman lived like she was already dead."

"You're dismissed," Florence said in a curt tone. "My brother told us all about you. You're working for Stan, hoping to blame one of us for dear Kimberly's death."

"If Miriam doesn't want me here, I'll leave, but I owe her an explanation."

Stella wrung her hands. "Oh my, Kimberly has gotten us all in trouble! I told that foolish girl to be patient, but she wouldn't listen. First my baby gets herself killed, and now this!" Her voice rose to a wail.

"Shut up," Florence said, her eyes glittering. "Marla, you are not welcome here any longer. Agnes will escort you outside."

"Hold on, dearie," warbled Miriam's voice from inside the room. "You don't leave until I say so. Come in, and close the door so those *yentas* don't hear us."

Gratefully, Marla rushed inside the bedroom, shutting the door with a loud bang. If she never saw the Pearl sisters again, it wouldn't be too soon. As for Agnes, maybe she was better qualified to take care of Miriam than Marla was, but Miriam shriveled under her care.

The old lady, sitting in a wingback chair, wore a shift dress and a cap over her newly permed waves. She gestured at Marla. "Sit over there, and tell me the truth. Morris says you're related to Stanley Kaufman."

Marla heard shuffling noises outside the door, as though the sisters were jostling for a position nearest the doorjamb. She hoped Agnes had left to accomplish her errands.

"I was Stanley's first wife," she began, pulling an armchair closer to the matriarch. She was glad to see Miriam, whose cheeks seemed rosier, out of bed and dressed. "When he was arrested, Stan called me. I'd helped the police solve a couple of cases before, you see."

"But you're not a detective, and neither are you a nurse's aide."

Marla glanced away from the old woman's penetrating gaze, effective even through her eyeglasses. "I'm a licensed hairstylist," she admitted.

Miriam's delighted laughter was not the reaction she'd expected. "And a damn good one, too!" the matriarch exclaimed. "Hee, hee. Don't think you're leaving here without giving me that coloring you promised."

Marla grinned in response and pointed to her bag on the floor. "I'm ready whenever you are. Shall we go into the bathroom and I'll continue my explanation while I work on you? Or do you want to go downstairs for dinner first?"

"I think it's best if we don't expose you to Morris again. Go ahead and call for two trays to be sent up. You can join me. Kathleen isn't here, and so Raoul's filling in."

Marla almost mentioned her appointment with Kathleen for Thursday but held her tongue. If anyone was listening outside the door, she didn't want to mention the maid's message. Continuing their discussion in the bathroom would help drown out listening ears.

She ordered their dinners. "Let me help you," she told Miriam who'd already started to push herself from the chair with difficulty.

"No, dearie, I have to start doing more things for myself. I thought of hiring a new nurse since you showed me what I've been missing, except Agnes is so good with bookkeeping. She goes over all the accounts with me. My reading glasses broke, you know, and she's promised to take me to the eye doctor, but we haven't made it there yet."

"I know an optometrist, if you need a reference," Marla murmured, remembering Barry Gold.

"At least I don't have cataracts." Miriam grunted, trying to lift herself and brushing away Marla's assistance. Shoving herself to a standing position, she wobbled in place until Marla stabilized her with a walker.

On their way to the bathroom, Marla glanced at a desk laden with papers. "I'll be glad to help you while I'm here. I have my own salon, so I'm accustomed to bookkeeping."

"Tell me about yourself, Marla."

"Just a minute. Let's sit you in the wheelchair." After Miriam was comfortable, Marla spread her supplies on the counter. She studied the old lady's skin, and selected a level-eight Framesi product. She'd brought a few choices just in case. Squeezing the tube's contents into a bowl, she added developer and mixed the compound with a stiff brush. Then she withdrew a royal blue cape from her bag and tied it around the matriarch to protect her clothes.

While she was working the coloring solution into Miriam's roots with a gloved hand, Marla spoke. "My salon is the Cut 'N Dye, located in Palm Haven. I have my own clients as well as managing the salon. It means I hardly have any time off, especially when I'm doubling as a health care aide."

She hesitated. "I'm really sorry, Miriam. I feel bad about deceiving you. Stan suggested I take this position, because he suspects one of your family members killed his wife."

A heavy silence followed while Miriam digested her remarks. "I know we have our problems, but no one in this family killed that poor child. For God's sake, she's our flesh and blood! As for you, young lady, I'm very disappointed that you lied to me." Her eyes blazed. "Can't say I'm sorry you came here to take care of me, though. I had nothing left to live for until you pushed me out of that bed. I feel like a new woman! Do you know, I called a friend of mine I hadn't seen in years. We made plans to meet in the mall next week. Our nurses will push us around in our wheelchairs, and we'll have lunch."

"I'm so happy for you." Finished applying the solution, Marla stripped off her gloves and set the timer for thirty minutes.

The old lady grasped her arm. "I regret that you tricked me, but not that you've given me a new lease on life."

Marla blinked at the sudden moisture that sprang into her eyes. Stooping, she hugged the old woman's frail shoulders while emotion choked her throat. "I've enjoyed these visits. I feel . . . you're like a grandmother to me. You may not believe this, but I care about you."

Miriam's voice quavered. "You make a better granddaughter than Kimberly ever did. I know you're being truthful." She gave her an affectionate pat on the back. "Now tell me who you think killed her."

"I'm not quite sure." Marla leaned against the counter, wondering how much to reveal. Was it necessary to expose Morris's gambling habit? Or Kimberly's pregnancy? Perhaps it was best to start with the one fact Miriam already knew. "I've learned about Jeremiah Dooley and his connection to the family."

Miriam's startled gaze met hers. "So I gathered when you turned on his television program," she said wryly.

"I interviewed him at his fish farm outside Tarpon Springs. He mentioned his acquaintance with Kim but not his relation to her. I don't suppose he'd want his constituents to find out about his illegitimate birth."

"That was a shameful episode in our family's past. Harris never could keep his eyes off other women."

"Did you know Colleen was pregnant when she left the household?"

"None of us knew anything about the pregnancy until Jeremiah presented himself to Morris one day and announced he was his half-brother. Jeremiah hadn't even known his true heritage until Colleen told him on her deathbed. He'd always believed he was Piotr's son, the man she married after leaving our service."

"I thought you'd dismissed Colleen because you'd found out about her liaison with Harris."

"I fired her when I realized she was his mistress. I wasn't aware she was carrying his child at the time. Harris must have had an inclination, because he settled tracts of property on Colleen. I believed it was just a payoff to get rid of her."

"So none of you knew anything until Jeremiah approached Morris?"

"That's right. You can't imagine the shock! Morris was afraid he'd claim part of Harris's estate."

"If that wasn't his purpose, why did Jeremiah expose his relationship?"

"He'd been given property adjacent to some of our coffee plantations, and he wanted to use our connections to establish his missions. Once his fish farms were operational, Morris put him in touch with our exporters."

"I see." She checked the timer. Fifteen minutes to go.

A knock sounded on the outer door, and she hustled into the bedroom to let Raoul inside, who'd brought their dinners. Noting the empty bed, he glanced toward the bathroom with a disapproving scowl. "Where would you like me to put your trays, miss?"

"On the dressing table, thank you." After he'd left, she wheeled Miriam into the room so they could eat during the remaining interval.

"I presume Morris told the rest of the family about Jeremiah?" she said, resuming their conversation between mouthfuls of meatloaf and mashed potatoes.

"He asked me if Jeremiah could touch Harris's trust fund. Apparently he told his wife, Barbara, who spoke to Florence. Florence came running to me, horrified that her friends would find out. A

Christian missionary who was a bastard offspring of Harris's affair! How disgraceful; it would ruin our sterling reputation in the community. None of us wanted to expose Jeremiah's relation to the family."

Satisfied that Miriam was able to chew adequately with her teeth in place, Marla dogged on after taking a drink of water.

"Then you, your children, and Jeremiah were in agreement."

"That's right."

"I understand that Elise Addison and Kimberly were neighbors. Elise reported seeing Jeremiah's Porsche in their neighborhood. Kim had told Elise about her rich Uncle Jerry. Do you suppose Elise snitched on her to Florence? The two of them work together for a charity organization."

Miriam nodded, her eyes wise. "That's not how Florence learned Kim had been seeing him."

"Oh no?" Marla had to wait for the answer because the timer rang. Back in the bathroom, she donned her gloves and worked the color through to Miriam's ends.

"How did you decide to become a hairdresser, dearie?"

"I always loved doing people's hair. When women look good, they feel better about themselves. It's all about image and self-esteem."

Their conversation focused on Marla's work while she proceeded through the shampoo, conditioning, and comb-out. Finally, she twirled Miriam in her chair to face the mirror.

"Yippee, I'm a blonde!" Miriam exclaimed, her eyes bright.

"Now you can have more fun." Marla plugged in a blow-dryer and curling iron. Sifting through Miriam's wet strands of hair with her fingers, she examined the results with satisfaction. A light golden tone suited the elderly woman's sun-starved complexion.

"You were telling me about Kimberly and Jeremiah," Marla prompted after she finished with the blow-dryer.

"Sorry. I'm forgetful at times," Miriam said, watching Marla's deft movements in the mirror. "Kimberly planned to redo our family albums that were falling apart. Florence told me she'd questioned certain photographs so she could label them. When she didn't get a response, Kim looked up birth records and mentioned finding out about Jeremiah."

"That must have upset Florence."

The old lady grimaced. "Because she'd been in love with the man Stella eventually married, Florence had always resented Kim. It's possible she told Morris about Kim's discovery. But neither of them killed my granddaughter, if that's what you're thinking."

No? Morris was afraid that revealing Jeremiah's blood relationship might entitle him to a share of their inheritance, while Florence feared besmirching the family's reputation. Did one of them silence Kim to prevent the news from leaking out?

"Kim was getting money from someone to pay her tuition at design school. She planned to leave Stan and found a financial source to help her. Do you think Morris had reinstated the allowance that you withdrew?"

Miriam's shoulders stiffened. "I never stopped that girl's allowance. I don't know what you're talking about! Maybe I didn't approve of her manner in getting what she wanted, but she was entitled to that money."

"From what I've heard, you cut her off. That's why she had to seek another source of support until her portion of the trust fund became available."

Miriam's sharp gaze speared her. "My daughters believe Stan killed Kimberly, because she'd mentioned finding a way out of her trap, as she called her marriage. Florence suspected she'd found another man."

Marla put down the curling iron and unplugged her devices. Armed with a teasing comb and hair spray, she quickly styled Miriam's blond wavy hair. "Kimberly had revived her relationship with Gary Waterford, the man she'd been dating before she met Stan. Gary got her pregnant, but he couldn't afford to pay her tuition. I thought Jeremiah must have been funding her, but it could've been one of your family members as well."

"That's absurd." Anger flashed in Miriam's eyes. "I provided for her. She should still have been getting my allowance."

An unpleasant possibility crept into Marla's consciousness. "Who wrote the checks and mailed them?"

"Agnes does my writing for me. My hand isn't so steady, and I don't see well close up even with my reading glasses."

"She signs your name?"

"Well, no, I sign a bunch of checks each month, and she fills them in. We go over the books together."

"Maybe you should ask Agnes where Kimberly's money has gone."

Chapter
Eighteen

Marla drove to her meeting with Kathleen on Thursday morning with high anticipation. Surely the maid would tell her what was going on in the Pearl household. She'd learned nothing new last evening. By the time Agnes returned, Miriam was asleep. She'd like to have been a fly on the wall when Miriam asked the nurse about Kimberly's allowance checks. Meanwhile, she'd left her cell phone number for the matriarch in case of an emergency.

Luckily, she'd eased off on her client load for today and could take a generous lunch break. Heading east on Sunrise Boulevard, she turned right into the parking lot across from the flea market. Finding a space was tough. Anytime the circus performed, a mob scene prevailed.

Outside, her nose picked up the impending scent of rain. A cold front was scheduled to move in, and heavy clouds scudded overhead in a stiff cool breeze. She stuffed a folding umbrella into her purse before locking the Camry.

She'd spoken to Vail earlier. He'd scheduled an interview with Jeremiah at his Margate residence today. She hadn't told him her plans; hearing his voice had reminded her guiltily of her inaction regarding Brianna's birthday party. What kind of mother would she make if she always put her own business first? Not a good one, she told herself, stepping along the pavement toward an escalator. It rose to a yellow skyway stretching across the busy thoroughfare.

She crossed the street on the covered elevated walkway, then hesitated. Ahead was an entrance into the building housing permanent stalls. Below on her left were outdoor amusement rides, an arcade, and a cotton candy concession stand, almost empty since it was a weekday. Farther along was a Farmer's Market that teemed with customers. She recalled Kathleen saying she bought papayas for Miriam. It was early yet; should she look for the woman there?

Her long skirt flapped about her ankles in the wind, which made the decision for her. Shivering, she hustled forward into the building's shelter, ending up in a corridor with a dirty linoleum floor. An eclectic furniture collection was on her right, an artificial-flower shop on her left. She glanced at a moving waterfall picture and wrought-iron bed frame draped in black and gold lace before moving past a women's dress boutique. The smell of incense reached her nostrils as she strode by a toy store. Shops selling belts and scarves, slot machines, lingerie, and pens tempted browsers with their wares.

Arriving at a central court, Marla stood a moment to get her bearings. Crowds jostled her as her ears were assaulted by blaring televisions and stereos and her eyes were stunned by flashing neon signs. The circus hadn't even started yet, and she felt as if she were in the middle of one. How would she ever find Kathleen in this mob?

It might be easier to find the housekeeper at the Farmer's Market than in this crowd. Glancing at her watch, Marla noted she had twenty minutes before the circus began. Plenty of time to search for Kathleen outside and grab herself a bite to eat.

She stopped at a food court and scanned the offerings. The cultural diversity of Broward County was well represented by the food choices: Jamaican meat patties, coco bread, Montreal smoked meat, Cuban sandwiches, pizza, potato knishes. Feeling the need for haste, she ordered a kosher hot dog and ate it on the run.

She found a rear door and exited to an outdoor section of the flea market. Loud gospel music mingled with chatter in foreign languages as she wound her way through a maze of stalls selling Hawaiian shirts, tacky Florida souvenirs, scooters, sportswear, and perfumes. At a toy stand, electronic bleeps competed with "Here Comes the Bride" from a bridal doll twirling on a pedestal.

Passing a group of alleys shaded by overhead tents, she reached the marketplace. Enormous papayas vied for attention with coconuts, mangos, plantains, juicy beefsteak tomatoes, glossy eggplants, and more. A nearby flower stall sold roses for five dollars per dozen. *No wonder Miriam sends Kathleen here for papayas*, Marla thought. *These prices are cheaper than Publix, and the produce looks fresher.*

Unfortunately, she didn't spot the auburn-haired maid anywhere in the crowded aisles. It was nearly time for the circus. She'd better get inside to look for the woman. A momentary alarm flickered through her. What if Kathleen didn't show up? Her news was dangerous enough that she hadn't wanted to be seen with Marla at the Pearl household. Maybe she'd discovered the murderer.

No sense worrying. Just find her.

The circus area consisted of two levels. For one dollar, people could sit at side rows of preferred seating overlooking the stage from the upper level. Marla cringed at the barrage to her eardrums. Explosions and gunfire from an arcade of video games punctuated the music blaring from a speaker system. Her gaze fastened on a worker in a red logo shirt who was occupied whitewashing the rail leading down a flight of metal steps. The noise didn't seem to bother him; he must be used to it. Below, bleachers facing an elevated stage cost two dollars for extravagant spenders.

As the music flared and the lights dimmed, Marla searched frantically for Kathleen. A few men returned her regard, and she quickly averted her gaze. For the most part, they were scruffy-looking individuals. She shuddered, wishing to complete this rendezvous so she could return to the salon.

Where was Kathleen? Marla didn't see her sitting in either of the side sections on the upper level. While the red curtain rose on a clown act, she scrutinized the people walking by. The hairs on her nape prickled, as an uneasy feeling swept over her.

She dropped her gaze to the lower section where she glimpsed Kathleen's distinctive silver-streaked auburn hair. Her breath caught, and she dashed for the stairs.

A security guard blocked her path. "Sorry, miss, all the seats are taken."

"I'm meeting someone. She's down there." Marla craned her neck, searching for her quarry.

A loud explosion made her jump, while smoke billowed from the stage. Motorcycles roared into the arena, belching fire. Out stalked a tiger, playing tag with the monstrous machines.

Pop, pop. Marla's attuned ears picked up the sounds. Was that part of the circus act? Her heart thumping wildly, she brushed past the guard and charged toward the row of seats where she'd spotted Kathleen a few minutes ago.

There she was! The maid sat rigidly in one of the bridge chairs in a side section. Bumping her way past several irritated patrons, Marla crouched in front of the woman, who appeared transfixed by the circus.

"Kathleen, what's wrong?"

The woman's eyelids fluttered, but she didn't raise her head. She moved her lips, and it took a few seconds for the words to come out. "Letter opener . . . I took it . . . missing from my room . . . Miriam is . . ."

A trickle of blood flowed from the corner of her mouth. Her eyes glazed, and she said no more.

"Miss, remove yourself from there!" ordered the guard, who'd followed her.

Marla ignored him as icy tendrils of fear clutched her heart. "Kathleen!" She clasped the woman's hand, feeling for a pulse. There was none.

A blurred shadow whizzed behind her. *Pop.*

She shot to her feet. *Oh my God, I've got to get out of here.* Avoiding the guard, she turned in the opposite direction and crashed her way through a jumble of legs and feet until she exited the seating area.

She wound up behind the stage, dodging restless animals and circus workers who screamed at her that she'd entered a restricted area. Her nose wrinkled at the stench of manure as she narrowly avoided getting kicked by a spooked horse. Grasping her purse, she vaulted over a low rail and ran for the rear door. Strangers gawked at her; the security guard doggedly pursued her, and from somewhere a killer chased her.

Turning a corner in the maze of outdoor stalls, she ducked inside a boutique and crouched behind a display of straw hats and swimwear. An idea took shape when she spied a selection of wigs next door.

Several moments later, Marla left the stall with a lighter wallet and a new look. Blending into the crowd, she smoothed her turquoise ankle-length beach robe and straightened the straw hat on her blond head. She put a jaunt into her step as she headed steadily toward the parking lot, careful to latch on to a bunch of tourists going in the same direction.

When she reached the safety of her car, she wished she had searched through the crowd for a familiar face. Maybe she would have identified the murderer. She couldn't think about what Kathleen had said yet. Her body shook so violently she had trouble fitting the keys in the ignition. Before pulling out, she called Vail on her cell phone.

"Go to your salon," he ordered after she related her news. "You'll be safe there. What time do you get off work today?"

"I won't finish until eight."

"I'll pick you up. I don't want you to be alone. Kathleen must have been followed, and you were seen with her."

Marla wiped sweaty palms on her coverup, glad she'd worn canvas shoes. They went well with her disguise. "Kathleen mentioned something about Miriam," she said, pulling off her wig and hat. "I'm concerned for her. If someone in their household . . ."

"Jeremiah Dooley wasn't home when I went to see him."

"What?" She turned on the engine and joined a line of vehicles exiting the parking lot. Although she kept checking her rearview mirror, she didn't notice anyone hanging behind when she proceeded onto Sunrise Boulevard.

"Remember, I was scheduled to meet him today?" Vail's deep voice replied. "I haven't been able to locate the man." He paused. "I'll admit to being annoyed before, but now I'm worried. If someone got to Kathleen, maybe they took him out first."

"I don't understand the connection."

"You will. I'll tell you later. See you at eight."

Somehow Marla made it through her afternoon appointments, mostly by performing robotic movements that she could have done with her eyes closed. If her clients noticed she was less than usually conversant, they didn't mention it. She couldn't help sliding frequent glances toward the door, expecting Kathleen's killer to charge through the entrance. Her slippery fingers kept dropping instruments, and once she left a client's highlights on too long so the hairs came out carrot-colored.

A shock jolted through her when the man of the hour appeared at six o'clock. He slammed open the door and barged inside, thick brows drawn together in a scowl.

"What are you doing here?" Marla asked, blurting the first response in her head.

"You killed her," Jeremiah Dooley shouted. "The wrath of the Lord will visit you for what you've done!"

She felt herself go pale. All voices in the salon fell silent, and several pairs of eyes turned in their direction.

She'd been cleaning her counter before the next customer arrived, and now she held the spray bottle in front of her like a weapon. "I don't understand," she began, but he cut her off.

"I told her not to meet you. Stupid woman wouldn't listen. She must have been followed."

"Look, do you mind if we take this outside?" She nodded to Nicole. "Come get me when Michelle arrives. She usually shows up late anyway."

In front of the salon, Marla motioned to a bench. Jeremiah was too agitated to sit. They stood facing each other, two combatants ready for battle. Thanks to her marriage with Stan, Marla possessed skills in verbal sparring. It was also thanks to Stan that she found herself in this predicament, Marla reminded herself with a wry grin.

"Why are you smiling?" Jeremiah snarled. "My sister is dead, and it's your fault. May the good Lord have mercy on her soul."

"Kathleen was your sister?"

"I didn't think you were smart enough to figure it out."

"Katie ... Kathleen. I should have guessed! She was born to Colleen and Piotr, then," Marla said, untangling the family threads in her mind, "whereas you were Harris Pearl's illegitimate son. I found out about Harris's affair with his Irish maid."

Hostility fled from Jeremiah's expression. "For years, I believed I was Piotr's son. Not until my mother was dying did she tell me the truth."

"Why did you reveal your identity to Morris?"

He flashed a brief, mirthless smile. "I showed up in his office one day and announced I was the son of his father. You should have seen the look on his face! I showed him my birth certificate as proof. Colleen had never let Piotr see that his name wasn't on the document."

"Morris was afraid you'd stake a claim on the family fortune." She scanned the parking lot, but didn't see Michelle's red Volvo. Traffic roared by, fumes and dust reaching her nostrils. A cool, stiff breeze chased the water-laden clouds to a slate gray horizon. In true tropical fashion, patches of rain thundered by in short, angry bursts.

"I'm not interested in their money, although Morris lives in fear of the day when I ask for my share," Jeremiah confessed. "He's afraid he'll have to explain where all the company funds have gone. His misdeeds won't go unpunished. I'll see to it." His face darkened, and he clenched his fists. "All I wanted was his help establishing my missions. He already had connections in the Latin markets. I needed to set up export routes for my fisheries."

"So basically, the two of you kept your connection under wraps," Marla concluded. "What happened when Kimberly learned about

you through her genealogy research?" Tired of standing for most of
the day, Marla leaned against an exterior wall.

Jeremiah paced the pavement. "She contacted me and threatened to expose my background unless I helped her."

"I don't imagine she referred to her spiritual requirements,"
Marla said in a dry tone.

"She required money to enroll in design school. When Kim realized she wouldn't deceive her husband for long, she demanded her
own apartment and a regular allowance. I warned her about becoming too greedy."

"Is that why you killed her?"

He put his hands together in a prayer position. "I do the Lord's
work, not Satan's. Despite our dubious connection, I regarded her as
my niece. Someone else silenced her. If I knew who it was, I'd recognize Kathleen's killer." Lowering his head, he muttered a verse
from a psalm.

"Have you any idea what Kathleen wanted to tell me?"

"She said she'd discovered something important that you should
know. I warned her to stay away." His anguished gaze met hers, and
she realized how painful it must be for him to lose the one relative
to whom he had felt close.

"Why was she working in the Pearl household?" Marla asked,
needing to clarify the point. "Did you settle her there to spy on
Morris?"

"I didn't trust Miriam to keep her mouth shut. I knew he'd told
her. Morris didn't want to expose his association to me any more
than I did. But Miriam had no such scruples. I couldn't risk the news
leaking out. Imagine the reaction from my congregation! They'd
condemn me for having tainted blood, for being spawned from an
immoral relationship. My position as missionary leader would be
jeopardized."

"Especially if they examine your take of their contributions,"
Marla muttered. Maybe that's what concerned him more; that any
publicity might expose his high-spending lifestyle.

He ignored her remark. "Kathleen served as my early warning

system. She was adamant about helping me continue my good deeds. It was her idea to take employment in the Pearl household to keep an eye on their family. I told her she had to curb her destructive impulses, or she'd draw attention to herself. Her sinful behavior didn't go unnoticed."

"What do you mean?"

"She liked to collect things. You know, small items from around the house. It was a devilish compulsion she couldn't expel no matter how hard she prayed. Our Lord evoked a harsh punishment for her." His voice cracked, and he bowed his head.

"I'm sorry."

"If she hadn't called you, my sister wouldn't be dead," he said, raising eyes tinged with moisture. "Whatever she'd discovered, she should have told me first."

Oh, yeah? Then you'd have buried it along with your identity. Doesn't truth and justice mean anything to you?

"Here comes my next customer," she said, spotting Michelle in the parking lot. "I believe you had an appointment with Detective Vail earlier, for which you didn't show. It might be a good idea for you to get in touch with him."

He gave her an enigmatic glance. "The Lord summons me elsewhere. I must obey His Word first."

Before she could ask him more, he stalked off.

While she worked on her last customers, Marla felt haunted by something the televangelist had said. She couldn't place what it was until later, when Stan phoned her for a progress report. Relating her conversation with the minister, she stopped when he gave a snort of laughter.

"You'd think that woman was working here, with all the things missing around this house! Kimberly would have known where everything was kept. I can't find the silver millennium pen she gave me, my pocket watch, or my autographed baseball. I'd been planning to ask Kate this afternoon, but she didn't show."

"Who's that?"

"Our cleaning lady. She always comes on Thursdays. I don't understand why she didn't call. She's been very reliable since Kim hired her a few months ago."

A frown creased Marla's brow. "What's her last name?"

"Sebastian. Not very Irish, eh? She has a lilt and red hair. Said her mother came from the homeland."

Her eyes opened wide. "You hired an Irish housekeeper whose name was Kate Sebastian?"

"What are you getting at?" Stan snapped.

"I'll bet she took your missing items. Jeremiah said she had a compulsion." Her mind raced forward. "Your letter opener! She must have brought it to her room at the Pearls' house. Tell me, did Kathleen have a key to your place?"

"How else would she get in when I'm at work? Kimberly usually left the house by nine, too. What does that have to do with anything?"

"I'll tell you later. Bless my bones, I have to warn Miriam. Bye." Excitement shook her voice. It was all coming together now.

She finished by seven-thirty, a half hour remaining before Vail arrived to escort her home. Alone in the salon, she picked up the extension by the front desk.

No one answered at the Pearl household.

How odd. They should be having dinner now.

Before she could decide what to do next, her cell phone rang. She snatched it from her purse, hoping it was Dalton.

"Hello?"

"It's me, dearie," warbled a feeble voice.

"Miriam? I just tried to call you."

"I couldn't reach the telephone. Marla, I'm worried. Agnes isn't here, and there's no one answering from downstairs."

"What do you mean?"

"Agnes went to get my dinner and never came back. I gave Raoul the night off. Pressing personal business, he said. Normally Kathleen would be here. She has the day free and goes to the market for me, but she didn't return by her normal time."

"Isn't the cook there to prepare dinner for the family?"

"I don't know. No one answers on my service line."

"Dear Lord. I meant to warn you."

"About what? Wait, I think someone's coming. Oh, it's you," she heard Miriam say. "What are you doing? Can't you see I'm on the phone? Oh, my. Marla—"

The receiver went dead.

Chapter
Nineteen

M arla waited in her Camry with the engine running until Vail arrived. After he'd parked his vehicle and strode over, she gestured for him to get in her car.

"Miriam is in trouble. I just spoke to her, and we were cut off." Switching gears, she pulled onto the main road and headed south. "I think I figured it out."

His solemn gaze raked her. "That's what I like about you, brains to go along with beauty. What's up?"

"Did you find out anything about Kathleen?" she countered.

"She'd been shot from behind. No one around her noticed anything unusual with all the noise from the circus."

At Broward Boulevard, she turned left to head east. Traffic was light toward downtown at eight o'clock; most people had already gone home. Orange streetlights provided a bright glow as they sped past empty storefronts and the interstate overpass. Puddles flanked the road, but the rain had stopped. Moisture clung to the air as though the night had perspired. She kept her wipers on, oblivious to their monotonous hum.

"Stan called me earlier," Marla explained after they'd crossed a set of train tracks. "He wanted to know how I was progressing with the case, then he mentioned not being able to find things around his house. He meant to ask his Irish maid about it, but she didn't show up today. Her name is Kate Sebastian. Ring a bell?"

"Kathleen?"

"You got it." She grinned at his bewildered look. "Jeremiah showed up at my salon, accusing me of contributing to his sister's death. That's what you were going to tell me, isn't it? That Kathleen and Jeremiah were related. He said Kathleen had a compulsion to take objects that don't belong to her. She also had a key to let herself into Stan's place when no one was home. What if she lifted his letter opener and brought it to her room in the Pearls' house?"

His gaze sharpened, and she warmed to his solid, stabilizing presence. "I see where you're going. Someone at Miriam's place took the letter opener and the key, someone who knew the victim's morning routine of getting up early to fix Stan's breakfast before he came downstairs. Either Kim unlocked the door to let in a person she knew, or the killer entered with a key. The perp stabbed her with the dagger, panicked and threw it in Stan's yard, kicked some dirt over it, then fled."

"Meaning it's someone from the Pearl household. Kathleen must have realized who it was, and that's what she intended to tell me. I hope nothing has happened to Miriam."

They arrived at the estate in record time. The Camry's brakes squealed when she stopped it in the circular driveway and shut off the engine. A few moments later, they charged up the front steps. The door was slightly ajar.

"Hold it," Vail commanded. Drawing a gun from his holster, he brushed past her and edged the door open farther. Dead silence greeted them.

"Shouldn't you call for backup?"

"We're in Fort Lauderdale, not Palm Haven," he whispered. "Maybe nothing's wrong, and Agnes got tied up talking to the cook. You can wait outside while I take a look around."

"Are you kidding? I have to see if Miriam's all right."

"This could be dangerous. Do what I tell you."

"No way. I'll be careful."

"Damn stubborn woman." He cracked the door wider. "Where's the butler?"

"Miriam said she gave him the night off."

"Peculiar. Isn't this about the time you said the family ate dinner?"

She nodded, her heart thudding wildly in her chest. Wiping sweaty palms over her long skirt, she stepped forward. Keys rattled in her pocket, and she clamped a hand over them. She'd locked her purse in the car, not wanting to be burdened.

"I'm going upstairs," she said without waiting for his permission.

A scraping sound off to the left caught their attention. "I'll check the kitchen," Vail rasped. "Holler if you need me."

Marla carefully ascended the steps, watching her footing so she didn't trip over the same piece of folded carpet as before. At the landing, she hesitated. The door to Miriam's room was closed. Dare she peek inside?

Concern for the old lady propelled her forward. *Please let Miriam be okay. Maybe she's just sleeping, and that's why it's so quiet.*

She tried to calm the tremors that shook through her, but her heart beat so fast that her teeth chattered. With icy fingers, she twisted the doorknob to Miriam's chamber.

Oh, no. The matriarch's still form lay on the bed. A pillow covered her face. Marla gasped, her indrawn breath the only sound in the room.

Rushing forward, she snatched the pillow away. To her relief, Miriam's eyes were closed. She would have fainted at confronting the sightless stare of the dead. The old woman's skin appeared translucently pale, blue veins throbbing at her temples.

Throbbing. She was alive, but unconscious. Someone had tried to smother her and failed.

Marla leaned forward to put her hand on a bony shoulder when several things happened at once. She heard a shout followed by a gunshot downstairs. The single lamp in the room went out, along with the hallway lights. Darkness descended, but not before she noticed a shadow hurtling at her from the doorway.

A scream tore from her throat. She dodged sideways, missing a blow aimed at her head. It grazed her shoulder, sending a searing pain down her arm. Lashing out with her foot, she felt a satisfying crunch when it connected with someone's leg. A yelp sounded, revealing her assailant's position. Before she could take advantage, her hair was caught in a viselike grip, her head jerked back.

"Interfering bitch," snarled Agnes's voice.

A sharp object jabbed her neck, pressing against her skin. She couldn't speak, could barely breathe. *Dalton!* her mind cried.

"Kathleen took this heavy onyx paperweight from Stan's house," the nurse said. "Do you know what a sharp point a narrow pyramid shape has? No?"

It punctured Marla's skin. She whimpered, and Agnes chuckled. It was a cold, calculating sound that chilled her blood.

"Kill her," urged a male voice from beyond the darkness.

Horror dawned in Marla's breast as she realized she faced two enemies who had her at their mercy.

"I'm having fun," Agnes said. "Miss Shore has been a thorn in my side, making Miriam ask me uncomfortable questions. The old bag even wanted to double-check my bookkeeping. How else do you think Miriam got wise to me? Oh yes," she said, yanking on Marla's hair until she moaned with pain. "I stopped sending those checks to Kimberly a long time ago. Built myself a nice nest egg along the way, until the smart-ass child figured out where her money was going."

"What about you, Morris?" Marla croaked, buying time. "How are you involved?"

Heat emanated from Morris's body as he joined them inside the room. "I couldn't let my darling niece expose Jeremiah's connection to the family. If my brother claimed his share of Harris's fortune, he'd find out it wasn't there. Mother would learn I've been covering my gambling debts by skimming money from the company, and she'd disinherit me."

"I noticed Morris's financial reports didn't jive with our accounts," Agnes said proudly. "When I realized he'd been dipping into the family funds, I confronted him. We ended up covering for each other. So you see, we had a perfect arrangement, until you came along."

"I took care of the cop downstairs," Morris said. "Get rid of her, or would you rather I do it?"

"Don't be in such a rush, darling. We'll be gone by the time your family returns from their concert."

Marla, who'd listened in rising panic, jabbed the nurse in the ribs with her elbow and stomped on her instep.

Agnes howled with fury but loosened her grip enough for Marla to spin away. Feigning to the right, she shot to her left as Morris lunged. The doorway loomed in front of her like a portal to heaven. She staggered into the hallway, cursing the pitch darkness. Dropping to her knees, she crawled in the direction of the staircase.

Then the lights switched on with blazing clarity.

Morris faced her, holding a familiar weapon in his hand. Dalton's gun. What had happened to the detective?

Agnes emerged from the bedroom, face purplish with fury. "Shoot her," she urged, spittle on her lip.

Marla glanced at the balustrade railing. She'd never make it down the stairs. Only one option presented itself to her.

Leaping to her feet, she vaulted over the railing and crashed to the marble floor below.

A sharp pain jarred her right hip upon impact. For an instant, she remained paralyzed, frozen with fear. At least all her limbs moved; she hadn't broken anything. Torn between checking on Dalton and escaping through the open front door, she hesitated. Maybe there was an exit through the kitchen. Didn't servants usually enter through a separate service door? It had to be in the rear somewhere.

While her instincts screamed at her to escape, she mustered her strength to dash into the kitchen. It became a limping marathon, because she couldn't put her full weight on the side where she'd fallen.

Her stricken gaze fell on Dalton flat on the tile but still breathing. A swelling bruise on the side of his head told the rest of the story.

"Dalton, please wake up!" She lifted his arm, attempting to drag him toward the rear door. At least she'd been right on that account.

Now if only he would budge, because she lacked the strength to move him. Her heart leapt when he moaned and his eyelids fluttered open.

A gunshot sounded, and a whoosh of air flew by Marla's head. Dalton rolled to his feet, swayed in place, and would have fallen if not for her supporting arm.

"This way," Marla indicated. They stumbled together out the door into the inky night. Now what? If they could make it to her car, they were home free. But as they staggered around the corner, she gave a gasp of dismay. All four tires had been punctured. Agnes grinned at them, waving a poker she must have retrieved from the fireplace.

Behind them, Morris chortled in triumph and fired a volley of shots. His aim went wild, but Marla didn't stop to thank her lucky stars. Grabbing Vail's hand, she pulled him toward the woods surrounding the Pearl compound.

He kept pace with her limping stride, but his constant blinking had her worried. From his dazed expression, it looked as though he was making a concerted effort to stay conscious. Oh joy, she thought, I can barely walk, and he can barely stay awake.

At least the clouds dissipated, revealing a full moon that provided enough light for them to discern a path through the forest. She urged him on, afraid Morris and his partner in crime would overtake them. Or else that one of his bullets would hit the mark.

"He's out," muttered Vail, hanging on to her arm. His added weight made her good side sag.

"Huh?"

"Out of ammunition. He stopped firing."

"Maybe he just wants to get closer. We have to get off this path if we want to evade them." She glanced at his empty belt, which usually held a cell phone. "If we can circle around to my car, I'll grab my purse. My phone is inside."

"Never mind. We have to separate Morris and the nurse. We'll have a better chance to take them on one at a time."

"Yeah, right. Like either of us is in a condition to fight."

"There!" Vail pointed to a spreading banyan tree that must have been hundreds of years old. Dead leaves and dried pine needles crunched underfoot as they struggled through the underbrush. Sea grapes competed for space with cabbage palms and live oaks in the semitropical hammock, redolent with the earthy odor of decaying vegetation. The hairs on her arms prickled in the cool breeze as footsteps thudded close behind.

Vail stooped to snatch a dead tree limb, fumbled it, and slid to his knees. "Dizzy," he grunted.

"Not now! We have to get up that tree." She wouldn't leave him on the ground to be beaten senseless by their adversaries. Or worse.

It would have been difficult under normal circumstances to scamper up the roots that reached from the branches to the ground. A tree house would fit in the network of intertwined limbs that stretched in a wide radius, and she wished for one now, with a convenient ladder. Lifting her leg brought a sharp agony to her right hip. She bit back an exclamation of pain, gritting her teeth as she clambered over the rough bark from one foothold to the next. Vail crawled after her, holding a club fashioned from a stump.

They crouched on a horizontal branch, waiting—two disabled prey hoping to turn the tables on their predators. The sounds of their soft breathing mingled with the crickets' nightly chorus.

"I'm sure they went in this direction," Agnes's voice sounded directly below.

"Dammit, I don't see them," Morris snapped.

"Maybe we should leave. If we make the flight, it doesn't matter what they report."

With a swing of his club, Vail cracked Morris on the head. The man crumbled like a wet noodle.

"Oh, what the hell." For the second time that night, Marla took a leap of faith that would have impressed even a man of spirituality such as Jeremiah Dooley. She landed on Agnes, knocking her to the ground. The poker dropped from Agnes's fingers, but the nurse was far from disarmed. A blade in her other hand gleamed in a shaft of moonlight.

"Marla, watch out!" Vail cried from above.

Beyond their twisting, struggling bodies, Marla caught a glimpse of his sickly expression. The effort of swinging the chunk of wood must have aggravated his head. Nonetheless, he hung his legs down in preparation to jumping.

A knee to her stomach forced the breath from her lungs. As she tried to draw air, Agnes rolled her onto her back. The nurse's leering face hovered above hers as their arms locked into a death match. While her heavy weight held Marla down, Agnes pressed a leg against her bad side, forcing a groan from her lips. Her arms weakened, and Agnes thrust the blade forward. Its sharp edge pierced her chin.

Beside them, she heard a thud. Dalton must have landed, she thought vaguely. Or fallen. She didn't sense any other motion nearby. It was just the two of them, and Agnes had the advantage.

Stones and twigs dug into her back through her sweater as she fought to keep the knife from slipping to her throat. Now that she'd regained her breath, she panted in short, hard bursts. Sweat dripped down her chest.

Agnes's onion breath washed in hot gusts over her face. The whites of her eyes showed in feral madness. Marla's arms ached from the difficulty of pushing against her superior strength.

Hell, I'm no lightweight. I lift hairbrushes all day! Mustering her energy, Marla shoved with all her might, at the same time sliding her good leg sideways and over. Her twisting motion took Agnes by surprise. She felt the nurse's grip loosen. Letting go of one hand, Marla groped in the soil. She hit pay dirt when her fingers closed around a rock.

Crack. Marla cringed when the rock connected with Agnes's skull. Relief surged through her when the nurse collapsed to her side, stunned.

Marla grabbed the knife from her momentarily nerveless fingers. Vail stirred, putting a hand to his head.

Hearing him rouse spurred Agnes from her prone position. "Morris!" she called, but her companion didn't answer. He remained sprawled on the ground, unresponsive.

Vail leveraged himself to his knees.

Uttering a cry, Agnes hauled herself upright, then sprinted away into the night.

"Is he dead?" Marla asked, fearful that Morris might rise again and pounce on her.

Vail crawled over and prodded him. "He'll live, but he's got more than a concussion. Are you all right?" He turned to her, eyes gleaming in a manner that brought warmth back into her chilled veins.

"Yes, and you?"

"My head feels like it was hit by a sledgehammer. Sitting up makes me dizzy."

"Then I'll have to help you."

Help wasn't what Dalton had in mind when his arms closed around her.

Chapter Twenty

Sunday morning, Marla reversed her Camry from the garage and closed the garage door with her automatic opener. While it lowered, Moss waved to her from the next yard. She kept her foot on the brake, waiting for the white-haired gent to saunter over.

"How ya doing?" he said when she rolled down her window. "I hear you and your detective friend caught those crooks who killed that young gal."

She smiled kindly. "The two of them are being held without bail. Morris had to be treated in the hospital after Dalton gave him a nasty crack on the head. Agnes was caught at the airport boarding a flight for Costa Rica."

"So why do you have that sad look on your face?"

Her shoulders sagged. "Morris's wife was shocked to learn her husband and the nurse were not only having an affair, but also were implicated in Kim's murder. Barbara was sharp enough, though, to approach Miriam with a business proposition. Miriam has agreed to let her run the family corporation."

"Bet your ex is happy."

"Stan is relieved that his slate has been cleared, but he's still depressed. He really misses Kimberly. I'm on my way to see him right now. He's signing over his share of our jointly owned property."

"That's dynamite, mate. Say, have you seen Goat lately?" Moss asked, crinkling his tanned face.

"No, why?"

"He planted our impatiens and said he'd water them, but they're wilting. His van has sat in the driveway since Friday, and no one answered when I knocked on his door."

"Have you tried calling him?"

Moss nodded, his captain's cap bobbing on his head of white hair. "Same luck. Do you suppose he's left town for the weekend?"

She met Moss's concerned glance. "I don't think Goat would leave his pets untended. Besides, he'd take his van, unless someone picked him up. If he has customers scheduled for tomorrow, he'll be here. See if he turns up on Monday."

"I hope you're right."

"Got any new limericks to show me?" she asked, hoping to erase the worried expression on her neighbor's face.

He smiled. "I'm working on them. Gonna bring your detective over to see me?"

She laughed. "Yeah, if we ever get any free time together. I'll see you later. Let me know if Goat turns up."

The drive to Stan's house took fifteen minutes. Marla was surprised to see him waiting outside by his front door. As she strode toward him, she glanced approvingly at his polo shirt and tan Dockers. He'd slicked his hair off his forehead and even shaved for the occasion. She caught a whiff of his favorite lime cologne as she greeted him.

"Come in," he said. "This won't take long."

Her low-heeled pumps echoed in the hallway as she followed him to the kitchen. The house remained eerily quiet. Nothing seemed to have moved since she'd been here last.

She curbed her impatience, accepting Stan's offer to sit at the kitchen table. "Here's a check for the full amount," she said after he joined her.

His eyes flashed surprise, as though he hadn't expected her to manage the funding. "Did you take out a second mortgage?"

"No, Miriam gave me a loan. Her only condition is that I continue to visit her. She hired a new nurse, you know. Linda Haines. Linda is a real *mensch*. She's already taken Miriam to the mall and brought her to my salon. She doesn't have a head for figures, though. Miriam has convinced Stella to review the accounts with her."

"What about your car? Your lease is up. Do you intend to buy the white Camry or lease a new one?"

"I'm going to the dealer tomorrow. I'll make my decision then." Her lips pursed. "The papers, Stan."

He pushed them across the table to her. "I'll miss that rental income."

"No, you won't. You make plenty of money."

"It wasn't enough for Kimberly."

"Kimberly wasn't used to having someone control her purse strings. You expected too much from her, from all of us."

"I took care of you. That's what you wanted."

"Look, I'm not here to review past history." She stuffed the papers in her purse after examining his signature.

"You came through for me, Marla." His expression softened. "You're special in that way. People can rely on you. I-I never appreciated how dependable you were, or how far you've come."

"That's for sure! You wouldn't admit I could accomplish anything without you."

"So I've made a lot of mistakes. A lot. I'm hoping we can fix things between us."

"Meaning what?" She gave him a suspicious glare.

"We'll go out together. I need you, babe. That's what you like now, isn't it? To take care of other people instead of being taken care of yourself?"

She shoved to her feet. "Our relationship was finished a long time ago, Stan. Don't delude yourself into thinking we can raise it from the ashes. Besides, Dalton and I . . ."

"Are you sleeping with him?"

"That's none of your business!" Slinging her handbag over her shoulder, she narrowed her gaze. "If you're looking to mend fences, why don't you consider Leah? I don't know if even she'd take you back, though. Good-bye, Stan. Don't bother me again."

Her next stop was Miriam's house, where she'd been invited for brunch. A new maid served the family in the dining room.

"Where are the boys?" Marla asked Barbara, whose demeanor had been subdued since they greeted each other. The other woman didn't hold a grudge, even though it had been through Marla's efforts that her husband's crimes were exposed.

"Fortunately, it's their winter break. They're visiting my brother in Tampa. We may move to the West Coast. It's not the best climate here for them right now."

Marla recognized she wasn't speaking about the weather. "I'm sorry."

"You shouldn't be," Stella cut in. "Although it was Agnes's hand that killed my child, Morris was just as guilty."

She and Florence were seated on either side of Miriam, who didn't need any assistance with her meal. The matriarch had grown stronger with better nutrition and a more active role. Linda, the new nurse, sat opposite Marla, while Barbara assumed a position at the far end.

"I still don't understand everything," Florence muttered, looking elegant in a designer dress.

"Marla, tell us what that policeman learned," Miriam demanded. Her sharp gaze swung to Barbara. "Unless you'll be too upset, dearie. We've got a good lawyer for my son. Don't you worry, it's that rotten nurse who will get full blame."

"Apparently Agnes had been writing checks to herself that should have been going to Kimberly. Miriam thought she was still paying Kim's allowance, but that wasn't so," Marla explained. "I guess Agnes needed the money to help pay for her sister's care. All the while, Kim thought Miriam had cut off her funding, and that made her feel trapped in a marriage where Stan controlled the purse strings."

"My baby. She should have come to me," Stella whined.

"If I recall, she asked you for money, and you refused her,"

Florence sniffed. "You felt she should learn to walk on her own two feet."

"I listened to your advice! I should have realized you'd be happy to throw her to the dogs. You've hated me ever since I married Douglas, and you resented Kimberly as our child."

Florence's eyes glowed like two flame throwers. "She should have been my daughter! You stole Douglas from me. I was prettier. Why would he even look at you?"

"Girls, stop it!" Miriam cried, her face a mask of distress. *"Kainer hot nit kain legoteh tsu hoben charoteh.* No one has a monopoly on regret."

"When did Morris start conspiring with Agnes?" Barbara directed her question to Marla. She'd been playing with her food, Marla noticed. Her plate of smoked whitefish, a bagel, eggs, and sliced tomatoes was barely touched.

"Agnes helped Miriam audit the family financial records, and she noticed discrepancies. She asked Morris about them, and he revealed he knew about her theft. They entered into an alliance which soon became more than a business arrangement. Morris needed money for his gambling debts."

"So why did Agnes murder my daughter?" Stella asked, her voice hoarse.

"Kim found out Agnes was stealing money from her grandmother. It had nothing to do with Jeremiah Dooley's existence, which was what I'd initially suspected. True, Kimberly blackmailed him. She threatened to expose the reverend to the media if he didn't pay her way out of Stan's house. Neither your family nor Jeremiah wanted his background revealed, but Kim wasn't killed for that reason. Greed was the motive. Morris extorted money from the company, and Agnes stole from Harris's trust fund. They had a cozy arrangement until Kimberly got wise to them."

"Is that what happened to Kathleen?" Miriam demanded.

Marla glanced at the new nurse, sitting white-faced in her seat. What a way to enter service, she thought, hoping the woman wouldn't quit. It wasn't an easy family group to join.

"Kathleen had a compulsion to take things. After Kim approached Jeremiah with her knowledge of their connection, Kathleen took a job at Stan's house on Thursday afternoons as their housekeeper. Apparently, she took Stan's letter opener and brought it to her room upstairs in your house."

"She spied on them, just like she did on our family." Miriam's tight-lipped expression held disapproval.

"Kathleen did it to protect Jeremiah's interests. She was devoted to him and believed in his higher purpose. Detective Vail told me his fish farms are legit. Jeremiah enjoys a luxurious lifestyle, but he still puts most of his money into his missions. Anyway, Agnes happened to notice the letter opener engraved with Stan's name in Kathleen's room. I guess she discovered the key to their house also. That's when she conceived of the notion for silencing Kim. Morris did nothing to dissuade her when she told him her plan."

"You see, it was all Agnes's idea," Miriam said.

"Morris didn't have the backbone to stand up to her. How did she know Kim would be downstairs that morning?" Stella asked, pushing away her untouched platter.

"When Morris learned of her relationship to Gary, he encouraged the repair man to talk about her. Gary told him how Stan made Kim get up every morning to fix his breakfast and how he expected her to wait on him."

"Morris didn't realize she was pregnant, did he?" Stella said, dabbing at her moist eyes.

"I don't think he understood Kimberly was that intimately involved with Gary, or he might have blackmailed her into silence. As for Kathleen, she must have figured out the nurse stole the letter opener from her bedroom. Agnes's prints were on a gun the cops found in the flea market where Kathleen was killed. It's a *shandeh* no matter how you look at it."

"How is Stanley?" Stella asked, her gaze downcast. "We were wrong to suspect him."

"In his own way, he loved Kimberly. He misses her. I've never seen him so depressed."

"I can't believe you were married to him."

"I'm sorry I tricked you. But just as you suspected him, he suspected one of your family. He thought one of you killed her for her share of the trust fund. What will happen to that money now?"

"It'll go to Morris's sons. They're good boys. I think you'd do better to move them away from here," Miriam said to Barbara. Her shoulders slumped, and in that instant she appeared her true age.

After all, Marla thought, what did she have left? If her only remaining grandchildren moved away, she'd be stuck with the two bickering sisters. At least Marla could be a friend to her.

"I'll bet Linda is going to keep you so busy that you'll barely have time to get your hair done at my salon every week, let alone phone your grandsons," she said encouragingly. "When you get your new eyeglasses, maybe you'll consider buying a computer. Everyone keeps in touch on the Internet these days."

"I'm too old to learn new tricks, dearie."

"No, you're not, Mother," Florence piped in. "We could all learn together. Right, Stella?"

Her sister gave a grudging nod.

As Miriam's glance met hers, Marla detected a sparkle of glee. The old lady had more strength than her children combined. She wouldn't let anything keep her down, now that she had people who cared about her.

"I'll look into computer classes at the senior center," said Linda eagerly, sitting forward in her chair. "We're going shopping tomorrow. Miriam wants to look spiffy when she meets your mom next week."

"Ma can't wait to meet you. I think you'll get along famously. I hope you don't mind that I've invited Dalton to join us for lunch."

"I'm delighted," Miriam said, "although I'll have a thing or two to tell him about letting you run around playing undercover detective."

Marla laughed, disregarding the frowns on the sisters' faces. Let those old prunes stew. It gave her great pleasure to brighten Miriam's life.

* * *

"She sounds like a charming woman," Anita said later when Marla dropped in and reported on her visit. "I'm looking forward to meeting her. How about some chicken soup with matzoh balls? I just made it last night."

Marla sat in the kitchen, across from her mother. She'd been glad to capture her alone, without her new boyfriend.

"No, thanks. I'm stuffed. I ate a bagel with Nova and cream cheese at Miriam's house."

"Then I'll put some into a container, and you can take it home for later. So, tell me, what's your status with the detective? Roger's son wanted to call you, but he got the impression you weren't interested."

"I'm not. Every time Dalton and I get together, it's been over a case he's investigating. I want to see what happens when neither of us is distracted."

"That sounds serious."

"Maybe it is. I don't know. There's still Brianna. I'm afraid I'm not very good as a mother figure. I've hardly done a thing about her birthday party."

"How do you have time when you have a business to run and spend your spare time chasing murderers?"

"Speaking of business, I found out why we've been getting so many no-shows lately."

"Oh?" Anita raised a penciled eyebrow. Even when she wasn't expecting company, she put on makeup, fluffed her white hair, and touched up her red-painted fingernails.

"You remember Carolyn Sutton? I worked in her salon for a couple of years before leaving to open my own place. She moved away, but her new location proved to be a bad choice. Now I hear she's leased a shop in the same shopping strip where I am."

Anita scrutinized her expression. "I gather this doesn't please you, *bubula.*"

"Why should it? She's doing it on purpose to get back at me. Carolyn felt I betrayed her, and she resented my success. She should have understood that I was ready to break out on my own. It wasn't anything personal."

"Competition is the way of the world," Anita commented.

"You got anything to drink? I'm thirsty." She shifted in her chair; just talking about Carolyn made her uneasy.

Anita handed her a can of ginger ale and a glass full of ice. "What does Carolyn have to do with your no-shows?"

"She's been offering free services to my customers. Somehow she got hold of our client list."

"Go on!"

Marla sipped her drink, the effervescent liquid sliding down her throat. "Oh, I know some clients will come back when Carolyn starts charging them. But some may remain, especially if her prices undercut mine. Cut 'N Dye has been the only hair salon in that area. I've worked hard to build up my clientele. I hate to think Carolyn is edging in on my territory."

She knew how petty it sounded, but she couldn't help the way she felt. Her salon had been the only kid on the block until now. All that time and money she'd spent promoting her salon's image would now have to be shared, and with someone who hated her.

"Have you checked with the landlord? Maybe there is a non-competition clause in your lease."

"Mr. Thompson could care less. I'll just have to deal with it. She'll be opening within the next few months. In the meantime, I've hired a couple of new employees. You should have seen some of the weirdos who applied for the jobs."

"Marla, you need to take some time off. You're too stressed out."

"Don't worry, I plan to relax." Her eyes twinkled playfully. "I've invited Dalton for dinner tonight. Just the two of us, no interruptions. Brianna doesn't have school tomorrow. It's a teacher workday, so she's sleeping over at a friend's house."

"I hope you won't do anything you'll regret," Anita admonished, wagging a finger. "You are on the pill, aren't you?"

"Ma! If you don't mind, that's private information." She chuckled. "And who are you to give me advice? How often are you seeing Roger?"

Her mother blushed. "We're going out tonight."

"Uh-huh. Well, you just be careful not to do anything *you'll* regret! Times have changed. Pregnancy isn't the only thing you have to worry about these days."

The only thing she worried about when Dalton showed up at her door at seven o'clock was how would he react to her suggestion. She broke the ice by offering him a glass of chardonnay while they munched on stuffed mushrooms in her kitchen. She'd put a brisket and potatoes in the oven, but they still had some time to go. Smoothing down her short royal blue silk chemise dress, she regarded him from under mascaraed lashes.

He'd dressed for the occasion in a button-down shirt with a pullover wool sweater and form-fitting trousers. His peppery hair, parted to one side, looked as though he'd used a styling comb. Her gaze sank from his hair to his eyes, gleaming like polished pewter. She choked down a piece of mushroom. Now that she had him all to herself, she felt suddenly shy.

"We promised each other not to talk about any of your cases," she said. "I don't know what to say."

They stood in front of the counter, facing each other.

"I've never known you to be tongue-tied." His mouth quirked in a half-smile.

"Uh, I made a few more calls about Brianna's party. We could do laser tag or bowling, or rent the pavilion at Flamingo Gardens. None of those costs as much as a catered affair. If she wants to go fancier, we could do a dance party at—"

"Never mind." He put his glass down, then reached for hers and placed it on the counter. Stepping closer, he put a hand on her shoulder. "I've solved the problem."

"You have?" Her breath came short at his nearness. The room seemed to shrink around them as they locked gazes. The scent of his spice aftershave mingled with the aroma of roasting wine-braised beef. Warmth coiled in her center, spiraling outward.

"I reserved a group of tables at Dave and Buster's," he said, his voice husky.

So he's affected by me, too. "That's the place with the video games?"

"Right, but they also have a dinner show. Brie loves the idea. It's an interactive murder mystery play, what else?"

"That's great." Grinning, she threw her arms around him. Thank goodness that chore was off her list!

"Umm, I like this," he said, pressing his body against hers.

She tilted her neck to regard him. "I have a proposition. How about if we put a hold on dinner and go straight to dessert?"

"Honey," he said, kissing her, "you've got a deal."

AUTHOR'S NOTE

I became interested in tilapia farming when I visited The Land pavilion at Epcot Center in Walt Disney World. This short boat tour, tunefully accompanied by "Listen to the Land," included an educational cruise through the Tropical Greenhouse and Vegetable Production House. These sections showed alternate methods of cultivating crops, while an Aquacell displayed the potential value of farm-raised fish. If you want to read more about these topics, check out the links on my Web site. Next time you sit down to a fish dinner with a cup of coffee, I hope you'll remember what you've read in BODY WAVE.

Coming next is HIGHLIGHTS TO HEAVEN. While Marla wrestles with the mystery of why her neighbor, Goat, has vanished, she mediates an authority struggle between Brianna and Vail. Marla aims to come out on top, but the handsome detective has another position in mind for her! Succumbing to his charms presents its own dangers, not the least of which is being distracted while another killer runs amok in sultry South Florida.

I love to hear from readers. Write to me at: P.O. Box 17756, Plantation, FL 33318. Please enclose a self-addressed, stamped #10 business-size envelope for a personal reply.

E-mail: *ncane@att.net*

Web site: *www.nancyjcohen.com*